ABOUT THE AUTHOR

Ali Smith was born in Inverness in 1962. She is the author of *Spring, Winter, Autumn, Public library and other stories, How to be both, Shire, Artful, There but for the, The first person and other stories, Girl Meets Boy, The Accidental, The whole story and other stories, Hotel World, Other stories and other stories, Like* and *Free Love*. *Hotel World* was shortlisted for the Booker Prize and the Orange Prize. *The Accidental* was shortlisted for the Man Booker Prize and the Orange Prize. *How to be both* won the Bailey's Prize, the Goldsmiths Prize and the Costa Novel of the Year Award, and was shortlisted for the Man Booker Prize. *Autumn* was shortlisted for the Man Booker Prize 2017 and *Winter* was shortlisted for the Orwell Prize 2018. Ali Smith lives in Cambridge.

ABOUT THE COVER ARTIST

Sarah Illenberger is a Berlin-based artist, illustrator and designer. Born and raised in Munich she studied graphic design at St Martins in London. She set up her studio in Berlin in 2007, where she creates illustrations and installations, using everyday materials and techniques. These are then photographed and printed in magazines and digital media or presented in public places such as shop windows and art spaces. Her visual language is defined by giving common things a new meaning.

PENGUIN ESSENTIALS

The Accidental

'Inspired . . . So far ahead in my personal reckoning of novels of the
year that it might as well sit on the shelf sprinkled in fairy dust'
Alex Clark, *Daily Telegraph*

'Sharp, original and breathtaking' James Naughtie, *Herald*

'A great, dazzling voice that fizzes like a long-burning fuse' *Saga*

'My book of the year. Ali Smith is one of the most inventive writers
we have. She jumps from high places and lands on her feet'
Jackie Kay, *Scotland on Sunday*

'Reminded me why Ali Smith has such a growing legion of fans.
She is a true original with stunning powers of observation'
Jamie Byng, *Scotsman*

'A lyrical, modern fable' Erica Wagner, *The Times*

'Exerts a strange spell long after you finish reading it'
Andrew Crumey, *Scotland on Sunday*

'Dazzling' Philip Hensher, *Spectator*

'An account of a disintegrating family infiltrated by a mysterious stranger, it's
as brave, beautiful and funny as her previous books'
Maggie O'Farrell, *Independent on Sunday*

'Rightly singled out for praise. The sense of dislocation in the everyday,
and a unique narrative voice – spare and yet absorbing – make the book
a compulsive read' Iain Campbell, *Scotsman*

'A magical writer . . . flows beautifully' *Scotland on Sunday*

'Smith's language is endlessly imaginative' *Time Out*

ALI SMITH

The Accidental

PENGUIN BOOKS

PENGUIN ESSENTIALS

UK | USA | Canada | Ireland | Australia
India | New Zealand | South Africa

Penguin Books is part of the Penguin Random House group of companies
whose addresses can be found at global.penguinrandomhouse.com.

First published by Hamish Hamilton 2005
Published in Penguin Books 2006
This Penguin Essentials edition published 2020

001

Copyright © Ali Smith, 2005

The moral right of the author has been asserted

Printed and bound in Great Britain by Clays Ltd, Elcograf S.p.A.

A CIP catalogue record for this book is available from the British Library

ISBN: 978-0-241-98911-1

acknowledgements and thanks

Thanks to Carla Wakefield for the original accidental.

Thank you, Charlie, Bridget, Kate, Woodrow, Xandra, Becky, Donald, Daphne and Stephen.

Thank you, Andrew and Michal, and Simon and Juliette.

Thank you, Kasia.

Thank you, Sarah.

The extract from Antal Szerb's *Journey by Moonlight* is reproduced by kind permission of Pushkin Press.

The extract from Nick Cohen's *Cruel Britannia* is reproduced by kind permission of Verso, London.

'What will survive of us is love' by Philip Larkin is reproduced by kind permission of Faber & Faber Ltd.

The extract from John Berger's *The Shape of a Pocket* is reproduced by kind permission of Bloomsbury Ltd.

All efforts have been made to contact holders of copyright; in the event of any inadvertent omission, please contact the publisher.

for
Philippa Reed
high hopes

Inuk Hoff Hansen
far away so close

Sarah Wood
the wizard of us

Between the experience of living a normal
life at this moment on the planet and the
public narratives being offered to give a
sense to that life, the empty space,
the gap, is enormous.

John Berger

Shallow uniformity is not an accident
but a consequence of what Marxists
optimistically call late capitalism.

Nick Cohen

The whole history dwindled soon into a matter
of little importance but to Emma and her
nephews: – in her imagination it maintained its
ground, and Henry and John were still asking every
day for the story of Harriet and the gipsies, and still
tenaciously setting her right if she varied in the
slightest particular from the original recital.

Jane Austen

Many are the things that man
Seeing must understand.
Not seeing, how shall he know
What lies in the hand
Of time to come?

Sophocles

My artistry is a bit austere.

Charles Chaplin

My mother began me one evening in 1968 on a table in the café of the town's only cinema. One short flight of stairs away, up behind the balding red velvet of the Balcony curtain, the usherette was yawning, dandling her off torch, leaning on her elbow above the rustlings and tonguings of the back row and picking at the wood of the partition, flicking little splinters of it at the small-town heads in the dark. On the screen above them the film was Poor Cow, with Terence Stamp, an actor of such numinousness that my mother, young, chic, slender and imperious, and watching the film for the third time that week, had stood up, letting her seat thud up behind her, pushed past the legs of the people in her row and headed up the grubby aisle to the exit, through the curtain and out into the light.

The café was empty except for the boy putting chairs on tables. We're just shutting, he told her. My mother, still blinking from the dark, picked her way down the scuffed red stairs. She took the chair he was holding and put it, still upside down, down on the ground. She stepped out of her shoes. She unbuttoned her coat.

Behind the till the half-submerged oranges in the orange

juice machine went round and round on their spikes; the dregs at the bottom of the tank rose and settled, rose and settled. The chairs on the tables stuck their legs into the air; the scatters of cake crumbs underneath waited passive in the carpet for the vacuum cleaner nozzle. Down the grand main stairs leading out on to the street, where my mother would go in a few minutes' time with her nylons rolled in a warm ball in her coat pocket, swinging her shoes in her hand by their strappy backs, Julie Andrews and Christopher Plummer smiled out from behind their frames exactly like they'd still be smiling, faded and glamorous, a decade out of date, at the blaze of light that blackened the staircase five years later when the junior projectionist (cheated out of a job he believed was his; the management had hired a new projectionist from the city when the old projectionist died) gutted the building with a tin of creosote and the dropped end of his cigarette.

The expensive Balcony seats, where smoking was forbidden? Up in smoke. The Stalls with their deep-seated leathery smell? Gone forever. The velvet drapes, the glass-bowl chandelier? Blowaway ash, a sprinkling of tiny broken shards of light on the surface of local history. Next day's newspapers were adamant, an accident. The man who owned the cinema claimed the insurance and sold the demolished site to a cash and carry warehouse called, rather unimaginatively, Mackay's Cash and Carry.

But that night back in 1968 in the nearly closed café the voices were still booming modern love behind the walls. The music was still soaring out of nowhere. Just before the part where the filth get Terence Stamp and put him where he belongs she had fastened her heels behind his back and my father, surprised, had slipped and grunted into her, presenting her with literally millions of possibilities, of which she chose only one.

2

Hello.

I am Alhambra, named for the place of my conception. Believe me. Everything is meant.

From my mother: grace under pressure; the uses of mystery; how to get what I want. From my father: how to disappear, how to not exist.

The beginning

of things – when is it exactly?
Astrid Smart wants to know. (Astrid Smart. Astrid Berenski.
Astrid Smart. Astrid Berenski.) 5.04 a.m. on the substandard
clock radio. Because why do people always say the day starts
now? Really it starts in the middle of the night at a fraction
of a second past midnight. But it's not supposed to have
begun until the dawn, really the dark is still last night and it
isn't morning till the light, though actually it was morning as
soon as it was even a fraction of a second past twelve i.e.
that experiment where you divide something down and down
like the distance between the ground and a ball that's been
bounced on it so that it can be proved, Magnus says, that the
ball never actually touches the ground. Which is junk because
of course it touches the ground, otherwise how would it
bounce, it wouldn't have anything to bounce *off*, but it can
actually be proved by science that it doesn't.

Astrid is taping dawns. There is nothing else to do here.
The village is a dump. Post office, vandalized Indian
restaurant, chip shop, little shop place that's never open,
place for ducks to cross the road. Ducks actually have their
own roadsign! There is a sofa warehouse called Sofa So

Good. It is dismal. There is a church. The church has its own roadsign too. Nothing happens here except a church and some ducks, and this house is an ultimate dump. It is substandard. Nothing is going to happen here all substandard summer.

She now has nine dawns one after the other on the mini dv tape in her Sony digital. Thursday 10 July 2003, Friday 11 July 2003, Saturday 12, Sunday 13, Monday 14, Tuesday 15, Wednesday 16, Thursday 17 and today Friday 18. But it is hard to know what moment exactly dawn is. All there is when you look at it on the camera screen is the view of outside getting more visible. So does this mean that the beginning is something to do with being able to see? That the day begins as soon as you wake up and open your eyes? So when Magnus finally wakes up in the afternoon and they can hear him moving about in the room that's his in this dump of a substandard house, does that mean the day is still beginning? Is the beginning different for everyone? Or do beginnings just keep stretching on forwards and forwards all day? Or maybe it is back and back they stretch. Because every time you open your eyes there was a time before that when you closed them then a different time before that when you opened them, all the way back, through all the sleeping and the waking and the ordinary things like blinking, to the first time you ever open your eyes, which is probably round about the moment you are born.

Astrid kicks her trainers off on to the floor. She slides back across the horrible bed. Or possibly the beginning is even further back than that, when you are in the womb or whatever it's called. Possibly the real beginning is when you are just forming into a person and for the first time the soft stuff that makes your eyes is actually made, formed, inside the hard stuff that becomes your head i.e. your skull.

She fingers the curve of bone above her left eye. Eyes fit the space they are in, exactly like they were made for each other, the space and the eye. Like the play she saw with the man in it whose eyes were gouged out, the people on the stage turned him so the audience couldn't see, then they gouged out his eyes then whirled the chair round and he had his hands up at his face and he took them away, his hands were full of red stuff, it was all round his eye sockets. It was insane. It was jelly or something similar. It was his daughters who did it or his sons. It was one of Michael's tragedies. It was quite good though. Yes, exactly, because at a theatre the curtain goes up and you know it's the beginning because, obviously, the curtain's gone up. But the way the lights go down, the audience goes quiet, and right after the curtain goes up, then the air, if you're sitting near the stage, you can actually smell a different other air with bits of dust and stuff in it moving. Like when Michael and her mother made her go to the other tragedy that was completely insane about the woman who loses it and kills her children, but before she does she sends them, two boys, really small boys, off the stage, they actually come down into the audience and walk through it, the mother has given them poisoned clothes etc. to give to the princess their father is marrying instead of her and they go to a house or a palace somewhere behind the audience, this doesn't happen on the stage, it doesn't happen anywhere except in the story i.e. in your head but even though you know it doesn't, you know it's just a play, even so, somewhere behind you the princess is still putting on the poisoned things and dying a horrible death. Her eyes melt in their sockets and she comes out in a rash like if terrorists dropped spores on the Tube. Her lungs melt and

Astrid yawns. She is hungry.

She is starving, actually.

9

It is literally hours till anything like breakfast even if she wanted to eat anything in this unhygienic dump.

She could go back to sleep. But typical and ironic, she is completely awake. It is completely light outside now; you can see for miles. Except there is nothing to see here; trees and fields and that kind of thing.

5.16 a.m. on the substandard clock radio.

She is really awake.

She could get up and go and film the vandalism. She is definitely going to do it today. She will go to the restaurant later and ask the Indian man if it is okay to. Or maybe she will just film it without him knowing in case he says no. If she went right now there would be nobody there and she could just do it. If anybody happened to be up and around at this time of the morning (nobody will, there is nobody awake for miles but her, but if there were, say there were) they would just think oh, look, there is a twelve-year-old girl playing with a dv camera. They would probably notice what a good model the camera is, that's if they knew anything about cameras. She would tell them if they asked that she is a visitor for the summer (true) filming the scenery (true) or that it is for a school project (could be true) about different buildings and their uses (quite good). And then maybe there will be vital evidence on her mini dv tape when she gets home and at some point in the investigation into the vandalism someone in authority will remember and say oh that twelve-year-old girl was there with a camera, maybe she recorded something really what is the word crucial to our enquiries, and they will come and knock on the door, but what if they aren't still here for the summer, what if they've already gone home, some investigations take quite a long time, well then the authorities will trace her back home with their computers by looking up Michael's name or by asking the people who own this substandard house and, because of her, things will finally be put right and a mystery like who is responsible for the vandalism at the Curry Palace will actually be solved.

This is a quintessential place. Her mother keeps saying so, she says it every evening. There don't seem to be many other people here on holiday regardless of how quintessential it is, maybe because it's not actually holiday time yet, officially. People in the village do a lot of staring even when Astrid isn't doing anything, is just walking about. Even when she isn't using her camera. But it is nice weather. She is lucky not to be at school. The sun has come out on most of the dawns she has recorded. This is what a good summer is like. In the past, before she was born, the summers were better, they were perpetual beautiful summers from May to October in the past apparently. The past is a different century. She herself will probably be the one to live longest into the new century out of all the people here in this house right now, her mother, Magnus, herself, Michael. They are all more part of the old century than she is. But then again her whole life, mostly, was lived in the old century. But then again their whole lives were too, and percentage-wise she has already lived 25 per cent of hers in the new (if you start at 2001 and allow for the next six months of this year now to have already happened). She herself is 25 per cent new, 75 per cent old. Magnus has lived three out of seventeen in it so comes out at. Astrid works it out. Magnus is 17ish per cent new, 83 per cent old. She is 8 per cent more in the new than Magnus. Her mother and Michael are way out there on a much much more significantly small percentage in the new, a much much more significantly large percentage in the old. She will work it out later. She can't be bothered now.

She shifts on the substandard bed. The substandard bed

11

creaks loudly. After the creak she can hear the silence in the rest of the house. They are all asleep. Nobody knows she is awake. Nobody is any the wiser. Any the wiser sounds like a character from ancient history. Astrid in the year 1003 BC (Before Celebrity) goes to the woods where Any the Wiser, who is really royalty and a king but who has unexpectedly chosen to be a Nobody and to live the simple life, lives in a hut, no, a cave, and answers the questions that the people of the commonweal come for miles around to ask him (most probably a him since if it was a her she'd have to be in a convent or burnt). People who want to know answers to things have to knock on the door of the cave, well, the rock outside, she picks up a rock and knocks it against another rock, this lets Any the Wiser know that someone is waiting. I brought an offering, Astrid calls into the dark of the cave. She has brought an offering of croissants. You probably can't get good croissants in the woods, like you can't get them out here. Both Michael and her mother have been complaining about no croissants since they got to this substandard village which is typical and ironic since they're the ones who wanted to come here and have made her and Magnus come and made her even more weird and unlike everybody is supposed to be than she already is, though with any luck by the time school starts again in September Lorna Rose and Zelda Howe and Rebecca Callow will have forgotten about her being taken out of school early two months before.

Astrid concentrates them out of her head. She is at the door of a cave. She is carrying croissants. Any the Wiser is delighted. He nods at Astrid to come forward.

He glints at her through the darkness of the cave; he is old and wise; he has a fatherly look in his eye. Answer my question, oh revered sage and oracle, Astrid begins.

But that's all she can say because she doesn't have a

question. She doesn't know what to ask him about, or for. She can't think of a question, not one she's allowed to say inside herself in actual words to herself, never mind out loud to a complete stranger, even a stranger she's made up.

(Astrid Smart. Astrid Berenski.)

She sits up. She picks up her camera, turns it over in her hand. She shuts its screen away, ejects the beginnings tape, slides it into its little case and puts it on the table. She clips the non-beginnings tape into the camera instead. She lies on her back then shifts over on to her front. By the end of their time here she will have sixty-one beginnings, depending on if they go home on the Friday, the Saturday or the Sunday. Sixty-one minus nine, i.e. still at least fifty-two more to go. Astrid sighs. Her sigh sounds too loud. There is no noise of traffic here. It is probably the fact that there is no noise that is keeping her so awake. She is completely awake. In a minute she will go and film the vandalism. She closes her eyes. She is on the inside of a hazelnut; she fits against the shell perfectly, as if she was born in it. Her head has it as a helmet. It fits the curve of her knees. It is completely enclosed. It is a complete room. It is completely safe. Nobody else can get inside it. Then she worries about what she will do about breathing, since the nut is completely sealed. She begins to worry about how she is doing any breathing now. There is obviously a finite amount of air, if any, inside a hazelnut. Then she begins to worry that Lorna Rose and Zelda Howe and Rebecca, if they were ever to find out she had ever had a thought like that she was inside a hazelnut, would think she was even more laughable and a mental case. Lorna Rose and Zelda Howe are playing a game of tennis on a public court in a park. Astrid walks past with Rebecca. Rebecca and Astrid are still friends. Lorna Rose runs across to the fence and tells Astrid and Rebecca they should come and play on the court next to the one she and Zelda Howe are playing on, and then the winners of each game will play each other to find who out of the four of them is the best. Astrid looks at the court she and Rebecca are supposed to play on. Its surface is all pieces of broken glass. She is about to say no but Rebecca says yes. But look at the glass, Astrid says because it is insane. Coward, Zelda Howe says. We knew you wouldn't do it. They have put the broken glass there on purpose as a test. If you want to play on broken glass you're an idiot, Astrid tells Rebecca. Rebecca goes into the court and crunches about on the broken glass. A man comes. He is one of their fathers. She is going to tell him about the glass but before she can he calls everyone except her over to the fence and breaks a Cadburys fruit and nut bar into four equal pieces. He gives a piece to each of them. She looks to see if he's eating the fourth piece himself but she can't make out his face, he is too far away. There is something in her hand. It is her camera. If she can get this on film she will be able to show someone everything that's happening. But she can't lift the camera. It is too heavy. Her arm won't work. A doorbell rings, miles away. It is at home. There is no one at home but her. The hall is as big and empty as a desert. Astrid runs along it to answer the door. The hall seems never to end. When she does get to the door she is doubled over, she has run out of breath and she is frightened that whoever is behind it will have gone by now because she took so long. She opens it. A man is standing there. He has no face. He has no nose, no eyes, nothing, just blank skin. Astrid is terrified. Her mother will be furious with her. It is her fault he is here. You can't come in, she tries to tell him, but she has no breath. We're not here, she breathes. We're on holiday. Go away. She tries to shut the door. A mouth appears in the skin and a great noise roars out of it like she is standing too close to

14

an aeroplane. It forces the door back. She opens her eyes, rolls straight off the bed on to her feet.

She is on holiday in Norfolk. The substandard clock radio says 10.27 a.m. The noise is Katrina the Cleaner thumping the hoover against the skirting boards and the bedroom doors.

Her hand is asleep. It is still hooked through the handstrap of the camera. She unhooks it and shakes it to get the blood back into it.

She puts her feet on top of her trainers and slides them across the substandard carpet. It has had the bare naked feet of who knows how many hundreds of dead or old people on it.

When she looks in the mirror above the sink she sees the imprint of her own thumb below her cheekbone where she slept on her hand ! ! She is like the kind of pottery things her mother buys that have been made by real people (not factories), actual artisans working in hot countries who leave the actual marks of their hands in it as their signature i.e. she has signed herself in her sleep!

She presses her thumb into the indentation it made. It fits perfectly.

She flicks water over her face and dries it on the sleeve of her t-shirt rather than the horrible towel. She pulls her trainers on properly. She picks up the camera again and lifts the latch on the door.

There are two ways to watch what you're filming: 1. on the little screen and 2. through the viewer. Real filmmakers always use the viewer though it is harder to see with it. She puts her eye to the viewer and records her hand making the latch go up then down. In a hundred years' time these latches may not exist any more and this film will be proof that they did and will act as evidence for people who need to know in the future how latches like this one worked.

The battery sign is flashing. The battery is low. There is enough power to record Katrina the Cleaner gouging with the hoover tube at the inside of each stair. Katrina is something to do with the house. She comes with the package. Her mother and Michael have a joke they whisper when she's round a corner out of earshot, or even when she's not in the house and wouldn't hear even if they shouted it, Katrina the Cleaner in her Ford Cortina. The Ford Cortina is a car from the 1970s; it is probably an oik car, though Astrid doesn't get the joke; Katrina doesn't actually seem to have a car; she carries the cleaning stuff along the road to the house from her own house in the village then carries it back again when she's finished. They always act so juvenile as if they are being really the worst they can be, saying something really risky. Personally Astrid is above such things. People are just different from other people, is what she thinks. It is obvious. Some people are naturally not as suited to living the same way as other people, so they make less money and live a different, less good kind of life.

There isn't much light on the stairs. It will be quite an interesting effect. She watches the top of Katrina's head through the viewer. She films her cleaning the stair. Then she films her as she moves down and cleans the next.

Katrina the Cleaner shifts to one side, not looking up, to let Astrid pass.

Excuse me, Katrina, Astrid shouts politely. Can I just ask you something?

Katrina the Cleaner bends away from Astrid and switches the hoover off. She doesn't look up.

Can I just ask you how old you are? Astrid says. It's for my local researches and archive. (This sounds good. Astrid tries to memorize it so she can use it to the Indian man at the Curry Palace.)

16

Katrina the Cleaner says something downwards. It sounds like thirty-one. She definitely looks that old. She has switched the hoover back on again. Thirty-one is tricky. Astrid rounds it down. 10 per cent new, 90 per cent old. She films all the way round Katrina then films her own feet going down the rest of the stairs.

This footage will come straight after the dead thing she taped on the road when she was walking back from the village last night. It was a bit like a rabbit but it wasn't a rabbit. It was bigger than a rabbit. It had small ears and smaller back legs; it had been mangled by cars; its fur was matted with mud and blood. Four or five crows rose off it when she went towards it; they had been pulling scraps off it. She had found a stick on the verge and poked it with it. Then she had filmed it. At some point she is going to leave the camera on the table in the substandard lounge at exactly the right place on the tape and Michael will definitely pick it up and look at what's on it, he is bound to, and he is such a loser he is really squeamish about things like that if they are happening in real life and not like on a stage or whatever.

She stops, stands in the hall. The dead thing. What if it was alive but unconscious and she had poked it that hard and it wasn't dead at all, it could still feel her poking it and only seemed dead because it was in a coma?

Well but maybe it would be okay because maybe if it was in a coma it wouldn't have felt it so much as it would have if it had been awake. In the four-wheel drive on the way here her mother and Michael did their usual Peep for Sheep game where Michael hits the horn whenever they pass sheep and they did their usual clenched fists in the air that they do whenever the car passes roadkill. It is supposed to honour the spirit of the dead thing. It is juvenile. Astrid liked it when

17

she used to be upset by the dead things. But now she is twelve and they are just dead things for God's sake.

It is very unlikely that it felt anything when she poked it.

She poked it for her researches and archive.

Astrid puts her eye back behind the camera. Also it is important to look closely at things, especially difficult things. Astrid's mother is always saying so. Astrid goes through the dark hall and into the front room. But the camera viewer floods with light so bright that she can't see. She has to look away from it quick.

She blinks. It was so bright it was almost sore.

There is the shape of someone on the sofa by the window. Because of the light from the window behind the person, and because of the flash of light still filling her own eye with reds and blacks, the face is a blur of light and dark. Astrid looks down at the carpet until her sight comes back. She can see bare feet.

It will be someone to do with the house, an oik from the village. It will be one of Michael's students. Astrid blinks again and turns her back. She ignores that side of the room. She switches off her camera very attentively and collects the charger and the other battery from behind the horrible old paperbacks in the bookcase thing. She carries them through to the kitchen.

Michael is peeling a pear on to a plate. The plate has been used hundreds of times by who knows how many people who have been in this house. He is peeling the pear with a knife which has a wooden handle. The wood of that handle has all the dirty washing-up water of all the times it has ever been washed by the hundreds of dead old people who lived here or holidayed here seeped into it.

The toaster also has old other people's crumbs in it. Astrid puts her camera stuff down by the chair, unrolls some kitchen

foil and breaks a piece of bread off the uncut end of the loaf.
She covers the substandard grillpan with the foil and lays the
bread under the grill, which she lights. Then she sits on the
chair by the door, swinging her legs.

Who's the person in the front room? she asks Michael who
is cutting the pear into neat white slices.

Something to do with your mother, Michael says. Her car
broke down.

He takes the plate with the pear on it and goes through to
the front, humming a tune. He is humming that Beyoncé song.
He thinks he is so now, i.e. he is completely embarrassing.

Astrid knocks her hand against the side of the chair to see
if it will hurt. It does, but not very much. She knocks it again,
harder. It hurts more. Of course science can prove, typical
and ironic, that her hand is not actually hitting the chair by
dividing down the distance smaller and smaller. She hits it
again. Ow.

She waits for the bread to singe a bit.

She can hear Michael in the front room talking in a loud
voice. She opens the bin. The pear skin is coiled on the top
of the remains of last night's dinner. Its insides are bright
white. She picks it out. He has peeled it in one complete
piece. She holds it in her hand so that it fits back together
again in the shape it took before he peeled it. The flap with
the stick attached sits on top like a hat. It is an empty pear!

She lets the skin drop back into the bin, lets the lid fall.
She washes her hands at the sink. Michael comes back
through. She can see the smile he had on for the person in
the front room fading as he does.

That's burning, Astrid, he says.

I know, she says.

He takes the grillpan out, opens the bin and throws in the
toast, black side up, on top of the pear peel.

If you'd cut it neatly in the first place, he says, it wouldn't have caught like that.

I like it burnt, she says under her breath.

He cuts another couple of slices off the loaf and drops them in the toaster.

No thanks, Astrid says.

Michael doesn't hear. He is such a wankstain. He is doing something with a cafetiere. His second name is stuck on the end of her first name and she has no say about it at all. She picks up her camera stuff and goes through to the hall. But she has no idea where the plug sockets are in the hall of this substandard house. She can't see one. She knows where the sockets are in the front room and in the lounge part of the front room. Or she could go back upstairs, but typical and ironic it sounds like Katrina and the hoover are in her bedroom now. It doesn't actually make much hygienic difference just vacuuming over a surface. Old people have licked the furniture with their dead tongues and ingrained the banister all the way up the stairs with skin flakes off their old hands.

She goes back through into the lounge. The plugs by the tv are all being used. If she unplugs one she will probably be in trouble for something.

The sound of vacuuming stops suddenly. The French windows are open. The room fills with the sound of the garden i.e. birds etc. She crosses back into the front bit of the room and unplugs a standard lamp. She plugs the charger in and stands up.

In the yellow rectangle of sunlight coming through the high front window the person is lying stretched out on the sofa. Her bare feet are up on it like she lives here. Her eyes are closed. She is actually asleep.

Astrid comes closer to the sofa.

She is kind of a woman but more like a girl. Her hair is supposed to be blonde but Astrid can see much deeper dark in her hair at the roots of her parting. Her feet are up on the cushions. The soles of them are quite dirty.

This close up she is younger than Astrid's mother, younger maybe than Katrina, but definitely too old to be a girl. She isn't wearing any make-up. It is weird. Her underarms aren't shaved. There is hair there, quite a lot. Her shins and thighs and the backs of them are also not shaved. It is unbelievable. They are sheened with actual hairs. The hairs are like hundreds of little threads coming straight out of the skin.

Less than a foot away from Astrid's face the girl, the woman, whatever, has opened one eye and is looking straight at her with it.

Astrid jumps back. There is a plate on the floor by the sofa. She picks it up as if Michael has sent her through for it. Carrying the plate ahead of her she marches across the room and straight out through the French windows into the garden and round the corner.

She is out of sight of the house before she stops. Her breath is high and funny. It is weird to look at someone. It is weird when they look back at you. It is really weird to be caught looking.

The plate is sticky with something. Astrid sucks a finger. It tastes sweet. She puts the plate down on the grass near the rockery. She dips her hand into a watering can to get rid of the stickiness. Then she wonders if it was water in the watering can. It might have been insecticide or weedkiller. She brings her hand up to her nose but it doesn't smell chemical. She puts her tongue out and tastes it. It doesn't taste of anything.

She goes down the garden to the summerhouse. The summerhouse is just a big shed though it was advertised as a summerhouse; her mother and Michael have been complaining about it since they got here, since one of the main reasons for coming to this boring nowhere is so her mother can work in a summerhouse all summer like some writer from the past used to. She can hear her mother inside it from as far back as here. She is very loud, even on a laptop keyboard. She is writing and researching about people who died last century again. She types with two fingers incredibly hard like she is angry, though she generally isn't, it just sounds like it.

Astrid stands outside, by the door on which there is to be no knocking except in an emergency. She stands in this garden with all its old trees and bushes and all the fields and woods that go on and on beyond the house. She is not being disturbing in any way. Compared to those trees round the summerhouse she is the kind of meaningless tree that gets planted in the grassy areas of the car parks of supermarkets.

The typing noise has stopped.

What? her mother shouts in the summerhouse.

Astrid takes a couple of steps back.

I can hear you, her mother shouts. What?

Nothing, Astrid says. I was just standing.

Her mother sighs. Astrid hears the chair grind back. The door opens. Her mother comes out into the sunlight. She squints her eyes, steps back into the doorway and lights a cigarette.

There, she says, and breathes out. Now. What?

I didn't want anything, Astrid says. I was just here.

Her mother sighs again. A bird sings somewhere above them.

Did you see that thing that happened to the Indian restaurant yet? Astrid says.

Her mother shakes her head. Astrid, I can't think about anything else just now, she says.

She is always having to think about dead people from sixty years ago. They take up her whole mind when she is writing about them. Personally Astrid thinks there would be a lot more usefulness in finding out about things that were happening now rather than people who died i.e. more than half a century ago.

When I woke up I had like a thumbprint here where I slept on my thumb, Astrid says. It was amazing.

Mm, her mother says not looking at Astrid, who has her thumb on the place in her face where the imprint was.

Like the blue pottery at home, Astrid says. You know how it's got the thumbprint in it from the artisan who made it.

Her mother doesn't say anything. The bird is still singing, the same three notes over and over.

It's a really nice day, isn't it? Astrid says.

Mm, her mother says.

This is how summers used to be, isn't it, before I was born? Astrid says.

Mm, her mother says.

Like with days like this going on for months, like all the way from May to October some summers, i.e. like summers were perpetual in the past? Astrid says.

Her mother doesn't notice. She doesn't react at all. She doesn't even say Astrid stop saying i.e. like she usually says. She leans on the doorframe and carries on smoking. Astrid feels her own face redden. Cigarettes are completely insane. They are harmful. They smell terrible. They typically cause all sorts of diseases and not just to the person smoking them.

She kicks at the tall grass round the wall of the summerhouse. She knows better than to say out loud the thing about not smoking. It is a thing you can only say at certain times.

Who's the person? she says instead.

What person? her mother says.

In the house, Astrid says.

No idea, her mother says. Is Michael still here?

Uh huh, Astrid says.

Is Magnus up? her mother says.

Don't think so, Astrid says.

Remember, if you go anywhere this afternoon take your mobile, her mother says.

Uh huh, Astrid says. Her mobile, switched off, is in the bottom of one of the litter bins at school, at least that's where she left it three weeks ago. If her mother and Michael knew this they would literally have kittens; they are still paying rental. Her mother thinks she is always safe carrying it, because of being able to call, obviously, but also because people can always be geographically pinpointed by the police by their mobile phones if they go missing. THINK UR SMART ASTRID SMART. U R A LOSER. UR NEW NAME = ARS-TIT. FACE LIKE COWS ARS 3 HA HA U R A LEBSIAN U R WEIRDO. It is dangerous, to bully. A girl died last term at Magnus's school because of internet bullying. A letter came from Magnus's school about it. You are supposed to tell people if you are being it. But that was at Magnus's school. At some point soon Astrid will tell her mother that her mobile phone has been stolen.

Have you eaten something? her mother is saying.

I had some toast, Astrid says.

Don't do that, Astrid, her mother says.

Astrid doesn't know what it is she's supposed to not do. What? she says.

Kick like that, her mother says.

She stops kicking. She stands with her arms out from her sides. She looks at her mother. Astrid is personally never going to be a size fourteen. It is gross. Her mother is gently tapping the end of the half-smoked cigarette on the frame of the door. When the cigarette has gone out she scrapes with her foot at the ash that fell, puts the half-cigarette back into the packet, goes inside the summerhouse again and shuts the door.

Astrid waits for the noise of typing to start. It takes a moment for it to. Then it does.

She looks at the way the sun comes through the leaves above her head i.e. the story of Icarus who had the wings his father made which the sun melted when he flew too close. She wonders what the difference would have been if the father had made the wings for a girl instead, who maybe would have known how to use them properly. But probably this would depend on how old the girl was, because if she was Astrid's age it would be okay. But if she was any younger it would be dangerous, she would be too young, and if she was any older she would be worrying about people seeing up her skirt and the sun melting her eye make-up.

Astrid also knows from somewhere, Magnus probably, that it is supposed to take twenty-eight seconds of looking straight at the sun to make a person go blind. What would it be like to be blind? You couldn't go to a play, or a film; there would be no point. A tv might as well be a radio. She shuts her eyes. How do blind people decide where the beginning of the day is if they can't see if it's light yet or not? if they can't see the difference between the light and the dark that happens every day?

She wonders what would happen if she were to stand here and make herself look at the sun for twenty-eight seconds.

Her eyes would melt.

There would be doctors and ambulances etc.

She steps into the blaze of sunlight between the two old trees. She opens her eyes wide and looks directly up. One, she counts. One second is too much. Her eyes clam shut. Inside them is all flashing light. When she opens them she can't see anything except the circle of the sun she looked at, bright orange. She closes them again. The outside world shifts on her eyes, like an inside photograph. Then the inside photograph is laid over the outside world when she opens them. If she could take photographs with her eyes it would be amazing. If she could do this and she had wings i.e. in the myth with the wings, she could take aerial photographs. She would soar over everything like in a helicopter. The substandard nothing of the village would be obvious. The smallness of these massive trees she is standing under would be like obvious. She could fly over home. She would be able to hold the whole house in the palm of her hand. She would fly over the whole school in a fraction of a second. All the people in the classrooms doing French right now, and the sports field, the playground, the streets around the school, would be like nothing, smaller than the palm of her hand and getting smaller and smaller depending on how high in the sky she chose to go.

It is too hot in the garden. She walks towards the house. That's her bedroom, there. She would fly up and go in through the window. She would never have to touch the carpet with her feet again. She would be inches off the ground all the time. She would fly up to Magnus's window now and peek below the blind. (Magnus Smart. Magnus Berenski. Magnus is not even bothered. Why should I care about him when he clearly doesn't give a fuck about me, he said once. But Magnus can remember him. He put me on his shoulders and we walked along the beach, he told Astrid one night in the treehouse. He let me spoon sugar into his tea.) The blind on Magnus's room is always down. He doesn't ever have a bath or a shower. He doesn't get up until two in the afternoon most days and only comes downstairs to bring down dirty dishes, collect his dinner in the evening and take it back upstairs with him and lock the door again. Their mother and Michael are losing their patience. But even though they are annoyed with him he still gets to do it. Because typical and ironic, when Astrid tried taking her dinner up the stairs as well all hell broke loose.

The four-wheel drive is gone from the front. There is an old white car in the driveway. The kitchen is empty. The tv is on by itself in the lounge. A man has gone missing on the news, and the police have found a body. Astrid puts today's newspaper on the armchair and sits on it, keeping her arms and hands tucked into herself away from the arms of the chair. The newscasters and the people they are interviewing keep saying that a man went missing and that they have found a body, but nobody will say that the body is anything to do with the man who went missing or vice versa though it is obviously what they mean. It is something to do with the war. The prime minister comes on surrounded by cheering Americans and having his hand shaken by men in suits. After the news a woman in a tv studio talks for ages about what happened to her bowel movements since she started putting her food into special combinations. Not just a pretty faeces, the woman presenter says. Everybody in the studio laughs. It is juvenile. A man phones up the programme and says he has been drinking his urine. The people in the studio discuss whether it would make you feel better to drink your own urine. Astrid is glad that Michael isn't here since he would probably think the urine thing was a good idea and make them all do it.

This tv only has thirty or so channels on it and most of them are rubbish. It is typically substandard. There is a 1980s music video show on another channel. It is okay to watch it because neither of them is around to act like a loser going on and on about when pop music was political or do the stupid jerky dance. The video comes on about the girl who is in a café having a cup of coffee and reading a comic then the comic comes alive and she becomes part of the story. The boy from the strip cartoon winks at her, then he holds out his hand, right out of the picture into her world and she takes it in her real hand and goes inside the cartoon world and becomes an illustration like him, but out in the real world the woman who owns the café can't work out where the girl has gone and is angry she left without paying for her coffee so she screws the comic up and throws it in the bin which in comic world is i.e. a total disaster and makes men with crowbars break in and start being violent. So the boy actually rips his world open for the girl (his world is made of paper) so she can escape through the ripped paper of the comic back into her own world. The woman in the café in the real world finds the girl, who's real again, collapsed on top of the café rubbish bin behind the counter. So the girl grabs the comic all crumpled out of the bin, goes running out of the café, runs all the way home and sits in her bedroom and tries to smooth it out. The end of the video is the boy from the comic (who is the lead singer from the pop group too) trying to smash his way through into the girl's real world to become real, not just an illustration.

Astrid goes through to the kitchen and breaks the loaf in two without touching anywhere any knife will have been. She fists out the bread from the inside. She eats it. On her way back through she pulls her t-shirt up over her mouth and breathes into the cotton, then smells the cotton where she breathed. It smells quite nice. She wonders if this is what she would taste like, this sweet breath-smell taste, if she could taste what it was she tasted of, or if someone else was maybe to. But what if she tastes disgusting? She worries about tasting disgusting through two more videos. Then she switches the tv off.

She fits the battery into the camera and checks it's working. She tucks the charger, still charging the other battery, in behind the old horrible crime and mystery paperbacks on the lowest shelf of the bookcase. She listens in the hall but there is no sound of Magnus. She leaves the house by the front door. Her mother and Michael keep saying how amazing it is to be in the country where you can trust people and leave your car unlocked and the doors of the house unlocked or even wide open. Astrid checks that the front door is locked behind her. If people want to rob the house they can go through the open French windows in the garden and her mother can be to blame. They won't find the charger unless they've come specifically to steal old Agatha Christie novels, which would be an excellent ironic crime.

She walks down the lane that leads to the road that leads to the village. It is very hot. She thinks of the house behind her, sitting there full of all its horrible things, and all their holiday things there too, arranged and different, like things floating on a too-hot surface. It is the moment before burglars walk in through the garden and just help themselves. But, since it's the moment before this happens, the rooms downstairs are all empty, nothing in them but things, like the rooms are holding their breath in this hot summer air. Magnus told her that idea about how something on a film is different from something in real life. In a film there is always a reason. If there is an empty room in a film it would be for a reason they were showing you the empty room. Magnus held up a pen, then dropped it. He said if you drop a pen out of your hand in real life, that's all it is, a pen you dropped out of your hand there on the ground. But if someone in a film drops a pen and the camera shows you the pen, then that pen that gets dropped is more important than if it's just a dropped pen in real life. Astrid knows this is true but she is not completely sure how. When Magnus is speaking to people again she will ask him. She will also ask him, if she can remember to, about why she poked the dead animal with the stick without even thinking. Magnus will know the reason she wanted to and will explain it. That would be amazing, if she had had film of that animal, not dead yet but just before it was run over, the minute before it was run over. There it would be, sitting at the side of the road, whatever it was, a rabbit, or a cat, just sitting there with its eyes and paws etc.

But it would only be really amazing if you watched it knowing what happened after it. You would know, but the animal wouldn't. If you knew *this* and had film of *that* it would be exactly like if you were looking at a room before it was burgled. You would know, but the room wouldn't. Not that a room can know things, as if a room could be alive, like a person. Imagine a room alive, its furniture moving round by itself, its walls calling across the room to one another. A living room, ha ha. Imagine if you were in the room, the living room ha ha ha, and you didn't expect it to be alive and you went to sit down on a chair and the chair said get off! don't sit on me! or it moved so you couldn't sit on it. Or if walls had eyes and could speak i.e. you could come into a room and ask it what had happened in it while you were in another room and it could tell you exactly what

Hello, someone says.

Hello, Astrid says back.

It is the person from this morning who was lying on the sofa in the front room.

She is walking alongside Astrid. She has two apples in one

hand. She weighs them both, looks them over, chooses which one to keep for herself.

Here, she says.

The apple comes at Astrid through the air and hits her quite hard in the chest. She catches it in the crook of her arm between herself and her camera.

Astrid, the person is saying. Astrum, astralis. How does it feel to have such a starry name?

Then she starts talking about stars. She says that because of light pollution from cities and streetlights, the night sky can't be seen properly any more and that all over the western world the sky now never gets properly dark. In more than half of Europe, in America, all over the world, people can't see the stars any more in the same way as they were able to in the past.

She has a way of talking i.e. Irish-sounding, or maybe a kind of American. Though Astrid hasn't said anything about how she's going to the Curry Palace, she starts talking about it. She says has Astrid seen it and that it is a blatant act of local crime. Why else would anyone throw black paint at the door and windows of the only ethnic restaurant in the village? The only ethnic restaurant for miles around?

Astrid holds her camera higher, then up near her eye, though it's off and its lenscap is on. She hopes the person will see it and ask her about it. But the person has stopped talking now and is walking faster, a little ahead of Astrid. Astrid lowers the camera. She starts eating the apple. She hadn't realized how hungry she is.

How did you know? she calls. I mean about the restaurant? She hurries to keep up.

How did I know? the person says. How could you miss it? How could you not know?

Are you something to do with the house? Astrid asks.

The person has stopped in the road. She is looking hard at the ground. She suddenly crouches down. Astrid sees a bee there, crawling on the rough tarmac, the large kind of bee, the furry kind. The person gets something out of the back pocket of her cut-offs. It is a little packet. She rips it at its corner and empties something out of it into the palm of her hand. She folds the corner of the packet and slips it into her back pocket again. She spits into her hand. It is gross. She is rubbing spit into her palm with her thumb. She scrapes her spit on to the road just along from the bee, which has stopped still now because something is close to it that's bigger than it.

The person gets up and walks on, licking her palm and rubbing it on the denim of her cut-offs.

Astrid thinks about asking her how old she is. She looks at the person's legs with the hair on them. It is obscene. She has never seen anything like it. She looks at the bare feet, walking on the road surface.

Is it sore walking on your feet like that? she asks.

Nope, the person says.

Did your car break down? Astrid says.

They are on a road Astrid doesn't recognize now.

Cars are a very bad idea in such a polluted world, the person says.

Did you rent us the house? Astrid says.

What house? the person says.

The house we're renting, Astrid says.

The person finishes her apple and tosses the applecore into the air and over a hedge.

Biodegradable, she says.

Why did you do that back there, near the bee? Astrid asks.

Resuscitation, the person says.

She takes the sachet with the folded corner out of her

pocket, makes sure it's tightly folded down, then tosses it to Astrid. It is the square kind they have in café sugar bowls, the kind that has random information on it like the dates of birth of classical music composers or famous writers or the names of famous cars and horses that won races. On one side it says WHITE SUGAR. On its other there is the ripped-through picture of a fighter plane and the words 'LD WAR 2 1939– 1945 An Estimated 55 Million Lives Were Lost'.

Keep it, she says.

Astrid balances the apple and the camera and tucks the sugar into her own back pocket. All along the new strange road the person is talking about how, after the summer, the worker bees throw the drone bees out of the hive because there's not enough food for all the bees for the whole winter otherwise and the drones' usefulness in the hive is finished now that the queen has been fertilized, and the running of the hive is changing because of the summer being over, so what the worker bees do is chew off the wings of the drones then let them drop out of the hive on to the ground.

What happens to them then? Astrid says.

Birds eat them, probably, the person says.

The drones do their best, she says, to hold on to the bees that are ejecting them; they hook on with their feet as their wings get chewed off. But for now, she says, the drones are safe. It's only the beginning of summer.

She is some kind of a bee expert. She is whistling now. She puts her hands in her pockets and walks along the road ahead of Astrid, whistling a tune like a boy would. Astrid is going down a road that she doesn't know with someone she doesn't know, and her mobile phone is buried in rubbish and she is now officially untraceable.

How do you know my name is Astrid? she calls at the back of the person's head.

Well, that's easy. The man told me, she says.

What man? Astrid asks.

The man. The man at your house, the person says. The man who's not your father. I don't have a father either. I never even met mine.

Astrid drops the half-eaten apple. It rolls off the road on to the verge. She almost drops her camera, but catches it against her as it slips. She stops. She stands in the middle of the road.

Car, the person says as a car rounds the corner ahead of them. Astrid jumps to the side. She tries to remember what she's said so far out loud. It wasn't anything about anything. She never said anything. She never mentioned a father or not a father. The car swerves round her and she feels the air as it passes. It is as if a car engine is roaring in Astrid's ears and eyes, though there's no wind at all and the noise of the car is gone and it's a completely calm, completely sunny, ordinary July day.

The person has carried on walking. Come on then, if you're coming, she calls without turning.

She is now going quite fast. Astrid starts to run. But it's as she catches up that it dawns on her. The whole point of being awake first in the morning is that there is nobody else about, just Astrid, yawning, near-asleep, leaning out of the open window, steadying herself with her elbows on the sill to film the light coming. All there is is the waking-up birds, all there is is the trees moving in the wind, the crops moving, no cars on the near or the faraway roads, no dogs barking, no nothing. But on one of the mornings Astrid, through her camera lens, which has a very good long range, has seen her.

It was her.

It was definitely her.

It was far away, there was someone sitting on the roof of

a car, a white car, Astrid is sure it was a white car, parked at the very far edge of the woods. She seemed to have binoculars or maybe some sort of camera, like a birdwatcher or an expert in some kind of nature. Funny that she was watching the only other person awake, who almost seemed, typical and ironic, to be watching her back, and now when Astrid catches her up on the road she talks as if they're midway through a conversation and as if she takes it for granted that Astrid understands exactly what she's talking about.

Because listen. If you tell anybody at all, the person says, I'll kill you. I mean it. I will.

The person turns and looks at her. She starts to laugh, as if something has delighted her, something so funny that she can't not laugh. She makes a wide-eyed face at Astrid and Astrid realizes that the reason the person is making this face at her is that her own face is so wide-eyed. Her eyes have gone so wide open that she can actually physically feel how wide open they are.

The person, still laughing, reaches out her hand, puts it firmly on the top of Astrid's head then raps twice, hard.

Anybody in? she says.

For quite a while after, Astrid can feel the place where it knocked. The top of Astrid's head feels completely different from the rest of her, like the hand is still there touching her head.

Something has definitely i.e. begun

the beginning of this = the end of everything. He was part of the equation. They took her head. They fixed it on the other body. Then they sent it round everybody's email. Then she killed herself.

That noise outside is birds. It is swifts. They are making their evening noise. Birds are pointless now. Evening is pointless. They took her head. They put it on the other body. They sent it round the email list. Then she killed herself.

It was a Tuesday. It was just a Tuesday. Magnus knows there will never be just a Tuesday again. There used to be just days in the week where everything felt like normal. It is astonishing now to think of that feeling. They walked along the corridor, just walked down the main stairs then along the corridor like it was any old Tuesday. He was wearing what he'd put on that morning. It was just clothes. The clothes didn't mean anything other than clothes, then. Was he wearing those socks? He knows he was wearing those trousers. He was definitely wearing those shoes. Those are his school trousers. Those are his school shoes. It was just a joke. They were all laughing about how funny it would be. He was laughing. He was the one who pushed the door open.

He can still feel the door now pushing hard back at him on its fire hinge. They used one of the new scanners. A child could have done it, though, even on old equipment. It was a pretty easy procedure. But they were both computer-stupid. They couldn't have done it if he hadn't shown them. First they scanned her. Then they scanned the other picture. Then they dragged the head on to the other picture. Then they emailed the jpeg round the email list. Then they went on doing things, clothes, shoes, school corridors, home, days of the week, day after day, for days. On one of those days, she killed herself.

Is it light? Magnus blinks at the blind pulled down over the window. You can pull down a blind but it's all still there behind it. Light makes all his muscles like they've been drugged. It makes his legs not want to do anything. It makes his arms like they're set in stone. If it's light, it'll darken. They took her head. They put it on a different body. They sent it to people. Then she killed herself.

He sits up, holds his stomach. He squints in the light, the dark. Far far away, as if he is looking down the wrong end of a telescope, he can see a boy. The boy is the size of a small stone. He is shining, as if polished. He is wearing his school clothes. He waves his arms the size of spiders' legs. He speaks in a squeaking voice. He says things like *well cool, quality, quite dodgy really*. He talks all about things. He talks as if they matter. He talks about calculus, about how plants grow or how insects reproduce or about what the inside of a frog's eye is like. He talks about films, computers, binaries. He talks about how holograms are produced. He himself is a hologram. He has been created by laser, lenses, optical holders, a special vibration-isolated optical table. He is the creation of coherent light. He is squeaking about it now. He says coherent light is well cool. He is quality. He contains all the necessary information about his shape, size, brightness. He is sickeningly excited about himself. He is quite dodgy really. He only seems to be dimensional. He is a three-dimensional reproduction of something not really there. He was never really there. Look at him. He's lucky. First of all, he doesn't exist. That's lucky. Second, he is so small. He could slip away under a door. He could slip away through a crack in a wood floor. Third, he is back then, before. The real Magnus is this, now, massive, unavoidable. The real Magnus is too much. He is all bulk, big as a beached whale, big as a floundering clumsy giant. He looks down at his past self squeaking, shining, clambering about on his own giant foot as if the foot is a mountain, an exciting experiment or adventure. Hologram Boy has no idea what the foot belongs to. Hologram Boy could never even imagine such monstrous proportions. First they. They then. Then they. Then she.

Magnus lies on the floor face down. If he were really a whale, even a beached whale, it would still be possible. If he were a fish, any kind of fish, in or out of water. It would be possible to go on breathing. Or it would be a relief, the flap, the panic, the not being able to breathe any more. If he were just the water or air that passes through the gills of a fish. Or if he were a dog, any dog, on or off a lead. If he had paws with pads leaving galloping trails of pawprints along a beach in the sand. If he were a dog with a dog-brain. He could be a dog from now on. He would be loyal. He would wait all day in a house for nothing but someone to come home. He would enjoy the waiting. He would eat from a bowl. He would drink with his tongue. He would do as he was told. He would do stupid tricks. It would be brilliant. He could be any animal. He could be a badger. He could live in the ground. He could eat worms. He could dig with talons. There could be earth in his talons. He would gladly be a badger.

Bad ger. Even the word is lucky. It is only half bad. Magnus himself is all bad. He was bad all along though he didn't know it. He believed in his own coherent light. He was wrong. He was bad. He was bad all through. He is like a rotten fruit hanging off a branch. If anyone picks him, splits him open, they'll see. The world with its Tuesdays, holograms, whales, fish, dogs, frogs, snuffling wet-eyed badgers, reels away from him. It reels away by itself as if he is watching down the telescope an old-fashioned film of a foxhunt in old England, all jolly hunting horns in its fading soundtrack as the fox disappears then the backs of the horses, the backs of the huntsmen recede. Hologram Boy smiles a boyish smile, waves his handkerchief as if goodbye, then all the Christmases, Easters, half-term breaks, summer holidays flicker away, gone. Magnus pulls the duvet off the bed. He rolls it, heavy, over his head but he can still breathe, even against the weight of it. Worms are eating her. There is earth under his nails. The bone, the muscle that held her body on her head were snapped. The end. It is because of him. He showed them what to do. They did it. They put her head on another body. They sent it round the email list. She killed herself.

Magnus is shocked every time he thinks it. What really shocks him is that nothing happens. Nothing happens every time he thinks it. Didn't it matter? Doesn't it? They took her head. They put it on the other body. Even though it was a lie it became true. It became more her than her. When he got home that Tuesday he checked his mail. The message flashed up. He was on the email list too. He clicked on her. There she was. It was funny. He laughed. He thinks of it now. He gets stiff. Up he comes, up he goes. Every time he thinks of himself standing looking at the picture they made, on his own, in his room. He was in on the whole thing. Every time, up he comes again. Ah. He is so fucking monstrous. He can't stop. He has tried. Try harder, ha ha. It was hilarious. The way her head was on the neck. The way the breasts were angled. The way hardly anybody knew. But he knew. Now he is laughing again, stiff as hell. He is foul. He changed himself when he changed her. He snapped his own head off without even knowing. It transplanted itself on to a body he doesn't know. If he looks in the mirror he looks the same as before. But he isn't the same. It is a shock to see how like himself it looks. She saw herself changed too. She never knew who did it. It was him. He did it. Magnus is God. There is actually no God. There is only Magnus. Hologram Boy believed God probably existed. Hologram Boy saw God as more human than human, moving among subhuman beings like the weekly celebrity among the Muppets on The Muppet Show. Hologram Boy was the form captain. He made the speech in Assembly on Remembrance Day for the dead soldiers in the world wars. It was Hologram Boy's job to lay the wreath, lead the squeaking prayers, lest we forget. But Hologram Boy was all forgetfulness. He was lucky. Hologram Boy's brain was all blank light. There will be no forgetting now. There will be no forgetting ever again. The remembering is like the darkening. The darkening is now happening more. It is like the way having the flu made light go dark. It is almost exactly like when he had flu in December 1999 January 2000. The old series about the Germans down below in the submarine was on tv every night, the pressure, whether or not they'd survive being that low. The first time it happened was two days after he knew she'd done it. He was standing, just standing, by a bus stop by a tree. The tree had a sticking-out branch. Above the tree, round the branch, the sky got darker. Then everything got darker. But nothing had changed. The sky was blue. There were no clouds. There was no change in the air. It just carried on, getting darker. It went away after he slept. Then it came back again the next week in the café. Then it went away. Then it came back, darker. There is no warning. It is like when you are at a cinema waiting for the lights to go down. Something inside your brain knows that at any moment the lights will dim. So sometimes you feel them go dim when they haven't done anything, haven't changed at all. It keeps happening to him. It is caused by causal effects. He has caused it. He has changed the way the world is. They played about with her head until they were happy. They shifted it about on the neck. Then they delivered it. Then she killed herself.

Forty people in the upper sixth probably saw that picture. Twenty-six people in the lower sixth probably saw it. Magnus can't calculate how many other people possibly saw it, or can still see it. There was a lecture about it at Assembly, after. Milton said the people who sent it should come forward. It would come to light, he said. When it did it would be worse for them then if they didn't come forward now. But it can't be traced. There is no way the email can be traced back to them. Anton found a zipcode from somewhere in the States. He got it out of the back of the magazine. The message was sent from 'Michael Jackson'. When Magnus checked his mail that Tuesday night that's the name that came up. He had laughed. He had thought it was well cool, to be part of it. He was in the common room when Jake Strothers first came in with the photo. Jake Strothers stole it from the school office. Jake Strothers had been sent to deliver a note but when he got there the office was empty. The filing cabinet was wide open. Jake Strothers looked in it. He found the photo on her file. She was in the lower sixth. She was near the front of the Ms. Jake Strothers came into the common room, showed it to Anton. Anton had the magazine in his locker. He fetched it out, folded the photo on to it. Jake Strothers went crazy. Don't for fuck sake you're bending it. Jake Strothers had wanted to go out with her. That's why he stole it. He didn't want a phone photo. He wanted a photo taken unsneakily. Then Jake Strothers actually looked at the composite Anton made by folding it. They both laughed. He asked them what they were laughing at. They wouldn't tell him or show him. They knew he hadn't ever done it yet. They could sense it like it was written on his forehead. Anton said: I'm not responsible for what happens to homosexuals. Magnus said he wasn't. Anton said: I believe you, honest. But I'm not responsible either for what happens to innocents who see things they're not ready for yet. Anton was right about that. Hologram Boy was so fucking pure. Hologram Boy noted his own stiffs like interesting science experiments. At this point he was still Hologram Boy. At this point Hologram Boy was still under the illusion that he was Magnus Smart. It was still an ordinary Tuesday. Magnus Smart knew something they didn't know. A child could do it for fuck sake. Anton, Jake Strothers, hadn't a clue. They were computer illiterates. Magnus Smart told them there was something he could really show them. It was after school hours. There was hardly anybody about. They walked along the corridor past the cleaners. They went down the main stairs. The school was empty, hollow, big as a whale. They walked through it like they were inside its ribs. But now Magnus is bigger, more bloated than the school. He knows more than the whole school does. They pushed the door open. What is it you see when you see a photo of someone? There was an article in the paper. It said: the tragedy of the loss of Catherine Masson who went to Deans. A happy generous well-loved person a polite bright girl a good friend whose friends would all miss her a keen member of the Lapidary Society. The photo in the

42

paper was the school photo. It was the same one. Magnus knows more than she knew. Magnus knows more than her family knows, even now. All the people who got the email, all the people who read the paper, Magnus knows more than them all. Anton knows. Jake Strothers knows. Nobody will know Magnus is anything to do with them. They are known as bad. He is known as good. They met at the side gate as if by chance they were just walking along at the same pace going home from school. Anton was looking at the ground as he walked. He said nobody was to know, nobody was to say. They all agreed, they nodded without saying anything, no one would know. But Magnus knows. He is all swollen up with knowing.

He did it.

They did it.

Then she did it.

She killed herself

Magnus shakes his head hard inside the duvet. He says the words to himself again. She. Killed. Herself. Nothing. Words are pointless. They mean nothing. They don't do anything. He pulls the duvet off his head. He is still in this room. They are on holiday in Norfolk. Is it dark yet? Doesn't matter. Catherine Masson. He says her name to himself. Catherine Masson Catherine Masson Catherine Masson. Doesn't matter doesn't matter doesn't matter. She was happy, generous, well loved. Her friends loved her. He puts his head inside the duvet again. She was bright. She was polite. She went to the Lapidary Society. At the Lapidary Society they polish stones to make things, like jewellery or cufflinks. She would have kept the things she made on her dressing table in her bedroom. There she is, at a computer, in her bedroom. It is a girl's neat bedroom. It has posters of singers, pictures of tv personalities, cut-out pictures of horses, baby animals,

43

tigers, polar bears. It is the moment she opens an email saying it is from Michael Jackson. She clicks on it. She stares at the screen. Ah. Doesn't matter. Doesn't matter. He passed her one time in the corridor. He is not even sure it was actually her. She was just a girl. She was in a bunch of loud laughing girls. They were terrifying. They were going to French. They were eating crisps, jostling each other through the classroom door. They were shouting about how stupid the French word for tyres was. *Les pneus*. Was it her? If that girl was her then they passed within about half a metre of each other but they didn't know. She didn't know who he was. He didn't know it either, who he was. She is lucky. She is dead. She can't feel anything. He can't feel anything either. But he isn't dead. After, the rumour went round the school. A girl from Deans had killed herself in the bathroom in her house. Her mother or her brother had found her. He heard the rumour in Maths. Charlie wants to add an extension with a floor area of 18 metres squared to the back of his house. He wants to use the minimum possible number of bricks, so he wants to know the smallest perimeter he can use. Write down an expression for the area in terms of x, y. Calculus is the mathematics of taking limits, especially with reference to rates of change. There was nearly a war over who discovered it first, whether it was Leibniz or Newton. Leibniz invented the = sign. Maths = finding the simple in the complex, the finite in the infinite. He sits on the carpet, holds his feet. It was a Tuesday. The whisper said she hung herself. Sarah walks with her brother Steven from home to school every day. One day they time themselves. When Steven gets to school he says: it takes me 6 mins 8 seconds. When Sarah gets to school she says: it takes me 6 to 7 minutes. Whose answer is more likely to be true? Hologram Boy, who was going to University, squeaked inside his head that hanged was more correct than hung.

Correction. There is no University. University is not more likely to be true. University is laughable. Calculus is laughable. Everything is a joke. Even the days of the week are laughable. It was a Tuesday when he heard it. If, that other first Tuesday, he just hadn't been in the common room after school. If he hadn't known so much. If he had just not. If they hadn't. Then they hadn't. Then she wouldn't have. Then she might still.

That noise is someone knocking on the door of this room. He lifts his head out of the duvet. Above the door is the jut of a roofbeam. It is probably not original. His jeans are in a pile on the floor. His long-sleeved shirt is piled next to the jeans. All the clothes he brought here are in a pile by the sink. She goes through the door of a bathroom. She sits on the edge of a bath. She is surrounded by shower curtain. What would there be a smell of? Toothpaste, soap, clean things. There would be carpet under her feet. Maybe the carpet would still be damp from the last person who had a bath or shower. She must have been quite resourceful. There aren't that many obvious places in a bathroom. It is a strange room to choose when you first think about it. But after you think about it for a while it makes perfect sense. You go in then you go out of a bathroom. You don't stay for any length of time. It's where you empty all the shit out of yourself. It's where you get clean. She looks at him from the edge of the bath. She is polite, bright. She is wearing her school clothes, like in the photo. She looks straight at him. She nods. It is the least she can expect. She expects it. No she doesn't. She's dead. She isn't looking at him, she can't look at anyone. But there she is, sitting on the edge of the bath, looking at him. She holds up the showerhead like it's her who's got the stiff, not him. She waggles it at him. She gives him the eye.

45

That noise is someone knocking again. Someone is shouting something. It sounds angry.

Right, Magnus calls. All right.

His voice sounds strange. It seems to come from his stomach. It is surprising to him that there is still a connection from his middle to his head.

Magnus, the voice behind the door had called. How long ago did it call? It had been his mother's voice. The words weren't angry in themselves but the sound of them was. Come downstairs now. All right. All right. It is all he has been saying for days. He is monstrous, a liar. All right.

Magnus gets up. He feels dizzy from standing. He walks across to the door. Then he notices his bare arm above his hand. He notices his chest. He looks down. He isn't wearing anything. He turns back into the room. He pulls on the shirt. He takes a button, lines it up against a buttonhole in the shirt's other side. But he can't get the button to go through the buttonhole. He can't get his hand to do it. He pulls on the jeans. He tucks himself in. He takes the zip, finger there, thumb there. He makes an effort. The zip goes up.

He unlocks the door. Above the keyhole the door has a latch. It is pretending to be an authentic old latch. The door is pretending to be an authentic old door. Maybe everything there is isn't authentic any more. Maybe everything there is is a kind of pretending. Magnus opens the door. The hall is too bright. This is the kind of bright that goes dark. Over there is the door to the bathroom. It has a little rectangular plaque stuck on it that says the word Bathroom in swirling writing with an illustration of a watering can next to the word. Flowers are growing out of the word, through the letters, the capital B. Magnus shuts his eyes. He is sweating. He feels across to the wall with his hands, feels with his toes for where the floor turns into the stairs. He opens his eyes a crack when he knows he must be past the bathroom door. He goes down the stairs.

Down in the hall he turns to face the door of the room where they eat every night. He steps towards it, stands in front of it. He raises his chin off his chest. All right. He opens the door.

There's his mother. She doesn't know anything. She is saying something. Magnus nods. He picks up the plate from a place at the table with no one sitting at it. His sister takes the plate from him. She doesn't know either. She is putting something on the plate out of a dish on the table. It smells of fish in the room. Michael is saying something. He doesn't know anything. He is pointing at something. Magnus nods. He hopes that this nodding is what they need. He nods several times, as if he is very sure of what he is nodding about. Yes. Yes, definitely. No worries. He takes the knife then the fork from the place setting. He slides them against himself where his back pocket should be. They must have gone in. There is no sound of them hitting the floor. He can feel the cold of them against his back. The cold is astonishing. It is astonishing to feel anything. The feeling won't last.

If you don't mind, I'm going to take this up to my room, Magnus says. Please excuse me. Thank you very much.

He is polite. He is like her. She was polite, bright. *Les pneus*. His mother says something. It sounds like an exclamation mark. His sister hands him his plate. He takes it in both hands so as not to drop it. The fish on it is dead. It is headless.

The door swings shut behind him. Ahead of him are the stairs. They are deep in shadow. The door with the word Bathroom on it is at the top of them.

Magnus walks to the front door. He puts the plate down on the carpet. He opens the door, picks up the plate again. It is so bright outside. It is unbelievably bright. He hunches his shoulders. Any minute now it will darken. That noise is just wind in leaves, the noise of birds. The birds are like a nightmare. They are making the same noises, again, then again, then again. The leaves are hissing. Birds are pointless. They make a noise to reproduce for their own genetic ends. Leaves are pointless. Trees are pointless. They sustain the lives of insects which die almost as soon as they're born. The leaves help to produce oxygen that keeps people breathing, then people stop breathing. Insects pollinate a third of the food that people who are horrible to other people, people who are going to die because of it, eat. Hologram Boy: *a purpose-bred silkworm moth in caterpillar form can transform the mulberry leaves it eats into half a mile of unbroken silk thread stronger than a steel thread of the same thickness would be*. Information is a joke. It is laughable. It is so meaningful it is meaningless. The other noise is the crunch of his own feet on gravel. It doesn't hurt enough. He looks down at the ground moving under him. It doesn't hurt now because he is walking on grass.

He is on a little bridge. Under it is a clogged river. He leans over, scrapes the fish off the plate with his hand. Most of it lands in the water. Part of the tail-end breaks off, lands in a bush on the bank. He drops the plate in after the fish. Then he gets the knife out of his back pocket, then the fork. He drops them over too.

The bush is a scratchy one. He leans right into it to reach the bit of fish that got away. When he has it, he goes to the river's edge. He wades in, then he cups the broken pieces in the water. He lets them float out of his hands. They waver then sink, flaking apart, settling round his feet.

Magnus sits down on the bank in the litter, the weeds. His jeans are wet up to the thighs from the river. Once last year

two girls from school came round looking for him. It was a
Wednesday. He was at Chess Club. Astrid told him
afterwards. She had been in the garden. Two girls had put
their heads over the gate. Was this where Magnus Smart
lived. Was she his sister. What girls? he asked her. He couldn't
believe it. It was unbelievable. What did they look like? Don't
ask me, Astrid said. I didn't recognize them. They were a lot
older than me. They were like your age, sixteen at least. One
had her belly button done. But what did they want? he said.
Hologram Boy. He was all shiny with amazement. They
wanted you, Astrid said, but you were out. Why would they
want me? (Hologram Boy. He was so brightly shining.) Well
duh, Astrid said. She was throwing her powerball at the wall
by the Egyptian prints, an illegal thing to do if Eve ever knew,
catching it, throwing it again, catching it, throwing it again.
The prints shook as the ball hit the wall. No, really, what?
he said. I told them you didn't live here, she said. I told them
you have a body odour problem you have to go to the doctor
about. I said you were at a special clinic taking medication.
I told them your nickname was Wankstain. I told them you
were gay. They were both really ugly. The one with the belly
button was infected. One of them had a scar like this all
down her face. They both smelt disgusting of dead fish.

He caught her powerball in mid air. He ran up all the stairs
to the second floor with her screaming give it back all the
way up past the bedrooms, grabbing at his arm when he went
up the ladder to the loft. He threw it out of the velux, it fell
deep into the shrubbery where she'd never find it. She said
she didn't care about a powerball so he went to her room to
get her old Gameboy. He threw it out of the window down
into the bushes too. For nights he tried to work out who
those girls had been. He made lists inside his head of the ones
who had pierced belly buttons, at least the ones he knew

about. It was amazing that a girl with a piercing would want to come to his house. He had lain in bed doing it with a sock, imagining one of those girls was Anna Leto. A girl like Anna Leto would never have come to his house looking for him, would she? She definitely had a piercing. It was legendary. She ran the hundred metres. Athletes aren't supposed to have them. They tried to give her a hard time about it but because she kept winning things for the school they couldn't. After the soldiers went into Iraq Anna Leto was still anti-war. This made a lot of other people be it. Hologram Boy believed in order vs chaos. Obviously some countries knew more about good order than others. But if Anna Leto was anti-war then it wasn't all wasters desperate to get off classes on protests who were it. Even Hologram Boy was nearly persuaded. Magnus thinks of the moment when Anna Leto stood up in class to tell them to be anti-war.

But he daren't remember properly. He doesn't dare let it into his head in case. Because there they all are by his garden gate. They're waiting for him, the girls. All the girls he will ever know. Every girl he is ever going to look at. Every girl who is ever going to look at him. They all have it, her face, the school photograph face.

He glances up at the sky, then down again. Bright means dark. At his first Assembly on the first day of the school year Hologram Boy read out the reading about how the earth was a formless void. There was deep darkness. God said let there be light. There was light. God used the light to divide the day from the night. Anton had a new phone. It lit up. It played a dimensional tone. He was using it to take photos of bits of girls at Registration. He lined it up on passing girls, pressed the button. All the girls look the same this year, Anton said in his ear. He was pleased someone like Anton had singled him out to tell him something like that in his ear.

Look, Anton said. They all look like they're off porn sites. It was true. After you've looked at sites, all girls start to look like it. Commercials on tv begin to look like it. Singers on the music channels all look like it, well, the girls anyway.

He could ask Eve when he gets back if he could borrow her laptop. He could ask Michael, if she is busy on hers or doesn't want anyone to touch it. He can work out the email, it is people's names plus sp for school pupil dot deans dot co dot uk. Dear Catherine Masson. I am. I hope you don't mind me. Please don't mind me emailing you but. You don't know me but. You have no idea how. I wanted to say I'm really. I'm so. Magnus is sick on to the grass by his hand. Nothing much comes up. For a moment he feels much much better. Then the good feeling goes. She walks into a classroom but all the faces are strange to her. She can't make them out. They used to be her friends. Now she doesn't know any more. There's no knowing. For all she knew it could have been any one of them. She walks down a street she knows or into a shop she's been in a thousand times. It's strange to her, it's changed. She sits at home. Her family, sitting in the same room, is in a different world, one where things haven't changed. She sits on her bed. Catherine Masson. Doesn't matter. Here it comes, the darkening, it comes down on him, the grass he's sitting on turns grey. He shakes his head, closes then opens his eyes. The leaves above him are black. The river is black water. It ends in a massive smashed black ocean. It doesn't matter any more what numbers add up to. All the billions of electrical impulses, billions of messages sent in miraculous nanoseconds at the flick of a button or a key or a switch across grey miles, countries, continents, the whole wide world: this is all it adds up to. He did it. They did it. She got the message. She killed herself.

He gets up. He walks back over the bridge, retches again.

51

He holds on to the wall of an old white building. He has the slightly better feeling again. He thinks he could stay like this for a while, head down, shoulders against the wall, looking at the rubble, the weeds pushing out of the place where the building meets the ground. But a man comes out. He shouts at Magnus until he gets up. All right, Magnus says. He nods sorry to the people through the big window in the front of the building. They are looking at him in amazement. There is a vase of flowers on the table between them. Magnus crosses a road. He walks past a chip shop. Some boys are standing outside it. They shout something after him. He wonders how it would feel, to be kicked to death by them. He tries to remember a prayer, but the only thing that will come is the words for now I lay me down to sleep I pray the Lord my soul to keep if I should die before I wake I pray the Lord for them to come after me, knock me down then kick me until I'm dead. But they don't, because there is no God. They shout something else but they don't come after him. Never mind. Magnus feels better. He knows what to do. He has known all along, really.

He walks back to the house. It is the correct house, the house he left, because its front door is still open. He can see Eve, his mother, sitting in the front window. She is holding a wine glass. He can see the colour of the wine in it. It is dark. Winedark! Hologram Boy squeaks. It makes Magnus laugh. His stomach hurts. His family is laughing at something too, something else, in the front room of this strange house. He can hear Astrid, his sister, laugh. She has no idea. After all, Hologram Boy is saying, why get three yobs outside a chip shop to do it when nobody's better at doing things than you yourself are? Absolutely, Magnus agrees. Absolutely. He says it every time his foot hits a step all the way up the stairs. BATHROOM. It is on there for the benefit of all the people who temporarily pass through this rented holiday house. He is level with the picture of the watering can. He puts his forehead against it. He pushes open the door with his head.

It is a very plain bathroom. It is so meek, mild. There's the white bath with the rough-rubber grips in the shape of a large foot with toes, stuck to the bottom of the bath's insides so people won't slip getting in or out. There's the power-shower. There's the pink bathmat folded on the edge. There's the shelf of towels, the spare pink soaps. There's the sink. He has only come in here when he hasn't been able not to. He has urinated in the sink in his room. He has kept his eyes shut when he absolutely had to come in here, when he needed to

Excrete, Hologram Boy says brightly.

He sees himself in the mirror. He looks remarkably like himself. It is a joke. The towels on the shelf are folded so neatly. The walls have more of the little plaque-pictures of garden things on them, flowers, wordless pictures. A cheap amelioration of a room which we like to pretend is nothing to do with the cloacal. Hologram Boy says the words amelioration then cloacal in his unbroken voice. He waits, head cocked, for Magnus to say absolutely back.

Fuck off out of here you fake little shit, Magnus says to Hologram Boy.

Hologram Boy fizzes a little, as if overloading. Then he snaps into nothing in an instant like someone unplugged him.

Magnus breathes out hard. He looks at the ceiling above the bath, at the fake beam. He wonders if all the rooms in the house have them. He stands on the edges of the bath. He tests the beam with his weight by hanging off it by his arms. It holds, firm enough. He takes off his shirt, ties one arm of it to the beam with a slipknot. He tugs on the other arm to tighten it.

The girl in the magazine had breasts that were angled as if

coming at you out of the picture. There was no escape from them. They were like two stupefied eyes looking at you. They were quite big, with lighter-darker tan marks over their nipples. She had dark hair. He can't remember what kind of eyes. Her nipples were large, hard. Her mouth was red, open. Her wet tongue was there, her teeth. Her body was arched so you could see into all her holes.

Catherine Masson was wearing her dark blue school pullover. It had the shield embroidered into it on the left side of her chest, with its words in it, Endeavour With Concord, the Deans motto. She was wearing a tie with a full-looking, soft-looking knot. She was wearing a white school shirt with its lapels tucked neatly into the pullover. She was smiling a friendly smile. Her mouth was closed. Her skin was clean-looking. Her brown hair was shoulder-length. Her fringe was quite far down over her eyes. You could still see her eyes quite clearly. They were deep brown.

He used one of the new scanners with a Mac. First he scanned both using Photoshop. Then he clicked on the marquee tool. He showed them how to select the head, copy then make a new layer with the body. Then he showed them how to cut round her with the lasso. He showed them the background eraser. He explained pasting the head, dissolving the edges, blending it normal. He showed them save, then how to send it as a jpeg, then finally how to delete.

Magnus puts his arms around himself. He is shivering. He is freezing cold. He stands in the bath on the rubber grip. Reaching up, he ties a slipknot in the other arm of the shirt. He stands up on the edges of the bath again. He loosens the knot until it is big enough. He pushes his head through it. It hangs loose all the way round his neck. Its cuff juts into his ear. He is at the angle of depression. Conduct an experiment to discover how a beam will progressively sag with a loading upon it where m = the load in tonnes, where n = the sag in mm. He takes one foot off the edge of the bath. He holds it in the air. He should say a prayer. Now I lay me down to sleep. He is shaking. He puts the foot carefully back on the edge again. He can see the dust on the top of the beam, the places whoever painted it black missed with the brush. He is level with the lampshade. He can see the cobwebs on its upper rim, the dust on the top of the lightbulb. He can't work out why the lampshade isn't shaking too, why the whole room isn't shaking.

Meanwhile someone has come into the bathroom. It is his own fault. He should have locked the door. He didn't remember to lock it. He is such a failure. He can't even do this properly.

It is an angel. She stares up at him.

It was just a joke, he says.

I see, she says. Is this a joke too?

She leans on the towel rail, watching him. She has yellow angelic hair.

It's my fault, he says. Because first I showed them how to. Then they sent it round the list. Then she. I have to.

He starts to cry. He holds on to the beam.

I understand, the angel says.

It was an accident, he says.

Okay, the angel says.

The wrong thing happened, he says.

I get the picture, she says.

She is nodding. She is very beautiful, a little rough-looking, like a beautiful used girl off an internet site. She is all lit up against the wipe-clean wallpaper.

Do you need some help? she is saying. When you're ready I can knock myself against you here so you lose your balance.

She has him by the leg; she is holding very tightly round it with both her arms. Her arms are bare. The leg she is holding is shaking against her chest, her face.

Just say when, she says into his jeans.

He swallows. He is crying. His face is all snot or sweat. Sweat or snot is all up the cuff of the shirt by his nose.

Come on then, she says. Ready when you are. You want to?

He nods. He tries to say the word yes. He can't. Sweat or crying, he doesn't know which, falls from somewhere, hits his chest.

Are you sure now? the angel who's holding him says

the beginning again!

Extraordinary. Life never stopped being glorious, a glorious surprise, a glorious renewal all over again. Like new. No, not just like new but really new, actually new. Metaphor not simile. No *like* between him and the word new. Who'd have believed it? That woman, Amber, had just pushed her plate away, pushed her chair back, long-limbed and insouciant and insolent as a girl, and had stood up and left the table, left the room, and Michael, now that all that was opposite him was her empty chair, could stop, breathe out, wonder whether Eve, who was scraping at breadcrumbs with her napkin, if she looked up, say she looked up and looked him straight in the face, would see the surprise of it written all over him. His face would have that astonished look more usually found on the face of a soprano hitting a high perfected oh.

Eve was looking up at him now. He straightened his mouth in case. The perfect pitch of her, in his ears and his head and jangling all through his blood, so that he leaned forward at the table then sat back again then couldn't think how to sit. What Apollinaire called 'that most modern source of energy – surprise!', words he wrote on the whiteboard at the start of every academic year, modernist literature being full of the energy of surprise, as Dr Michael Smart told the new third-years every first term. But Dr Michael Smart God bless him and all who sail in him had never before hit a note quite like this one for this startling a quality, this piercing a newness, this jolt of an oh.

He sat forward, leaned on his hands on the table. He sat back again. His arms and legs were acting new to their sockets, his hands had never before been at this loss as to what to do with or where to put themselves. But he felt so exceptionally good. He felt remarkable. He drummed at his legs; they felt good. He stretched out in his chair. Every muscle felt strange, new, good. Eve was still speaking, oblivious, good. She was clearing plates, telling Astrid something. They were saying something about spoons. Spoons! There was a world, with spoons in it, plates, cups, glasses. He held his wine glass out in front of him, swirled the end of the wine in it, watched it settle. It was good. It was Gavi, from Waitrose.

If he were this wine glass there would be hairline cracks holding him together, running their live little electrical connections all over him. Oh. To be filled with goodness then shattered by goodness, so beautifully mosaically fragmented by such shocking goodness. Michael smiled. Eve thought he was smiling at her. She smiled back. He smiled at Astrid too. She gave him a murderous look and scraped a plate. Good for her! Obnoxious little creep. He laughed out loud. Astrid glared at him and left the room. Both Eve's children needed therapy. Magnus was a case in point. To refuse to eat with them was one thing. To refuse, though, to acknowledge a guest in the room, to act as though she weren't there, to refuse to say a simple hello, as he'd just done, was quite another kind of rudeness, deeply reprehensible no matter how profound the adolescent hell angst etc. and Michael, who generally kept well out of that side of the parenting thing, was actually going to make a point of talking to Eve about it later in bed. But now a large moth had come in through the open window and was hanging around the lit candle. Moths couldn't help it, *like a moth to a*, they were genetically programmed to be attracted by light, of course they saw all light as love-light. When they swam through air drunk towards it it was because they believed, genetically, that they'd found their Übermoth, the one moth in the whole world especially for them. They would even try in a clear night sky to fly as far as the moon if the moon was full.

No preamble – this one went straight into the flame and dropped on to the table with an audible thud. It was a brownish moth. Over it went on itself, and again, and again. He could make out the furred blur of its facial features as it flopped itself round on its damaged wing (he had always had excellent eyesight, good eyes; well into his forties and no need at all at any point in it for glasses or contacts or whatever). Moths and candlelight! Like a moth to a flame! Dr Michael Smart had been reduced to cliché!

Deeply exciting, though, cliché was, as a concept. It was truth misted by overexpression, wasn't it, like a structure seen in a fog, something waiting to be re-felt, re-seen. Something dainty fumbled at through thick gloves. Cliché was true, obviously, which was why it had become cliché in the first place; so true that cliché actually protected you from its own truth by being what it was, nothing but cliché. Advertising, for example, loved cliché because it was a kind of pure mob truth. There was a lecture in this, maybe for the Ways To Read course. Source? clearly French, he would look it up. Larkin, for instance, the Sid James of English lyric poetry (now that was quite a good observation, Dr Michael

Smart firing on all cylinders) knew the power of cliché. *What will survive of us is love*. His old racehorses in that horse poem didn't 'gallop for joy' but for *what must be* joy. Larkin, an excellent example. Comic old sexist living all those years in the nether librarian circles of Hull, no wonder he was such a curmudgeon, but he could crack a cliché wide open with a couple of properly pitched words. Or when Hemingway, for example, wrote it before anyone else had even known how to think to express it, *didst thou feel the earth move* (or however it was he faux-peasantly put it in the not-very-good For Whom the Bell Tolls, 1941 Michael believed), could he have had any idea how his phrase would enter the language? Enter! The language! Cliché *was* earth-moving, when you understood it, when you felt it, for the first time. Earth and movement, an earthquake, a high-pitched shattering shift in the platelets far down in the heat, below the belt, beneath the feet. Moth plus flame. Right here, right now, Michael had seen and felt and heard the precise drama of the moment when that moth wing singed and went brittle in the candle. He had felt the whole substantial impact of individual moth hitting individual table. He had felt these things, yes, more acutely, more truly, more *surprisedly*, than he had maybe felt anything since he was, oh, he didn't know, a fresh-faced (cliché!) twelve-year-old, and not a twelve-year-old like that one over there either, he thought to himself, casting a glance over the top of the bland combed hair of the head of Eve's curmudgeonly girl, not a twelve-year-old now, when nothing was new and everything was so already known and been and done and postmodern-t-shirt-regurgitated, no, he meant a back-then tank-topped twelve-year-old at the side of deep water, lying deep in the long grass and the noise of summer, the sweet core-line of a piece of the grass in his mouth, when for the first time he saw two insects, two flies of some kind, long-legged water-flies, a metonym you might say for the whole of summer, and the one was on the other's back in a sheer frenzy of what Michael knew for sure, for the first time, the most innocent time, was entry.

Entry! It was a wonderful word. The fly in the fly. The boy in the grass. The grass in the boy. The boy deep in the day and the day deep in the boy. He particularly liked the word sheer too; as a word it was calmed and smoothed yet still so bloody boyishly enthusiastic, it still went as far as it could. The sheer surface of the water, imagine, then someone diving right into it, unabashed.

She had entered him like he was water. Like he was a dictionary and she was a word he hadn't known was in him. Or she had entered him more simply, like he was a door and she opened him, leaving him standing ajar as she walked straight in. (Ajar! When is a door not a door? Terrible joke from boyhood television which he was never supposed to watch, it was never funny, that joke. Not till now. He had never been open enough to it till now, ha ha!)

Who is she? what's her name again? Eve, taking him aside before supper in the kitchen, quietly asking him. It was unlike Eve to forget such things or be cavalier with the details of made appointments; he was suddenly pleased, it made him feel good about his own organizational clarity. He had been dotting the insides of a trout with knobs of butter. Too much and it's spoilt. Too little and it's spoilt. Well judged. Amber something, isn't it? he'd said, poking butter in under the slit.

She had rung the doorbell this morning. He had opened the door and she'd walked in. Sorry I'm late, she'd said. I'm Amber. Car broke down.

Dessert, is there any? Eve was saying now, passing through the room. She was smiling her persuasive smile. She was in a good mood. The fish, by the way, was perfect, she said as she leaned across him.

Yes, he said. It *was* good, wasn't it? (She had liked it; she had liked everything he put on the table, she had wolfed it all down so, well, wolfily, fishskin and all, that Astrid had stared at her and Michael had found himself wanting to stare too; he had forgotten what it was like to have what you made be quite so physically appreciated. Nobody ate like that any more, like they were hungry, like what they were eating was good.) I thought Pears Belle Hélène, he told Eve. I just need to heat it. I'll do it in a minute.

Eve took the last of the plates, took the plate from between his hands. She kissed him as she did; he kissed back, light but pressing; she put her hand to the back of his neck then went through again. The sun was gone but the evening was warm. She would come back into the room any moment now. Any moment now she would come down the stairs, turn towards the door and enter and sit there opposite him again and he'd glow inside his clothes like a reddening electric element. Would he start to smoke and smoulder? Would his clothes melt into his skin? Would his khakis start to singe where they stretched tight against his thigh?

He drummed his thigh again with his fists. Ha-ha! he said. Astrid gave him a withering look. He ignored her. He sang. *It's a Barnum and Bailey world, Just as phoney as it can be.* His voice sounded good. His reflection in the window made him look boyish. *But it wouldn't be make-believe.* The moth had stopped moving. He went to pick it up off the tablecloth and it moved again; it had only been resting. He got it; he held it close to his nose; he was tempted to put it in his mouth.

He was smelling a moth for the first time.

Moths didn't smell of anything.

It was fluttering inside his hand. Thank you, moth, for your excellent simile, he said as he closed his hand, leaned over, closed his eyes, put his hand through the open window and dropped the moth out, not looking to see where it landed.

Good luck, moth. *If you believed in me.*

Michael liked the old songs. They were lyric poems in themselves. He breathed in, deep. The air was new and clean to him. He had finally mastered an oven he didn't know, in a house that wasn't his, and an electric oven at that, always the worst. There was moth dust left on his hand; he wiped it on his jeans. The doorbell had rung. He had opened the door and in she'd walked. She had walked right past him. He had answered the door while he was still on the phone. Hang on, he'd said to Philippa Knott. Something's come up, can I call you straight back, Philippa? His own voice saying Philippa's name, he could hear it, gravelly, soft-rough, skin needing a shave, hotel afternoon skin, the promise of it going into Philippa Knott's ear. As he'd answered the door he'd been wondering what he'd call her, Pippa, Pip maybe. A pity she used her full name already, the full name was always more meaningful, more full; these other names were child names; pity; they tended to like to be asked to be adult. He'd ask her later what she'd like, which name she'd prefer him to use. She'd have been waiting for someone to ask her; they generally always were; generally loved to be asked.

Philippa Knott had known to return and hold his eye over the heads of the others in the second-year Victorian seminars; she was slim and dark, long dark hair with a very slight wave in it. Good dress sense, almost totally straight-A in her accumulative writtens for continual assessment, a couple of notably good second-year essays especially one on pre-Freudian suggestion in Robert Browning's monologues; she'd written very well about the surfaces of stone in Browning's poems, the way Browning made such sensuality of stone, he'd told her so in his office at the end of the summer term when she'd come to ask him to supervise her American dissertation. She'd looked him directly in the eyes then too; she was game, that was good. Excellent, he'd said, are you here in town for the summer? because I'll be popping up and down, marking, office work, holiday home in Norfolk, have you got a mobile number, or? He'd put his hand on the small of her back as she'd left his office and she'd let herself shift, just slightly, back into it. He'd phoned Justine to check her summer exam results, mostly beta-alphas; good, that settled it.

Then this happened.

Sorry I'm late. I'm Amber. Car broke down.

He hung up on Philippa Knott, *something's come up, can I call you back?* She walked straight in and sat down on the sofa. She looked at him, uninterested; she wasn't here for him. A bit raddled, maybe thirty, maybe older, tanned like a hitchhiker, dressed like a road protester, one of those older women still determinedly being a girl; all those eighties feministy still-political women were terribly interested in what Eve did. Hippie name. Amber. Ridiculous name.

I'm Michael Smart, Eve's partner, he'd said and held out his hand. She looked at his hand, looked back at him, blank. He held it out, up in the air for a moment more then dropped it to his side, cleared his throat.

Eve's in the garden, he said. She's working in the summerhouse. I'm sure she'll be here in a moment. She's expecting you, yes?

She was looking out of the window. She didn't say anything.

Perhaps I can get you something while you wait? Some fruit, or maybe a drink of something? (Inside he felt blustery, overdone.)

Hunky-dory, she'd said. Is there coffee?

Hunky-dory. He hadn't heard the words hunky-dory for years. She had an accent that sounded foreign. Scandinavian. It came into his head in the kitchen, how he used to cycle to the campsite and lean on his bike-seat over the fence watching the holiday people and it was the year of the two Swedish girls, their hair so light it was almost white, and the patchouli oil smell, and the friendship bracelets, the leather thongs they had round their necks, they had ankle bracelets too, and their toenails painted purple and black, and the way they strode laughingly between the tents and the taps where they filled their water-bottles, and they called to him over the fence and tempted him in through the unzipped front of their tent, so small from the outside like there'd hardly be room in its upside-down V for them both to fit in it, never mind him as well. Anna-Katherine, and the other one was Marta. He was ten. How old had they been? They can't have been more than nineteen, maybe twenty; they'd seemed unthinkably adult to him, he'd known for sure he'd never be the kind of age they were. Where were those girls now? What had happened to them in their lives? Thirty years ago. More. 1971. Like yesterday. The noise of the rain on the outside of the tent, the backs of his bare legs in his shorts on the warm damp of the groundsheet.

He hadn't thought of it for years.

Those girls had stayed at the site for a week. His mother had wanted to know where it was he was going on his bike every evening and not coming home till it was nearly dark. He wasn't supposed to hang around there; the kind of people who did things like going camping weren't ever going to be the right kind of people. He had said he was at Jonathan Hadley's house. (Jonathan Hadley was some kind of chief pathologist high-earner now with a big family and a three-and-a-half-million riverbank house in Walton-on-Thames.) So every night he took a book off the classics shelf, had it in full view casually under his arm, told her he and Jonathan Hadley were spending the evenings reading in Jonathan's bedroom. That was admirable. That was allowed. Great Expectations. *My infant tongue could make of both names nothing longer or more explicit.* The Mill on the Floss. Volume One, Book First, Boy and Girl. Vanity Fair. A novel without a hero. The Manager of the Performance. The smell of wet grass. The light filtering through the walls and door-seams of the tent. When those girls left, the patch of flattened grass where their tent had been was unbelievably small. The new people to take the space were from somewhere unpleasant, Bournemouth, Bognor Regis, a big family. The father's face was tough-looking as he erected the complicated framework of their tent, which took up three spaces. They were loud. They shouted across the grass to each other. He was nothing but a local boy leaning on a fence.

He had brought through a pear for her, elegantly sliced. She ate it immediately, one slice after the other. Did she notice it was elegant? She didn't say thank you.

So what happened to it, your car? he'd said.

She didn't say anything. Maybe she hadn't heard him because of the noise of the vacuum cleaner above.

Your car? he said again, louder. Broken? he said. Won't start, or?

She shrugged.

The battery? he said. He said it too loud into a pause in the vacuum noise.

She looked blank. Maybe she didn't know the word battery.

I put the key in, turn it, nothing, she said, looking away from him.

She had probably left the lights on overnight, he thought. Maybe the small ceiling light. There was probably no petrol in it.

He sat on the arm of the sofa. So, where are you from, originally? he'd begun to say, when she broke in with a shockingly long sentence:

But do you think it will be okay and do you think it's completely safe there just left abandoned in the middle of the road like that?

The sentence ended. The noise started again over their heads.

Well, I've absolutely no idea, he shouted. To be honest it doesn't sound safe at all, if it's as you describe. Where is it?

She gestured vaguely in the air, towards the window.

I mean, it's very quiet round here, he shouted against the vacuum roar. The incongruity made him laugh. She looked at him. He stopped laughing.

But what I'm trying to say is, he said, I wouldn't consider anything left in the middle of the road very safe. It depends how middle of the road you mean.

Yes, she said. Right in the middle. Just on a corner I had to leave it where it stopped. All night I was driving to get here.

She rubbed her eyes. She did look exhausted.

Everything's still in it, she said.

You haven't left anything valuable? he said. Like a laptop, anything like that?

She nodded, gestured at his mobile on the table.

Everything, she said.

You really shouldn't have, he said. Nowhere's safe these days. Not even out here in the middle of nowhere. Thieves everywhere.

She sank back into the sofa and closed her eyes, shook her

head. She rubbed her head with her hand. She seemed to be waiting for something.

Well, I –, he began. I don't know much about cars. I don't have much time. I've got to nip in to London in about an hour.

She looked utterly bored.

Where is it exactly? he said. If you like, I could take a –

She had already stood up, taken a car key out of the pocket of her shorts and was holding it out. She sat down again when he took it.

But will the coffee be very long? she said.

It was real coffee, he had wanted to tell her. He wanted her to know he was the kind of man who would never make instant. He couldn't imagine any way of saying it, though, that wasn't patronizing-sounding. She'd notice when she tasted it, he was sure. He called Philippa Knott on his walk down the road. He blocked the number first; never ever give out the mobile number. *Hello Philippa? Dr Michael Smart here*, the sound of his voice in the open summer air was strange, bombastic. He fixed their appointment for two p.m. Just on the bend of the road by the start of the woods was a square little Volvo of some kind, parked quite neatly by a ditch. It didn't look like it had been broken into. Nothing looked forced.

Its door was open. He let himself in, slid back the driver's seat. He knew nothing about cars. This might not even be her car. But he inserted the key in the ignition and the engine started first time. Magic, he thought. Magic touch. Stroke of luck. She'd probably flooded it, done something with the choke. Something like that. Maybe it had overheated. She'd said she'd been driving all night. He drove it up to the house rehearsing how best to say it. I turned it over a few times and it started sweet as anything. I had a poke about under there and it all seems okay now. I'm not much of a car expert, but I had a little look at it and now I think you'll find it's running sweet as a nut.

Sweet as a nut! Michael was still at the table, sitting back and sitting forward, shifting about in his chair. Eve and Astrid were in the kitchen arguing about something. She still hadn't come back in the room. She would, any moment. It was actually true, he thought. Nuts were sweet. No innuendo. It was innocent. It was an innocent fact. Nuts had a unique sweetness.

Philippa on the other hand had, as soon as she was kissed, put her hand inside his trousers and cupped his balls. She was an ambitious girl. Let's start at the very beginning, he'd said to her as he'd unbuttoned her top. It's a very good place to start. But she didn't get it. He was still explaining as she unzipped him and pulled him out about how it was a camp reference. She had had no idea what he was talking about. Oh, right, she said, that old film, then squeezed him so hard that he couldn't speak.

It was a little depressing; he couldn't help feeling misunderstood, cheated even, as he went in under her dress. He liked to give the little speech about Agape and Eros. He liked to tell the story, how he had admired her in class when she'd said ' '. (He'd been ready, and hadn't needed, to use the moment Philippa Knott had said the thing about Charlotte Brontë being Emily Brontë on valium.) He liked to describe it, how he'd been pacing his study, preoccupied, unable to sleep for nights on end because the witty or clever thing she'd said in the class had revealed to him out of nowhere, as if he had been struck by lightning, that he wanted to take her and have her right then and there regardless, in front of all the others. He liked to tell it like this then sit hangdog on the chair, not his chair at the desk but one of the

chairs they themselves sat in, ashamed of himself, shaking
his head at himself, looking at the ground. Then the silence.
Then the glance up, to see. One (was it Kirsty? Kirsty
Anderson, graduated high 2:1, 1998) he had induced
ingeniously; she had looked the type. He had recited the
fragment about Sappho, I am undone by a beautiful youth,
and told her in his quiet voice, I am myself a lesbian. Don't
laugh. I sense myself as feminine, my soul is definitely anima
and the thing is I can't help but love girls and women. (He
believed she was now working for the BBC.) They used to
like that kind of thing more; he used to use quotes from
writers like Lillian Hellman and Alice Walker, writers whose
reputations were clearly passing; now it was Philippa Knott's
proposed Contemp. Amer. III dissertation: 'The American
Presidential Erection: images of power in the novels of Philip
Roth'. He had sped there on the train thinking he could let
her gently know, before he touched her (if she let him touch
her), that she'd passed her exams. Pippa passes, he thought
he could say gently in her ear; witty and apt. But she'd
brought her own condoms and she rolled one on him herself
as she propped him back against his desk, leaving him feeling
weak, as if hospitalized.

Ten years ago it had been romantic, inspiring, energizing
(Harriet, Ilanna, that sweet page-boyed one whose name
escaped him now but who still sent a card at Christmas). Five
years ago it had still been good (for instance, Kirsty
Anderson). Now Michael Smart, with twenty-year-old
Philippa Knott jerking about, eyes open, on top of him on
his office floor, was worried about his spine. He closed his
own eyes. How disappointing it was, he thought, that the
film actress Jennifer Beals, whom he'd watched a late-night
programme about by chance a couple of months ago on one
of the endless channels they now subscribed to at home, had

clearly had facial surgery to make herself look like all the other Hollywood women.

He could see the rough wood on the underside of the desk. Maybe Philippa Knott had been the wrong choice. Maybe he should have gone, after all, for the shy redhead, what was her name, Rachel, from Yorkshire, who reputedly wrote poetry and whose dissertation subject was comforting: the importance of authenticity of voice in post-war British working-class literature. Would Rachel have been more authentic? Different from this. But then again. This had its satisfactions. Michael's brain emptied. He came.

When he could think again, when Philippa Knot climbed off, stood up and rearranged herself, he found he was thinking of Aschenbach in Death in Venice, the moment when he takes sly pleasure in the thought that the delicate beautiful boy will probably die young. She checked her mobile. She had missed a message. She combed her hair and redid her make-up in a hand-mirror she propped on his bookshelves, by the dictionaries. He got up with his back to her, tucked in his shirt, reholed his belt, straightened his crease. Had he had her or had she had him? The teacher fucks the student. The student fucks the teacher. He began talking, because the room was resounding with the little noises of Philippa Knott. Word order was crucial in English, he told her, in a way it wasn't, interestingly, in many other languages, for instance in German, because subject and object were signalled separately by masculine / feminine inflexion. There wasn't much call for accidence in English, which had lost its inflexion tendencies in the Middle English period. Accidence won't happen, he said, ha ha, as he folded the used condom into a sheet of A4 off the top of the pile of old Yeats handouts. O love is the crooked thing, the handout said halfway down. He saw the words. A stanza from one of the pre-

71

Responsibilities poems, from when Yeats was still young. Then the ageing Yeats, trying to restart the dodgy old motor of his virility. Yeats, the old monkey. Philippa was talking about results and degree projections. I did quite well, she was saying. Justine in the office told me. I'm really pleased actually. I got a projected 2:1 for my Shakespeare and a projected 1 for my Victorian and a. Michael had felt suddenly exhausted. Before she'd left she had sat down in her usual seat three along from his desk and got a pen, a foolscap pad and a clutch of shiny Roth paperbacks out of her bag. She sat, waiting. Terribly sorry, Dr Michael Smart said. But we'll have to do this next time, Philippa. I'm afraid I have other appointments this afternoon.

Okay, she'd said unconcerned, and fished in her bag for her diary.

After she'd gone he looked at his watch. It was 2.24. He stood for the next ten minutes at his window. It looked into an empty courtyard, nothing in it, brick on brick. He liked it, usually. He could usually make something of it. But today the courtyard was irrefutably nothing.

He switched his computer on and checked his email. One hundred and seventy-three new messages. The weight of admin in this profession was becoming more than a joke.

He walked the length of the department corridor and met nobody else; he listened at a couple of doors and heard nobody. Friday afternoon, post-exams, not exactly surprising. When he called in at the office for his snail mail Justine was polite but untalkative, seemed disdainful. Secretaries were the unacknowledged legislators of the world. He hated it when they took against him. It made it such hard work. Justine never liked him at the starts and ends of term. It was possible that she was jealous.

He washed himself in the staff toilet, dried himself off with paper towels. He looked away from himself in the mirror. Back in his room he went through the new emails and deleted without reading the seven messages from Emma-Louise Sackville, who had just graduated with a rather poor 2:2 and was at the needy, tearful stage. Even if her results had been better, no difference. He made it very clear. He took pains to make it clear all year. After graduation there were no more supervisions.

He switched off the computer. He locked his door.

He thought about going home, to the empty house across the city. There would be no maudlin kids there with their foreheads high and full of misery, there would be no preoccupied grumbling dark-eyed Eve. The house to himself. He looked at his watch. Too late. He walked to the station. The streets were full of irritating young and happy people. He sat down on the train. The carriage was sparsely peopled, unlike on the way in, when the train had been crowded and sun-flashy, the trees cornucopiae of summer greenness and his mood as buoyant as the trees were. He had shot into the city today like a fool, laughing to himself at the local villages' free paper left on the seat beside him. Coffee morning advertisement with an appearance by the Norfolk Beatles. The Norfolk Beatles! A report of local vandalism. Several angry letters about a group of travellers putting up semi-permanent caravans on some local fields. (Which begged the question: was there really such a thing as a semi-permanent caravan?) A column about the mystery of who could be stealing the council paper-recycling boxes from one particular village. He had been looking forward to telling someone, Justine, Tom, maybe Nigel if Nigel was in, how funny, how odd, how interesting a place it was they were staying for the summer from the point of view of social interaction and demographics, in terms of metaphor for the larger England.

He would have told the stories and everybody would have laughed.

But now that he was headed back there the untold stories made him feel dull and squalid inside. The train doors shut with a cheap beeping noise. He should have gone home when he thought about it, when he had the chance. They should have gone to Suffolk. Nobody went to Norfolk. Everybody went to Suffolk. Dr Michael Smart would never be head of department, not even acting head, via Norfolk. Tom was in Suffolk. Marjory Dint was in Suffolk. She had her own summer place there. Of course, the Dints were loaded. They could afford it. Several people he could think of were in Suffolk, and several others he didn't know about were probably there too. The train swung out of the station. It was one of those lightweight unimportant trains. His heart was heavy. It was heavier than the train. It was heavy all the way through the suburbs. His eyelids were heavy too. He fell asleep.

But it was when he woke up God knew where, in the middle of nowhere, that he saw the empty seat opposite him.

It was just a seat with no one in it, just an empty seat on a train. There were lots of empty seats exactly like it throughout the carriage; there was hardly anyone on this unpleasant train. The seat's fabric was worn and grubby, municipally brightly coloured, as if for children; these trains were an embarrassment when it came to design. But now something in him dismissed what it looked like etc., because what mattered more than anything was that he knew, from nowhere, as if he had been struck by, well, yes, lightning, that he wanted that woman Amber from the house this morning sitting there opposite him in the empty seat.

He shook his head. He laughed at himself. Struck twice by lightning in the one day. He'd just had a girl. *Dr Michael*

74

Smart here. Incorrigible. He settled back in his seat, closed his eyes again and tried to imagine that woman, Amber, sucking him off in the train toilet.

But it didn't work.

He actually couldn't imagine it.

How curious, Dr Michael Smart thought to himself.

He tried again.

He put her down on her knees in front of him at the back of a near-empty cinema. But all he could see was the shaft of light from the projector above him, the movement of lazy dust in it as it changed with the frames, and ahead of him a stray pinpoint of light reflecting back off the screen where the screen had been tinily pierced.

He put her down in front of him on the floor of a London taxi in winter. All he could see was how the lights of London streets and traffic coalesced in the pinpoints of rain on the car window.

Curiouser and curiouser, as the paedophilic mathematician wrote in his book for children, Dr Michael Smart noted cleverly to himself.

But actually it was a little disturbing that all he could picture her doing was sitting there, opposite him, on this train. That was possible. That was perfectly possible. There she was. She was looking out of the train window. She was examining her nails. She was examining the ends of her hair. She was reading a book in a language he didn't know.

He thought about how those two girls in the tent, when he was a boy, sat him down between them, fed him the minced meat and onion they'd fried on their blue-flamed primus stove and ignored him, leaving him dozing against them with his book open at page one in front of him, warm in their body heat as they talked to each other over the top of his head in a language he didn't recognize any of the words of.

Epiphany! dear God it was an epiphany! the empty seat filled with nothing but goodness was a holy moment! and on a filthy train crossing the filthy fens!

But here was a new truth for Dr Michael Smart – because who in the world gave a damn, when he was really alive, like this, about 'epiphany', in other words about what things were called, about devices and conceits and rules and the boundaries of genres, the learned chronologies, the sorted and given definitions of things? Now he had finally understood, now he knew for the first time, exactly what it meant, what the Joyce and the droney old bore of a Woolf and the Yeats and the Roth and the Larkin, the Hemingway, the authentic post-war working-class voices, the Browning, the Eliot, the Dickens and the who else, William Thackeray, Monsieur Apollinaire, Thomas Mann, old Will Shakescene, Dylan Thomas drunk and dead and forever young and easy under the appleboughs, and all of them, all the others, and every page he had ever read, every exegesis he had ever exegesed (was that even a word? who cared? it was a word now, wasn't it?) had been about.

This.

He had sat opposite her at supper. She looked the kind of girl, no, the kind of good full adult woman, that you'd pick up in a car on the road and give a lift to the next village, then she'd get out of your car and wave goodbye and you'd never see her again, but you'd never forget it.

She looked like the dishevelled, flower-strewn girl in Botticelli's Spring.

He had got off the train surprised at himself. He had stood for a moment in the sun. He had stood watching simple sunlight glinting off his car in the station car park. He had felt strange, different, shiny under his clothes, so much so that on his way home he had begun to think he should maybe take an antihistamine. When he got home the Volvo was still in the drive. He parked his car alongside it. He walked round the side of the house. She was lying on her front in the garden examining something, like a girl. When he saw her his heart was a wing in the air.

He had made supper. He had made an excellent supper. Is she staying for supper? he'd asked Eve when she came in. I've no idea, Eve said, have you asked her to? He'd called to her in the garden, where she was lying on the grass with Astrid. Would she like to stay for supper? Astrid, sweet Astrid, called back that she would. Now she had pushed her chair back and left the table, gone upstairs, and Michael Smart had opened his eyes into what he knew was light, like a coma patient after years of senseless dark. He could see Eve. He could see Astrid. He could see his own hands like he'd never seen them. He had seen the light. He was the light. He had been lit, struck, like a match. He had been enlightened. He was photosynthetic; he had grown green. He was leafy and new. He looked around him and everything he saw shone with life. The glass. The spoon. His own hands. He held them up. They floated. He was floating, he hovered in air here on this chair. He was a defiance of gravity. He was fiery, full of fire, full of a new and uncorrupted fuel. He picked up his glass again. Look at it. It had been shaped in an intense heat. It was miraculous, this ordinary glass. He was it. He was this glass. He was that spoon, those spoons there. He knew the glassiness of glass and the shining spooniness of spoon. He was the table, he was the walls of this room, he was the food he was about to prepare, he was what she'd eat, sitting opposite him, looking straight through him.

She had ignored him over supper.

She had ignored him the whole time.

She had sat opposite him as if he wasn't there. He may as well himself have been an empty chair opposite her, a space, an innocent nothing. But he had made her car start. He had made an excellent supper. He would make warmed pears in hot chocolate sauce and then he would watch her cut with the edge of her spoon, scoop it up, put her spoon in her mouth and chew and swallow something that tasted very good indeed, and scoop more food into her spoon and open her mouth for the spoon again.

Any minute now she would step back through the door into the room.

There she was now, in the doorway.

Oh

the beginning was keeping her awake. She by far preferred the edit, the end, where the work in the dark was over and you could cut and cut until you saw the true shape of things emerge.

Where was Eve, exactly? Eve was lying in bed in this too-dark too-hot room, completely awake in the middle of the night, next to Michael completely asleep with his head under his pillow.

No other reason she couldn't sleep? No.

Honestly? Well. That girl of Michael's was a little distracting.

What girl? The girl who had had the effrontery to turn up at their holiday house, eat their food, charm Eve's children, tell what Eve suspected was one of the most blatant packs of lies she had ever witnessed anyone straight-facedly tell. The girl who, at the end of the (actually rather pleasant) evening, for no reason at all, had taken Eve by the shoulders and shaken her hard.

She had what? She had physically shaken Eve and then she had stepped back, opened the front door, said a cheerful goodnight, shut the door behind her and gone out to sleep under the stars (well, actually under the roof of a Volvo parked in the drive, to be more measured about it).

She had shaken Eve? Yes. Outrageous.

Why had she shaken Eve like that? For no reason at all. For no reason Eve could think of. Eve had absolutely no idea.

Who was the girl? She was something to do with Michael.

How was Eve right now? She was very very awake.

Was it a little bit too dark in this holiday house? Yes. It was unnaturally dark for summer. The windows of this house were far too small. The curtains were far too thick.

In what way was the girl 'something to do with Michael'? She was clearly his latest 'student'.

Was Michael pretending she wasn't? Naturally he was:

Michael: (*already in bed, to Eve, as she takes off her clothes and gets ready for bed too*) How did it all go?

Eve: How did all what go?

Michael: What kind of questions did she ask you?

Eve: Did who ask me?

Michael: What's her name. Amber. Were they good ones?

Eve: (*deciding not to mention the humiliation of being shaken half an hour ago in the hall*) How do you mean, exactly?

Michael: You know. Genuine. Was she good? Is she clever? She seems quite clever.

Eve: Well you should know.

Michael: How do you mean?

Eve: Well, she's one of yours.

Michael: One of my what?

Eve: Your students.

Michael: No she isn't.

Eve: Ah. Right.

Michael: (*turning over*) She's here to do some kind of Genuine interview, isn't she?

What is the latest publication sensation to take the literary world by storm? It's the Genuine Article Series from Jupiter Press, a series of 'autobiotruefictinterviews' created by Eve Smart (42), who hit upon the original concept eight years ago when she published Genuine Article 1: The Story of Clara Skinner, a profile of real-life London barmaid Clara Skinner killed in the Blitz at the age of 38. (Other Genuine Articles feature an Italian POW, a cinema usherette, a fighter pilot and an infant evacuee.) Excitement over her most recent Genuine Article, The Story of Ilse Silber, has galvanized the former independent Jupiter Press, whose usual print-runs average five thousand and who have sold nearly forty thousand this spring alone of Silber and seen demand for the previous volumes rocket (one of the reasons for the spotlight purchase earlier this year of small press Jupiter by multi-conglomerate HarperCollins). 'It certainly caught us out,' says Amanda Farley-Brown, at only twenty-seven currently chief commissioning editor at Jupiter Press. 'We are still reeling. We can't believe our luck. We are crossing our fingers that Richard and Judy will feature a Genuine.'

What are these books about? Each takes the ordinary life of a living person who died before his or her time in the Second World War and gives him or her a voice – but a voice that tells his or her story as if he or she had lived on. 'I let them tell the story of an alternative aftermath – the story of how things could have been,' says Smart.

What's so new about these books? Each of the slim volumes is written in Question & Answer format. The 'speaker' in The Story of Ilse Silber, a German-born woman, secretly Jewish but outwardly a good Nazi mother even awarded the special Mother's Iron Cross by Hitler for giving birth to seven children (all of whom subsequently perished in allied bombing raids), is asked to describe the moment of her real-life death when her clothes caught fire in heavy shelling and she threw herself into the Wuppertal river. With the help of Smart's questions she goes on posthumously to describe what happened when she dragged herself out of the river, dried herself off, healed her burns with the help of a local farmer and carried on with life for another thirty years.

Why the Q&A gimmick? 'It's not a gimmick. Every question has an answer,' says Smart.

Don't living relatives have something to say about Smart digging up their dead? 'Usually relatives are delighted. They feel it is very positive attention,' says Smart. 'I always make it clear that the Genuine Articles are first and foremost fictionalization. But fiction has the unique power of revealing something true.'

Have the critics finally caught on to Smart's smartness? 'Ingenious and moving' (Times). 'A book which makes the metaphysical as much part of the everyday as a teacup on a saucer on a scullery table in the year 1957' (Telegraph). 'Brilliant, profoundly atoning. A deeply assuaging read' (Guardian).

Is this ecstatic reception unanimous? 'When will writers and readers finally stop hanging around mendacious glorified stories of a war which may as well by now have happened planets away from this one? Smart's Genuine Articles are a prime example of our shameful attraction to anything that lets us feel both fake-guilty and morally justified. No more of this murky self-indulgence. We need stories about now, not more peddled old nonsense about then' (Independent).

What's next? Speculations about whether Smart will seek a more lucrative publishing deal are rife; meanwhile, is she tucked away working on Genuine Article number 7? Who will she resurrect this time? Only Smart knows.

What does Eve Smart (42) know? God only knows.

Where was Eve Smart (42) right now? Lying next to Michael in bed in an insalubrious holiday house in Norfolk.

No, I mean where was she with her next project? Please don't ask.

Why? She was as useless as a blunt pencil on the floor of the 'elegant summerhouse with internet connection-point' in the 'mature garden' of this 'Tudor Farmhouse next to picturesque village on the Norfolk Broads'. The advert should have read '1930s swindle of a summer let off the Norfolk B roads, next to a near-slum full of houses that look like the kind on old council estates'. Someone had stuck slices of old railway sleeper across the ceilings throughout this house. Mock Tudor all right. Eve laughed, but to herself, so as not to wake him.

Why? Partly because she genuinely didn't want to disturb him and partly because she didn't want to have to have sex again. He was asleep with one of the pillows he'd brought from home over his head.

Why did he bring pillows? He was often allergic to pillows that weren't his own. Other than that he didn't find sleeping difficult. He didn't find beginning anything new difficult either. He was always 'beginning' something else, something new.

Why those little ironic '   '? Eve chose not to answer that question.

What was wrong with the village? Eve had imagined a picturesque place of big comfortable houses with recording studios in their barns, people summering on decking overlooking Norfolk's legendary big open skies. Norfolk did have very nice skies. But one of the village's two shops had a skull in its window with a plastic rat stuck in its eyehole.

83

Why didn't they leave? Eve had paid up front.

Why were they here, exactly? Break from routine. Change of scene.

Why else? To get away from 1. dead people's relations phoning and emailing all the time to agree or disagree or demand attention or money; 2. all the pitiful letters, calls and emails from people all over the country desperate for her to choose their dead relations to be brought back to life in her next book and 3. people from Jupiter phoning several times a week asking her how and where the book was.

How and where was the book? Please don't ask this.

Wasn't she working on it? Every night at six she came out of the shed, went back into the main house and changed, and ate as if a day's work had been done and everybody's summer wasn't being wasted in a Norfolk hell-hole. Today Astrid had come over the grass rather than up the gravel so Eve hadn't heard her, had only just seen the shadow cross the window and only just managed to get up off the floor and on to the old chair at the desk to make a noise at the keyboards of the off laptop. After Astrid had gone Eve had stared at the blank screen. Calm. Measured.

Was Eve Smart a fraud? She had lain back down on the dirty floor after Astrid had gone.

Was Eve, for instance, tired of making up afterlives for people who were in reality dead and gone? Eve chose not to answer this question. *Was she fazed by the popularity of the last volume, which really she should have known to expect given the distasteful rise in public interest in all things Nazi and WWII generally over the past few years and especially now that the UK was back at war again?* Eve chose not to answer this question. *Was it anything to do with that 'mendacious glorified peddled' review just quoted?* Eve chose not to answer this question. *Did Eve really remember the whole of that review off by heart, verbatim?* Eve chose not *was it anything to do with the fact that thirty-eight thousand wasn't actually all that many after all, not in bestselling terms, and now that the big time had arrived, it was disappointingly not that big a time?* No! of course not! Absolutely not. *Did Eve have a subject for her new unbegun book yet?* No. *Why was the very thought of starting a new book, which would bring in relative money and fame, enough to make her spend all day lying on her back on the floor of the mock summerhouse unable to do anything?* Good question. See if you can answer it from the answers already given. She had watched a woodlouse climb out of a crack in the floor and then back down into it again. She had wanted with all her heart at that moment to be a woodlouse with a woodlouse's responsibilities, a woodlouse's talents.

Call that working? Eve took a deep breath. It is very very hard work indeed, she answered, to be a woman and alive in this hemisphere in this day and age. It asks a lot, to be able to do all the things we're supposed to do the way we're expected to do them. Talent. Sex. Money. Family. The correct modest intelligence. The correct thinness. The correct presence.

Isn't that a bit feeble? Any more questions like this and Eve would terminate the interview.

Well, what kinds of question are acceptable? Good questions. Conceptual questions. Not the personal kind. What did it matter what colour Eve's eyes were? Or what gender she happened to be? Or what was happening in her private life or her family?

What was happening in her family? Well, Astrid, for one, was acting very adolescently.

And Magnus? Eve didn't know what to do about Magnus. The way he was acting was very worrying.

And her husband? Michael was fine. Really, he was fine. But these are personal questions. They're the wrong kind of question. The point was: Eve was an artist, and something was blocking her.

Okay, so, what did Eve believe in?

It's a straightforward enough question; what did Eve believe? What do you mean exactly, what did Eve believe?

What did Eve believe?

What credo did she live by?

Well?

What made her think?

What made her write?

What kept her motivated? Eve was motivated by Quantum.

As in physics? Theory? Mechanics? Leap? Quantum was the name of the make of running machine she used.

Running machine? Yes.

She 'believed in' her Quantum running machine? Yes.

Like other people believe in God, or chaos theory, or reincarnation, or unicorns? The Quantum running machine definitely existed. At home, when she couldn't sleep, Eve used the Quantum. On the Quantum she exercised both body and mind while everyone else was asleep, asking herself questions and answering them as she walked or ran in rhythm. (It's actually how she first came up with the Genuine Article concept.)

But there was no Quantum in Norfolk? No. It was at home, in Eve's study.

Why didn't Eve just go for a run, then, during the day, rather than lying about all day on the floor of the shed? Don't be ridiculous. Eve never 'went for a run', anywhere, any time. What a terribly public thing to do. It wouldn't be the same at all.

Why didn't she try it, go for a run, right now, in the dark, in the middle of nowhere, where no one would have seen her? Eve sat up in the bed. She folded her arms.

Okay, okay. Where were we, again? We were on the floor of the shed. Woodlouse.

And what happened then, after the woodlouse? After the woodlouse moment of revelation she had fallen asleep on the floor.

Was it any wonder Eve couldn't sleep now, with all that sleeping during the day? Listen. Eve was lying in this too-hot bed in this too-hot room in this too-hot too-dark part of the world. At home, when she was awake like this, at least there were streetlights.

Why had that girl shaken Eve? Jealousy? Intimidation? Malevolence?

Had it felt malevolent? Well, no. Not really. It had felt as if –

As if what? Well, curiously as if, when she took her by the arms, the girl was going to, well, strange as it sounds, kiss her.

But she didn't? No. She shook her.

If Eve got up and went to the window would she be able to look down and see the car there? The girl would be asleep on its back seat. No, the back seats would probably fold down into a reasonable-sized sleeping space. Or she might be stretched across both front seats. Or in the passenger seat, reclined. Eve lifted the sheet, slipped out of the bed, made her way across to the   ow f***

What was that? That was the dressing-table edge.

*No, what was that supposed word, f***? Can't Eve say the word fuck?* Not out loud.

Why not? Have you never had children? Eve rubbed at her thigh. She hauled back the curtain, holding her breath. Dust. These curtains were probably from before the war, and that was probably the last time they'd been laundered. When they left this house Eve intended to send Mrs Beth Orris a list of what had been unsatisfactory and a demand for some restitution.

Was the car still there? Yes, parked next to their own.

How did someone sleep in a car? How did someone do it every night? Did she do this in the winter as well as the summer? It would ruin your muscles and joints. Wouldn't you like to sleep in the house, Amber? Eve had said when it came to the time to leave and she got up to go. Eve was hospitable. There's plenty of room, she'd said. There's a spare room, nobody in it, I think the bed's even made up, it's absolutely no trouble, you'd be welcome to. No, she said, I like to sleep in the car, and she came forward in the hall as if to give Eve a perfectly mannerly goodnight and thank you for dinner embrace, or kiss, whatever, and instead she took Eve firmly by the shoulders, so firm it was on the verge of painful, Eve could still feel the hold now, and before she had had time even to realize what had happened never mind say anything or be outraged at the intimacy of it, the girl had shaken Eve, hard, twice, for no reason, as if she had every right to.

Why did she think she had every right to? Behind her, Eve heard Michael turn over. She watched him shrug the sheet further down his back. Eve had been sure to kiss Michael hard when his 'student' was out of the room.

Why? To let him know.

What? That it was all all right with her, whatever he was playing at now.

Wasn't the girl (well, hardly a girl, only about ten years younger than Eve for God's sake)

– wasn't her general rudeness to Michael this evening yet more proof of her being one of Michael's conquests? Yes, definitely.

Wasn't she a lot older-looking than his usual? Curiously, yes, and more salacious-looking, rougher-looking, with her high-cut shorts and her low-cut shabby shirt, certainly more shabby than Michael usually liked. She didn't look like a student. She looked vaguely familiar, like someone you recognize but can't remember where from, maybe someone who's served you at Dixons or at the chemist, who you see in the street afterwards. She was also one of the brave ones, brave enough or stupid enough to come to the house. Eve almost admired this.

Were they already sleeping together? Quite possibly, because Amber MacDonald was already nonplussed around Michael. She acted preternaturally coolly around him. She didn't even flicker when he filled her glass.

But when was the last time there had been a dinner like tonight's? with Astrid somehow reduced to sweetness, to red-faced childish hilarity, by whatever the visitor had been whispering in her ear.

When was the last time Eve had seen Astrid like that, like someone had tickled her into submission? God knew.

And how in God's name had she managed to persuade Magnus? She had gone upstairs and come downstairs again and he had been there behind her, she had him by the hem of his shirt, she led him into the room, I found him in the bathroom trying to hang himself, she said. Everybody round the table laughed. Magnus laughed too and sat down next to the girl. He stayed downstairs. He sat with them for the rest of the evening. He ate chocolate pears off the girl's plate.

Where had the strange air of celebration come from? Tonight there had been no yelling about Astrid obsessively filming the various courses of dinner because tonight Astrid's camera was who knew where and Astrid was acting like a civilized being again.

What was Astrid? Poised before her own adulthood like a young deer before the head of a rose. (Deer love to eat roses.) Standing there on her too-thin legs, innocent, unsturdy, totally unaware that the future had its gunsight trained directly on her. Dark round the eyes. Kicky and impatient, blind as a kitten stupefied by all the knowing and the not-knowing. The animality of it was repulsive. She didn't get it from Eve. She got it from God knows where. From Adam. She was so adolescent. Everything about her asked for attention, the way she walked across a room or a shop or across the forecourt of a petrol station, leaning into the air in front of her as if about to lose her balance, mutely demanding that someone – Eve, who else? – put out the flat of her hand and let Astrid push her forehead or her shoulder into it.

What had Magnus been, just a moment ago? Clear and simple as a glass of water. So certain about simplicity that he sat down (at Astrid's age, a moment ago? five years ago?) at the Victorian bureau in Eve's study and wrote to the Queen, Elton John, Anthea Turner, God knew who else, asking them to fight world poverty and help homeless people find somewhere to live. To The Queen, Buckingham Palace, to Elton John, Los Angeles, to Anthea Turner, c/o the British Broadcasting Corporation. The child-Magnus, a sweet pedant. He had had some very pleasant letters back, like the one from a lady-in-waiting somewhere in a palace office who presumably spent all day answering letters like his. *Her Majesty the Queen was very touched by and interested to hear of your concern.* Magnus: a happy accident, a happy unexpected pregnancy, the happy beginnings of an unexpected family. (Astrid, on the other hand: a meant pregnancy; meant, by Eve, to hold unhappy things together.) That happy child version of Magnus had been stolen, by thieves maybe, and a long, thin, anxious, mysterious, self-righteous, impertinently polite boy who took a lot of showers (or alternatively, like now, took none at all) had taken his place; a boy so strange and unfamiliar that he even announced himself, one night at the dinner table earlier this year, as pro the Iraq war – a war about which Eve still felt a bit guilty, albeit in a measured way, about not doing more, about not having concentrated on more, what with being so busy worrying about being unable to start the new book.

But Astrid, tonight? had cleared the plates and shared jokes with Eve like a normal daughter. *Magnus?* had almost looked his old self again. He had even gone through voluntarily, like in the old days, to help Michael with the washing up (since there were apparently no dishwashers in the swindle that was Norfolk). Then Astrid had forgotten her adolescent squeamishness about the house's furniture and had lain on the sofa (though she did fold a Guardian on the arm of it where her head would go) and was nearly asleep. Eve and the girl, Amber, stood in the warm at the open french windows.

What did Eve do then? Let's take a walk around the garden, Eve said. Calm, measured.

All right then, the girl said. That'd be a nice thing to do. Thanks.

They crossed the gravel. Eve talked generally, about flowers, about how to get things to grow in shade. They sat under one of the old trees.

What did Eve say to the girl in the garden?

You're Scottish, aren't you? I can hear it in your voice. I love Scotland. I haven't been for years. My mother was Scottish.

Ah. Where are you actually from, originally?

Can you speak that – I can't remember the name of it – that other language people used to speak up there?

What did you say? It sounds beautiful.

Translate it for me. What you just said.

Tell me a bit about yourself.

Well, anything, just general. What are you studying?

At university, I mean.

What did the girl in the garden say back?

I'm a MacDonald.

I am directly descended from the MacDonalds of Glencoe.

(Something that sounded like gibberish.)

(laughing) I was telling you some ancient Gaelic proverbs that everybody knows off by heart in the place I come from.

Okay. Roughly translated. One: there's many a hen that lays an egg. Two: the yellow will always return to the broom. Three: be careful not to let folk over your threshold till you're absolutely sure who they are.

What do you want to know?

What d'you mean?

(laughing) I'm not at a university.

What was practically the last thing Eve said to the girl in the garden?

We are a family, Amber, as you will have seen this evening. Astrid is only twelve and at a very difficult stage, and things with Magnus are a little adolescent. It's complicated, with family. You understand, I'm sure. Did Michael tell you you could come here?

And the last thing the girl in the garden said to Eve, smiling at her in the dark?

Michael who?

(She was good, the girl.)

Did he tell you that it was all right for you to come here? Eve asked. Because you and I know that it isn't simple, that it's very complicated, especially where family and children are involved.

Was Eve being patronizing? Only within her right.

What did the girl do? The girl made a little Scottish snort of a noise through her nose. She got up, shook her head at Eve, stretched her arms above her head and went off back towards the house. Eve stayed sitting under the tree. She checked her watch.

Was ten minutes enough time for them to sort it out? She would go in herself after the tenth minute and courteously offer the girl the spare room for the night, to show there was no ill feeling, because there wasn't, was there? and in the morning, with no ill will, the girl would leave. She let the seconds tick round, measured, even, calm.

But what happened when Eve came back into the house? Nothing. Not a thing. Michael and Magnus were still in the kitchen clinking dishes, drying things. Astrid was asleep on the sofa, with her feet up across Amber MacDonald's lap. Shh, Amber MacDonald said to Eve as Eve came in. She was holding Eve's daughter's feet.

Was even her shh a bit Scottish-sounding? Eve stood by the open window. She could see the roof of the car, but not into it, not whether she was awake or asleep or even in there at all.

Why had that girl wanted to shake her? She really didn't know.

What was the story, again, of the place Amber MacDonald said she was descended from? Eve couldn't recall. It was historical, or a song, or something about a battle and a Scottish family.

What was Scotland to Eve? Eve's mother knelt on the rug in front of the electric fire in the front room in the house in Welwyn Garden City playing records on the big box-shaped record player. The voices of men came out of the box. They sounded like they were dead already but that they'd died valiantly for love or for loss, that the breaking of them had been worth it.

What were these terrifying gentle songs? They filled her mother's eyes with tears.

How old was Eve? It was before school age. One of the songs was called The Dark Island. Though the fire gave off a glow there was darkness coiled snakily in the corners of the room. Eve (4) saw it. On Sunday evenings Eve's mother always made toast rather than a main meal and she and Eve ate it in companionable silence, listening to the chart countdown of the top twenty on the radio. When Eve thought of happiness this is what she thought of: the taste of toast and marmalade, early spring light, a radio on a table. If You Leave Me Now by Chicago was playing. It was number one. It was quite late in the chronology of things. It was in Eve's teens. Soon Eve would be coming home every weekday from school to her mother ill in bed in the afternoons.

Summer afternoons? Winter afternoons? All the light and the dark afternoons.

What happened at twenty past four every afternoon when she got home? Eve left her schoolbag by the phone-table, went to the kitchen, put a teabag in a cup, made a cup of tea and took it upstairs, still in her school blazer. Her mother's head was tiny at the top of the white expanse of the bedcovers. Is it you, love?

Was that a sort of Scottish way of saying things? Is it you? Yes it was. Eve's mother had gone into hospital and died. She had died of heart disease. Eve was fifteen. Eve's father worked in business in the States; he had his 'other' family there. When she died he came home briefly. He and Eve collected all her mother's things together and gave them away to neighbours and second-hand shops. Be calm, fifteen-year-old Eve told herself, packing the Scottish LPs into a cardboard box full of

94

cardigans. Look, just look. An LP in its sleeve was very thin, wasn't much thicker than a slice of processed cheese. There was snow on the top of the mountains on the front of one of the LPs. It's just snow on a mountain, she told herself as she slid the record down between the side of the box and the empty folded clothes. It's just a two-dimensional picture of a place I've never seen. Measured and calm. Eve by a window so many summers later was moved nearly to tears by her fifteen-year-old self. Her fifteen-year-old self, still in her school blazer, stared back at Eve, steely, disdainful, not-crying. Feeble, she was saying. As if anyone's childhood was an excuse for anything. Don't blame me for you. I'm not taking the blame. She took the transistor radio off the table, held it up by the handle and smashed it hard on the floor. The back came off it and its insides spilled out. Grow up, for fuck sake, Eve (15) snorted at Eve (42).

When in her life had Eve snorted like that? At the funeral, at the notion that there was a God who, even if prayed to, would do anything about anything. At her father, after the funeral, when he took her for an upmarket dinner in a London restaurant, as if a treat, before he flew back to New York State. At her father again, when he suggested over prawn cocktail that she might like to spend summers there with the 'other' family. She was sixteen in a month's time. She snorted. In one month's time she could do what she chose. (It was one of the times in her life when she was free to do exactly that.)

When else? At Adam when he announced that he was going to divorce her and marry 'Sonja' from 'Personnel' at the 'Alliance', whom he'd met when he went in to set up a 'joint interest paying current account' for him and Eve.

Are you joking? Was his name really Adam? Eve chose not to answer that question.

And what had Eve done in Michael's university office the

first time she understood, as she sat waiting for him to come back from a meeting, that the wallspace of the office and even the spaces between the bookshelves on the walls were covered with a mosaic of postcards, literally hundreds of them, reproductions of works of art, of posters from films, of famous photographs, of international landmarks, of beaches, cats curled in Greek sun, French monasteries, penguins etc. doing funny things, writers, singers, film stars, historical figures, and that probably every one of these postcards was from some girl he'd been fucking, I mean f***ing? One card had slipped down and fallen off the wall in front of her. She had leaned forward, picked it up, turned it over. A coloured line-drawing of two old-fashioned trains. On the back in handwriting was a tawdry message from a girl who spelled Freudian freuedian, who called herself his 'jaguar' and who used too many exclamation marks. Calm and measured.   Hxxxx   p.s. you get an Alpha   calm   ! ! ! !   measured. Eve was waiting for her husband Michael in his office at the university, where he held a prestigious position in the literature faculty.

Because what was Eve? Eve was a house and a garden and a four-square family and a fascinating writer in her own right and doing rather well albeit on a small scale and money coming in and the given shape of things.

And what was Hxxxx? Thin as a postcard, and an old postcard too, going by the date. PLEASE DO NOT PUT ANYTHING BUT WASTE PAPER IN THIS WASTE PAPER BIN. She stuck the postcard back on the wall, back in its given little space. She looked up the wall. Cards on cards on cards. She looked round at all the other walls. Cards. Eve tried it again, now, across the room from the sleeping Michael (she tried it quite quietly) and yes, she could still snort, and exactly like that girl in the garden had earlier tonight.

What else did Eve unexpectedly like about the girl? The comment the girl had made about Magnus in the bathroom. 'I found him trying to hang himself.' She was no fool, the girl, to see so clearly, to be able to sum up so well, the special mourning period that being teenage was.

Couldn't it sometimes take an outsider to reveal to a family that it was a family? Magnus had said goodnight like he used to. Astrid had kissed Eve goodnight. Michael had kissed Eve's back, between her shoulders. They had had quite attentive sex before he put his head under the pillow. As Eve thought this, another thought struck her. It struck her forcibly.

What if the girl had been telling the truth?

What if the girl was in reality nothing to do with Michael? What if, all night, Eve had been maligning the girl – and also Michael, sleeping so sweetly there beneath his goosefeather pillow? Oh dear God. Oh dear God. Eve was standing by the window. Oh dear God.

Was this possible? For instance. Think back. Eve had come out of the shed earlier this evening at the usual allotted time. At the door she had heard a curious noise. It was Astrid, sounding happy. Astrid seemed to be talking to someone, a young woman, a girl, who was lying on the lawn with her eyes shut.

And what now? Astrid was saying.

I can still see the outlines, but reversed, the girl was saying. The light and the dark are reversed.

Like a photo negative? Astrid said. Like the whole thing inside is like a photo negative?

Eve had known as she watched, she had known in the photoflash of the moment in which she stood watching and unperceived, that one day Astrid would betray her. She had known in the flash of the moment that Astrid doing the natural thing, simply growing older, was a helpless betrayal in itself.

Then Astrid saw Eve standing there.

Oh, hi, she said. She said it brightly, obliviously. She looked pleased to see Eve.

The girl with the closed eyes had opened them and seen Eve above her. She'd sat up. She'd shaded her eyes.

Hello, she'd said.

She had said it with nothing but friendliness.

Because

what if, all night, ever since that hello, and possibly because she had been feeling momentarily betrayed about something totally else, something completely unrelated – what if, because of all this, Eve had concocted a scenario of which the girl was totally innocent? Eve stood by the window in the dark. She rubbed her eyes.

But then, if she wasn't Michael's, what would that make the girl?

A tramp. She looked a bit like she could be a tramp.

A gypsy kind of a person.

A skilful freeloader who lived by charming her way into people's houses to eat. She was charming, it was true.

An anecdote for future dinner parties – the night a total stranger fooled us into serving her dinner when we were on holiday in Norfolk one summer. I thought she was one of his students and he thought she was something to do with me –

No, answer the question – what did it make the girl? What it made the girl was truthful.

For instance, had that girl actually asked them for anything? No. Not a thing. She had been invited to supper. She had been invited to stay the night.

So was it any wonder, then, that she had shaken Eve so hard? No wonder. Eve stood by the window. She looked

98

down at the car. She looked out at the night. She looked down at the car again.

So what would Eve do about it? Right. If it rained tonight, Eve was definitely going to go downstairs and tell the girl that under no circumstances could she sleep in a car in the rain, that she was to come inside. Eve would run downstairs and out the front door with a coat over her head and knock on the wet car window and insist.

But (she glanced at the maddeningly clear sky) *would it rain tonight?* No. It wouldn't. It was the perfect summer night. It was, though, far too hot tonight for anyone to be sleeping in a car. Dogs, for instance, were known to suffocate in cars with the windows not down on hot days. They died of dehydration.

What if that girl had gone to sleep and left no car windows open? Presumably if you slept in a car you had to keep yourself safe by keeping the windows tight closed so no one could break in and do whatever horrible unsafe things people would do to someone vulnerable sleeping in a car. But keeping the windows closed on a too-hot night like this would be at least dehydrating, at most seriously dangerous.

Eve leaned out of the window and looked at the car. From here she couldn't tell, because of the angle it had been parked at, whether its windows were open or closed.

Hadn't it been, after all, a friendly kind of shaking?

Hadn't the girl been sternly smiling, almost as if Eve was an old comrade?

What did Eve do now? Very quietly, she crossed the room and pulled her dressing gown round her shoulders. Very quietly, she opened the door.

Where was the girl? Not in the car at all. Eve looked in all the windows, but the car was empty.

She was in the garden. She was sitting under the trees they'd both been sitting under earlier. She was smoking. Eve could smell the smoke, then see it. Cigarette smoke curled up into the still air above the girl's head and disappeared.

Hello, she said.

She patted the ground beside her.

Eve tucked her dressing gown round herself.

Want one? the girl said. She shook one out of the packet and held it out. They were French cigarettes, Gauloises. The girl struck a match; as she lit Eve's cigarette her face was caught in the flare of it, concentrated and serious, and then the dark again.

I haven't been entirely straight with you tonight, the girl was saying.

You haven't, Eve said.

No, and I'm really sorry. I didn't tell you the, well, entirely the truth.

Ah. Right, Eve said.

Because when you asked me would I like to sleep in the house, the girl said, well, of course the answer is yes, like who'd choose a car over a bed? But. The thing is. This thing, it happened, and I can't, I made the promise, I made it years ago, and I won't, well, I can't.

What did she tell Eve? In the half-sentences of someone who finds something hard to say, this:

When she was in her twenties Amber MacDonald worked in the city in a high-flying position in investment assurance and insurance interests. She had a Porsche. It was the 1980s. One sleeting winter night, the week before Christmas, she was driving along a narrow car-lined street in a small town with the radio on playing a song called Smooth Operator and the windscreen wipers doing their rubbery swipe over the windscreen, and a child, a girl of seven wearing a little winter coat, its hood edged in fur, stepped between two cars on to the road in front of her and Amber MacDonald's car hit the child and the child died.

Since then, Amber MacDonald said, I gave up my job, my salary. I sold the car and I left most of the money I got for it, thousands, in a big pile of cash, like a hillside cairn, by the side of that road where it happened. I bought a second-hand Citroën Estate. And I decided that from then on I would never live in a place that could be called home again. How could I? How could I live the same way after?

They sat in the dark. It would soon be light. A single tear welled up and out of one of the girl's eyes, ran down the line of her nose and stopped, as if asked to, just below the curve of her cheekbone exactly halfway down her face. Gently she stubbed her cigarette out in the grass. She looked up, looked Eve right in the eye.

Well? she said. *Do you believe me?*

I was born in a trunk. It was during the matinée on Friday. I stopped the show.

I was born in the year of the supersonic, the era of the multistorey multivitamin multitonic, the highrise time of men with the technology and women who could be bionic, when jump-jets were Harrier, when QE2 was Cunard, when thirty-eight feet tall the Princess Margaret stood stately in her hoverpad, the année érotique was only thirty aircushioned minutes away and everything went at twice the speed of sound. I opened my eyes. It was all in colour. It didn't look like Kansas any more. The students were on the barricades, the mode was maxi, the Beatles were transcendental, they opened a shop. It was Britain. It was great. My mother was a nun who could no longer stand the convent. She married my father, the captain; he was very strict. She taught us all to sing and made us new clothes out of curtains. We ran across the bridges and jumped up and down the steps. We climbed the trees and fell out of the boat into the lake. We came first in the singing contest and narrowly escaped the Nazis.

I was formed and made in the Saigon days, the Rhodesian

days, the days of the rivers of blood. DISEMBOWEL ENOCH POWELL. Apollo 7 splashdowned. Tunbridge Wells was flooded. A crowd flowed over London Bridge, and thirty-six Americans made bids to buy it. They shot the king in Memphis, which delayed the Academy Awards telecast for two whole days. He had a dream, he held these truths to be self-evident, that all men were created equal and would one day sit down together at the table of brotherhood. They shot the other brother at the Ambassador Hotel. RIGHTEOUS BROS it said in lights, above the hotel car park. Meanwhile my father was the matchmaker and my mother could fly using only her umbrella. When I was a child I ran the Grand National on my horse. They didn't know I was a girl until I fainted and they unbuttoned my jockey shirt. But anything was possible. We had a flying floating car. We stopped the rail disaster by waving our petticoats at the train; my father was innocent in prison, my mother made ends meet. I sold flowers in Covent Garden. A posh geezer taught me how to speak proper and took me to the races, designed by Cecil Beaton, though they dubbed my voice in the end because the singing wasn't good enough.

But my father was Alfie, my mother was Isadora. I was unnaturally psychic in my teens, I made a boy fall off his bike and I burned down a whole school. My mother was crazy; she was in love with God. There I was at the altar about to marry someone else when my boyfriend hammered on the church glass at the back and we eloped together on a bus. My mother was furious. She'd slept with him too. The devil got me pregnant and a satanic sect made me go through with it. Then I fell in with a couple of outlaws and did me some talking to the sun. I said I didn't like the way he got things done. I had sex in the back of the old closing cinema. I used butter in Paris. I had a farm in Africa. I took off my clothes in the window of an apartment building and distracted the two police inspectors from watching for the madman on the roof who was trying to shoot the priest. I fell for an Italian. It was his moves on the dancefloor that did it. I knew what love meant. It meant never having to say you're sorry. It meant the man who drove the taxi would kill the presidential candidate, or the pimp. It was soft as an easy chair. It happened so fast. I had my legs bitten off by the shark. I stabbed the kidnapper, but so did everybody else, it wasn't just me, on the Orient Express.

My father was Terence and my mother was Julie. (Stamp. Christie.) I was born and bred by the hills (alive) and the animals (talked to). I considered myself well in, part of the furniture. There wasn't a lot to spare. Who cared? I put on a show, right here in the barn; I was born singing the song at the top of my just-formed lungs. Inchworm. Inchworm. Measuring the marigolds. Seems to me you'd stop and see how beautiful they are. I rose inch by inch with the international rise of the nose of Streisand, the zee of Liza. What good was sitting alone in my room? When things went decimal I was ready for it.

I was born in a time of light, speed, celluloid. Downstairs was smoking. The balcony was non. It cost more money to sit in the balcony.

The kinematograph. The eidoloscope. The galloping tintypes. The silver screen. The flicks. The pictures. Up rose the smoke. Misty watercolour memories.

But it's all in the game and the way you play it, and you've got to play the game, you know.

I was born free, I've had the time of my life and for all we know I'm going to live forever.

The middle

of the dual carriageway right in front of the cars! She sticks her arm up i.e. Stop. The cars coming towards her screech to a halt with their horns going like mad. Amber stands in the middle of the two lanes with her hand up to keep the cars stopped.

Now! she shouts over the noise, waving her other arm at Astrid. Astrid runs across, careful not to drop the camera.

Then when they're both on the central reservation Amber steps out exactly like she did before in front of the traffic coming in the other direction and the screeching to a halt and the horns all start again.

It is insane. It is really dangerous. It is a bit like the story from the bible when the sea parts in two, except it is traffic. It is like Amber is blessed with a magnetic forcefield from outer space or another galaxy. If she were a cartoon character she would be the kind of superheroine that can draw things to her and repel them away from her at the same time.

Personally Astrid thinks Amber should stop when she gets to the edge of a pavement or whatever. It is insane just to walk out. But that's what Amber's like. It is what her personality is like. It isn't so much that she's a retard about cars, it's that she really believes that she has as much right to the road as they do, maybe even more.

They stand together on the verge with all the cars roaring back up to speed behind them and people still shouting at them out of car windows. Amber ignores it. Now that Astrid can breathe properly again and her heart has stopped doing the scared thing and she can hear herself think, she wishes she'd filmed it, them crossing the road. It would have been an amazing thing to have on film.

She films Amber now. She has the field behind her. It is all golden.

Astrid also wishes someone else was filming them both from the outside. They would look like an older person and a younger person who are having a day out and are really good friends or maybe sisters, sometimes even walking about with their arms linked, because age, Amber says, is nothing to do with anything, it is just irrelevant.

There is a great view of the countryside and the edge of the town. Amber points at the wild flowers in the grass as they walk; long thin red ones, really pretty little blue ones. Astrid films them. When she is finished filming Amber is already quite far ahead, going towards the buildings in the distance. She films Amber from behind for a while, walking in the field, swinging her arms.

One of the buildings is a supermarket. It has the little pointed roof with a cockerel weathervane on the top. When Astrid catches her up and points it out, Amber says the weathervane is nothing to do with the way the wind blows. It is to make the supermarket look more old-fashioned, from the past, so that when people go shopping there they feel better about it like they're going somewhere that's something to do with a tradition, somewhere they think they recognize from their pasts even though their pasts almost definitely

110

never had anything like that in them. It is fiendishly clever how it works. It works subliminally.

Astrid still doesn't know where they're going. It would be uncool to ask. Bring the camera, Amber called up the stairs to Astrid this morning. This is their third day out filming important things on Astrid's camera. Amber is striding out now across the field, walking straight through all the stuff growing in it. Insects buzz everywhere and there are birds. There are fieldmice or rabbits or grass snakes probably, ricocheting away from them as they take every step. It would be amazing if they could actually see them shooting off away from the noise of Amber's and Astrid's feet i.e. she and Amber are giants in a different world and the ground is shaking under them and all the animals etc. radiating away from them. But the stuff growing in the field is jabby on Astrid's legs, and the soil where there's space through the stalks of stuff is dry and very uneven, and the field is huge, much bigger than it seemed from the edge of the motorway where it looked like it would be really easy to walk across, and it is very very hot because it is around noon.

Halfway over, Amber stops and waits for her. She unties her sweater from her middle and winds it round Astrid's head to keep the sun off, tying a knot in it with its arms to keep it on.

How's that? she says.

Astrid feels better.

At the other side of the field they go round by the road past a garage selling cars (cameras outside) and a massive Boots the Chemist (cameras outside), then across an industrial kind of place (camera) and into the supermarket car park (several cameras). The car park is quite busy with cars. There is shade again when they get to the door so Astrid takes the sweater off her head and gives it back to Amber and Amber ties it round her middle again. Amber is really quite slim. She is probably a size ten. She has long hands, long fingers, they are quite elegant-looking really. Amber, Astrid's mother said last night at dinner, you have piano player's hands. Yes, Amber said back, but what kind of a piano player, a good one or a rubbish one? Magnus laughed. Michael laughed for ages like a mad person. A good one, of course, Astrid's mother said. You've never heard me play the piano, Amber said.

Astrid looks at her own small hands now, at the camera in them.

Do you want me to film? she says pointing the camera at the first security camera inside the door.

Amber is standing at the door with her eyes narrowing, scanning the inside of the supermarket. She shakes her head. She does it slowly i.e. she is concentrating.

Go and find something for lunch, she says. Are you hungry?

Astrid nods.

Anything you like, Amber says. Definitely get some fruit. Get me a sandwich.

Astrid's mission is to get lunch. At the fruit place she chooses a couple of apples called Discovery. The sign above them says they are local and organic. It is better than them not being local and organic. Tasting is believing! a sign above the apples says. Another one says how good the supermarket is at selling really fresh fruit. Imagine if it wasn't fresh. Imagine if they were all old and manked, all these rows and rows of apples and oranges and nectarines and peaches. Would the sign still say fresh or would it say old and manked? Old manked fruit here for sale. Tasting is believing. Ha ha. She makes a mental note to tell it to Amber, and to Magnus when she gets home. She picks out a tuna and mayonnaise sandwich from the great wall of sandwiches on the refrigerated shelves at the front of the shop. The great wall of sandwiches – like the great wall of China! Imagine if the great wall of China was made of sandwiches. The tuna in the sandwich has been caught without harm to dolphins. It says so on the packaging, which has a picture on it of an island with a palm tree.

There aren't very many people shopping in the supermarket even though there were all those cars parked outside. Astrid looks above the shelves at the signs hanging from the ceiling for the hot food sign. The hot food is next to the deli counter. Another sign hung behind the hot food counter also says Tasting is Believing! She chooses a small rack of barbecued ribs for herself and a woman wraps them in packaging that will keep them warm, the woman says, for about half an hour.

Thank you, Astrid says to the woman.

You're welcome, the woman says.

A camera above their heads films it all: Astrid asking for the ribs, the woman wrapping them and telling Astrid (it will come out silent on the tape) how long they'll keep warm for. Astrid takes the package. She wonders if the woman serving her knows about the cameras i.e. of course she knows, it's obvious and she works here. But what about when she stops work and goes for a walk along the road and the other cameras that she passes just because of the way she's walking home video her going past them? Like they videoed that boy who died when Astrid was younger because he was stabbed; just before he did he went skipping past the Peckham library with its new architecture; and that girl who played the saxophone and did the ironing on the home video that her parents let the authorities show of her on the news, the girl who went missing on her way home from school.

Except that the video of this supermarket woman doing

113

her job and walking along a street or getting her car out of the car park or going to a library, whatever, is just useless recording, it doesn't mean anything, it'll never get watched unless something awful happens to her and then it will mean everything, which would be terrible, but important.

And then, if nothing terrible happens, when the woman gets home at night and sits at dinner or with a cup of coffee or whatever, does she realize she is not being recorded any more? Or does she think inside her head that she still *is* being recorded, by something that watches everything we do, because she is so used to it being everywhere else? Or does she just not ever think about it, is she just a woman who works in a supermarket and doesn't bother thinking about that kind of stuff?

The thought of it all makes Astrid feel weird. She looks at the package in her hand. She knows the ribs are warm inside though the package feels completely cool from the outside.

Astrid goes from aisle to aisle of supermarket stuff. She eventually finds Amber in the aisle with all the bathroom things and deodorants etc. Amber is taking packets off the little hook they're hung on and letting them drop to the floor as if the front packet isn't the one she wants, and neither is the next one, and neither is the next one. Packet after packet hits the floor. When Amber has completely cleared one hook she starts on the packets on the hook next to it and does the same thing again. She has unloaded the contents of a couple of hooks already.

Astrid goes over. Sealed packets of razor blades, the kind with the plastic handles, are scattered round Amber's feet. Amber pulls another one off the hook and lets it drop.

Astrid looks at her.

Why are you doing it? Astrid's look says.

Amber looks back.

But Astrid has no idea what the look means.

Is mayonnaise all right? Astrid asks.

Depends on whether it's been left out in the sun for any length of time, Amber says.

Astrid laughs.

I.e. in your sandwich, she says.

Amber lets the packet fall, unhooks another, holds it out and lets it fall.

Yes, Amber says. Id est, I like mayonnaise. As long as it's not just a mayonnaise sandwich, id est with nothing in it but mayonnaise.

Tuna, Astrid says holding it up.

My favourite, Amber says.

Astrid is very pleased. Pleasedness, or whatever the word for it is, goes all through her body.

Amber gazes for a moment at the empty hooks in front of her and the packets all over the floor and then she says:

Right.

She steps out over the circle of packets.

Checkout time, she says.

Three uniformed security men and two men in suits are standing on the other side of the checkout almost as if they're waiting for Amber and Astrid. Then Astrid realizes they are. Amber pays a girl for the apples and the sandwich and the barbecued ribs. The girl won't look up or at Amber or Astrid. She only looks at the things they're buying and the till she's barcoding and pushing the keys on. She asks all the cashback and petrol questions without looking at them too. She knows she is being watched and that something is up. The security men wait there for the paying to finish, like angry silent cowboys in a tv western. One of the men in the suits looks angry. The other one looks ironic. He looks directly at Amber and shakes his head at her as she and Astrid pass. But they don't do anything or say anything.

Amber and Astrid leave the supermarket.

Ribs, Amber says, peeking into Astrid's package. Her face looks like she doesn't like ribs much.

Don't you like ribs? Astrid asks.

Take them or leave them, Amber says.

Me too, Astrid says. I can take them or leave them too. I quite like the burnt way they taste.

Carcinogenic, Amber says.

Yeah, Astrid says.

She knows carcinogenic means something but she can't remember what.

Eating burnt things. Cancer, Amber says.

It is as if she can actually read Astrid's mind.

I know, Astrid says.

Then she worries, because if Amber can actually read her mind she will know she didn't know what it meant. She steals a glance at Amber, but Amber is pointing.

Lovely picnic spot, she says.

It is a horrible recycling-bin place. They sit on the grass at the edge of the car park in the smell of old wine and beer from the bottle bins. Our recycling project, a sign says by the bins. Success. Environment.

One of the security men is standing at the front door of the supermarket. He has been watching them since they left and he watches them the whole time they sit there eating their lunch. He is talking into a phone.

Astrid and Amber watch him back.

I suppose they saw you doing that thing with the razor blades, Astrid says.

They definitely saw me, Amber says. You might say they saw quite a lot of me.

116

She tells Astrid that this supermarket is testing a new way of stopping shoplifters. When someone takes a packet of razor blades off the hook a computer chip inside it instructs a camera to take a picture of that person so that the people at checkout can match the photo to the person buying it, so they can know who has and who hasn't paid for their razor blades and whether they're being stolen or not.

Astrid doesn't really get what the problem is. She thinks it's fair enough really, for the supermarket to do this. After all, it is to stop people stealing.

Amber gets a bit annoyed.

Astrid thinks about asking Amber about the supermarket woman and the being taped. But she knows that if she says the thing about the supermarket woman maybe not caring because she is just a supermarket woman, Amber will get even more annoyed. So she doesn't say anything at all about anything. She holds a rib up and picks round it with her teeth, trying not to get sauce on her face or any further up her hand.

Amber has finished her sandwich. She gets up. Astrid hurries to her feet too, holding her hands away from herself. Amber is dusting herself down and stretching. She waves goodbye to the security man who raises a hand to wave back, as if not sure, as if by mistake. Then Amber takes the camera because Astrid's hands are all barbecue sauce and they go back the same way they came, across the hot field (Astrid eats an apple then throws the applecore away, biodegradable) then cross the dual carriageway by a pedestrian walkway bridge which leads directly to the station and is clearly the way they were meant to go the first time instead of walking out into the middle of the road that insane way.

Halfway across the pedestrian bridge, above the roaring traffic, Amber stops. They lean over and look at the view and the countryside again. It is beautiful. It is really English and quintessential. They watch the cars beneath them going in and coming out, moving like a two-way river. The sunlight off the windscreens and the paint of the cars is flashy in Astrid's eyes. It is easier to look at the further-away cars fading into a see-through wall of more shimmering heat. Their colours melt through it as if cars aren't made of anything solid.

It is a beautiful summer afternoon, like perpetual summers used to be in the old days, before Astrid was born.

Then Amber drops the camera over the side of the bridge.

Astrid watches it fall through the air. She hears her own voice, remote and faraway, then she hears the plastic-sounding noise of her camera as it hits the tarmac. It sounds so small. She sees the truck wheel hit it and send it spinning under the wheels of the car behind it on the inside lane, breaking it into all the pieces which scatter all over the road. Other cars come behind and carry on hitting the pieces, running them over, bouncing them across the road surface.

Come on, Amber says.

She is striding off ahead and is already halfway down the steps towards the station. Astrid can see her back disappearing, then her shoulders, then her head.

It is unbelievable.

It is insane.

All the way home on the train, Astrid is thinking: it is insane. All the way walking home from the train station to the house, which is quite far, Astrid isn't speaking to Amber. All the way home she won't look at her either. When she does sneak one look, from under her fringe, Amber looks completely unbothered, like nothing terrible has happened, like she hasn't done anything even remotely upsetting.

It was a present from her mother and Michael on her last birthday.

She will be in terrible trouble.

It cost a fortune.

They are always talking about how much it cost. They are proud of how much.

It was a Sony digital.

It had footage from today, of those flowers.

It had Amber crossing the field with all the yellow and gold behind her head.

There was filming on it from the other day in Norwich and it might also have been the tape with the footage they took outside the Curry Palace etc. on it.

What use will Astrid be to Amber now, now that she can't record anything important?

The dawn footage is on the bedside table. But it stops on the day that Amber came. What if Astrid woke up and wanted to start that again tomorrow?

Amber will have to be made to pay for the camera.

Typical and ironic, no security cameras on the pedestrian bridge.

Nobody saw it happen.

Astrid can't prove anything.

All the way home she won't look or speak. Amber doesn't even notice. She whistles ahead, hands in her pockets. Astrid trudges after her on the opposite side of the road, her eyes fixed on the ground moving beneath her sandals. But Amber doesn't notice, or if she does she doesn't think it matters.

When Astrid gets home and goes upstairs and locks the door behind her in the room, she catches sight of herself in the mirror and her face is so white that she has to look twice. It nearly makes her laugh out loud, how small and white and angry the face in the mirror looks. It nearly makes her laugh out loud that it is actually her.

She stares at herself.

The part of herself that wants to laugh feels separate, seeing herself like that. It feels i.e. completely unbothered, or like a whole other different her.

She sits on the bed looking away from the mirror and concentrates hard on staying furious.

A couple of days later Amber asks Astrid if she can borrow her pad and her felt pen for a minute.

Astrid nods. She makes a noise that means yes. She still isn't really speaking to Amber.

Amber lies on the grass in the shade, drawing with Astrid's pen on Astrid's pad of paper.

After a bit, Astrid comes over and sits nearby. Then she moves a little closer still.

Amber is pretty good and very quick at drawing. She has drawn a picture of a small child. You can tell the child is in school because there is a desk and an old-fashioned blackboard is in the background with an old-fashioned teacher at it. The child in the picture is drawing too, on a piece of paper on an easel. Her picture has the word *Mummy* in child-writing above it, and then is the kind of picture children draw of their mothers, like a stick figure with its arms stuck stupidly out, funny jaggy hair and one eye much bigger than the other and a scrawl for a mouth.

Amber shows Astrid.

Then she tears the page out, turns it over, puts her arm over the pad like people do when they don't want people to copy their answers, and draws something else.

When it's finished she gives it to Astrid.

The second picture is of the gate outside the school (there is a sign saying School) with three mothers there waiting to take their children home. Two of the mothers look like real people. But the third mother is the spitting image of the mother in the child's painting in the first picture. Standing beside the real mothers she is all crazy sizes and jaggy hair and has one eye too big and the insane mouth-scrawl and the arms at their stupid angle i.e. the mother *really* looks like that in real life, is the joke.

It is the funniest thing that Astrid has seen in her whole life. She can't stop laughing. She can't believe how funny it is that the mother in the real life might actually really look like the mother in the picture the child drew. It is so funny and so really stupid that Astrid laughs till she is crying with laughter. Tears run down the side of her head, cold behind her ears, down into the grass. Amber is laughing too, lying on her back laughing like anything. They are both rolling about on the lawn laughing and laughing at the two pictures.

Example of very similitude, Michael says when he looks over her shoulder later at the piece of paper (she is showing Magnus).

Very funny, Magnus says. He is lying on the sofa staring at the ceiling. (He is nearly normal again, he is talking to people again, he is even taking baths etc. There is still some black round his eyes as if someone took a felt pen and smudged it in there.)

Did Amber do it? her mother asks. She's so talented. She's such a talented girl.

She is. Amber is really talented. For days and days the joke still makes Astrid laugh in the middle of something else, anything else, it doesn't matter what.

Nights later it still comes into her head and she can't help it, she starts to laugh all over again, it is the kind of funny that's so deep in your middle where your breathing starts that it feels like your insides are melting or you have been taken over by an alien which does nothing but laugh inside you and long after the actual pictures have got lost or tidied

121

up or maybe thrown away by Katrina the Cleaner Astrid is still laughing helplessly when she thinks of it, how funny it is, how clever the idea of it is, the mother standing waiting at the school gates looking like she exists in the real world exactly the stupid childish way she has been drawn i.e. as if the way the child drew her was actually true and real after all.

Astrid, her mother says one hot hot evening when Michael has made something that's supposed to be special and there are inedible flowerheads scattered in the salad. You should film us all at supper tonight. It's such a lovely night, it's been such a lovely day, and it's such a lovely supper, we should commemorate it. Go and get your camera.

Astrid doesn't say anything.

Astrid, her mother says. Go on.

Astrid looks at her plate.

Go on, her mother says. Go and get it.

No, Astrid says.

No? her mother says.

I can't, Astrid says.

What do you mean, you can't? her mother says.

I lost it, Astrid says.

You what? her mother says.

Astrid says it again.

I lost it.

Where did you, Astrid, lose the camera? Michael says.

Well if I knew that, Astrid says, it wouldn't be lost would it?

Amber laughs.

Astrid, that's enough, her mother says.

Astrid scowls at the pile of little flowers on the ridge of her plate.

But how, exactly, you could do this thing? Michael says.

Astrid, it cost two thousand pounds, you know it did, her mother says but she says it wheedlingly rather than angrily because Amber is here at the table and they are trying hard to be perfect in front of her, even Astrid's mother.

When? Michael says. Did you report it to the police?

Astrid, for God's sake, her mother says. Your camera.

Actually, Amber says as she helps herself to another slice of bread, it's my fault. I didn't like her carrying it around all the time. So I threw it off a motorway pedestrian bridge.

Everybody turns and looks at Amber. There is a silence that goes on and on, keeps going on until Astrid says:

No she didn't. It just fell off.

Oh, her mother says.

Ah, Michael says.

It was on the edge of the bridge. And it just – fell, Astrid says.

Oh, her mother says again. There is another silence, except for the noise of Amber's fork and knife on the plate.

Pedestrian bridge, Amber says. Over the A14.

It could have killed somebody, anything, Michael says. If it had hit a windscreen, anything.

Yep, Amber says.

But it didn't, did it? Astrid's mother says quick.

No, Astrid says.

Nobody died, Amber says tearing the bread in half. Anyway, it was my fault so don't give her a hard time about it. If you're going to give anyone a hard time, give it to me.

Astrid's mother dabs her mouth with her napkin and looks at Michael, then looks at her watch, then looks out of the window.

Insurance. I'll look into it, Michael says glancing at her mother then at Astrid then at Amber then at nobody, into thin air behind Amber's head. He reaches for the bottle to put more wine in the glasses. Be fine, he says nodding.

Her mother carries on eating like nothing has happened. It is so weird. Michael carries on eating. Magnus is looking down at his plate and chewing. All up the side of his neck and face is all red like a rash. But nobody says anything else about the broken camera. Nobody says anything else about it all night or the next day and by the third day Astrid is pretty sure they've all forgotten about it.

Id est is long for i.e. or rather i.e. is short for id est. It is another way of saying i.e. and comes originally from Latin, which is what id est is.

Astrid tells Amber about the mobile in the school litter bin with its rental still being paid and nobody knowing. She tells her about Lorna Rose and Zelda Howe and Rebecca Callow. She tells her about how she and Rebecca Callow used to be friends. She tells her about her father Adam Berenski's letters to her mother and how she found them under the birth certificates, car insurance, papers about who owns the house etc., in the bureau in her mother's study and how she took them and how nobody has even noticed that she's taken them and how she keeps them now inside a sock inside another sock inside the zip-up pocket inside the holdall under her bed at home. She tells Amber the beautiful things they say i.e. id est off by heart *you are for me the Beginning of Beginnings. You have taught me the meaning of faithful. If I had a film camera behind my eyes what I would do is film all the dawns of all the mornings of my life then give the finished film to you all spliced together* (spliced means married). *Then you would know what it's like to know you, to wake up with you. You are a perpetual beautiful summer, a summer that*

goes on for months, from May to October, day after day
after day of uninterrupted gentle sun and summer air. I am
the high-flying birds which skim your sky. You make me fly.
When I look at you I feel that I am the only man alive ever
to be able to fly so close to the sun. Don't melt my wings! (id
est Icarus who is the son of Daedalus in the Greek myth).

She describes the photograph of him in the blue car with
the door of it open. He has one leg out of the car on the ground.
He is wearing jeans. He has dark hair. He is thin. He is wearing
a blue checked shirt, you can see it through the car
windscreen. There are bushes behind the car and modern-
looking houses behind the bushes. There is the leaf on the
ground that fell off a tree before the photograph was taken.

His arms are folded. You can't see his hands. His eyes are
either smiling or shut.

He took sugar in his tea.

The words come out of Astrid's mouth like the kind of
heated-up stones they use at the place her mother goes for
massage, the kind that leave red places on people's skin after
they've been put on and taken off.

Amber breaks a tall stem of grass from the edge, puts the
stem in her mouth and lies back on the lawn. She looks up
at Astrid for a long time through eyes half-closed against the
sun. She doesn't say anything.

The tops of the trees shift all round them a moment before
they feel the actual breeze that shifted the leaves above them
that moment ago.

Amber is away for the day.

Astrid walks round and round the house. She walks round
the garden. Then she walks to the village. On the way she
thinks about when she and Amber went filming in Norwich.

Stand there, Amber said directly below the first camera she

125

pointed out, the one filming them at Norwich station as soon as they got off the train. And just keep filming it for a minute. I mean film it for a whole complete minute.

Astrid sits on the bench across from the village church. She watches the road. She looks at her watch for a whole minute, each tick of the second hand. In that minute, which feels like a very long time, not a single thing happens.

A whole minute? she'd said to Amber. Who's ever going to want to watch a film for more than like five seconds of a stupid closed-circuit camera just there on the wall doing nothing?

Amber rolled her eyes and looked at Astrid id est Astrid was being stupid and annoying so Astrid switched the camera on and autofocused it and started filming the other camera. It swivelled to look at her. The cameras were id est filming each other.

It is too hot sitting here in the sun. The sun is a huge red eye. Astrid gets up. She looks at the war memorial, with its faded old fake flowers on the two wreaths. She touches its stone ledge, so hot from the sun that she can't touch it for long. Since this war memorial was new the sun has heated it up every summer.

She tries the door of the church. It is locked. There is a notice on it saying who to ask for the key, Mr something who lives in the street at the second junction (there is a map).

Churches are usually locked. It stops vandalism.

But what if you were a vandal? You could just go and ask for the key.

But then they would know it was you who was the vandal.

But what if you said you'd had the key and dropped it somewhere, say, and that a vandal must have found it and gone in and done the vandalism?

Or – what if the person who *owns* the key is a vandal, and decides to do some vandalism and then just make up

126

afterwards that someone else came and borrowed the key and wrote with spraypaint on the walls or broke the seats or whatever's in there etc.?

It is actually not true that not a single thing happened in that minute she counted just now. There were the birds and things like insects flying. Crows or something probably cawed in the heat above her. They are doing it now. There is the tall white plant over behind the wall, cow something it is called. In sixty seconds it probably moved a bit in the air and it must even have grown but in a way that can't be seen by the human eye. There are bees etc. everywhere in the shade, working in and out of the flowers, on their way home to their hive where the drones still have their legs because it's still summer, all happening in its own world which exists on its own terms in this even if someone like Astrid doesn't know about it or hasn't found out about it yet. A heart-shaped stone next to the door says on it Died 1681. There really is someone under it who died in 1681 id est once he or she was alive like this and now he or she whoever it was (there is no name on it, just the date of it, and no month, just the year), what is left of him or her, has been under there for more than three hundred years, and once he or she lived and was actually alive in this village. The sun has been hitting that stone every summer all that time, right the way through the perpetual summers up to the ecologically worrying ones of now. Astrid has never really noticed how green things are before. Even the stone is green. The wood of the locked church door is brown-green, has a kind of sheen of green on it from just being there in weather etc. It is a really bright colour. If she had her camera she would have just filmed the colour for a whole full minute and then later she would be able to see what it really looks like, that colour.

She sits down in the shade by the door and looks hard at

the greenness of the green. If she looks hard enough she will maybe know or learn something about greenness or whatever.

But those people who died in those wars last century and the person under the stone shaped like a heart, is it the same thinking about them as it is about that boy who ran past the Peckham library or that girl they found in the woodland dead last year? Or people right now in places in the world who haven't enough to eat so are dying right now as Astrid sits here thinking about a colour? Or animals in countries where there's not enough food or rain so they die. Or the people who are in that war that's supposed to be happening, though not very many people seem to have died in it, not as many as in a real war.

Died 2003.

Astrid tries to imagine a person, a child maybe, or someone Astrid's own age, in the dusty-looking places from tv, dying because of a bomb or something. She imagines Rebecca Callow on a hospital bed in a place that looks like it has no equipment. It is quite hard to imagine. And at school teachers are always going on about the environment and all the species of things that are dying out etc. It is all everywhere all the time, it is serious, animals with ribcages and children in hospitals on the news with people somewhere or other screaming because of a suicide bomber or American soldiers who have been shot or something, but it is hard to know how to make it actually matter inside your head, how to make it any more important than thinking about the colour green. The Curry Palace i.e. it was easy to make *that* matter because here it is, right here in front of them. But when she and Amber went and asked the Indian man he shook his head and said it was just local high spirits having a bit of fun and not vandalism at all and certainly not racist and there was definitely nothing he wanted them to film and asked them to go away. The whole time he did he was looking over their shoulders at the boys standing watching them outside the chip shop across the road from the Curry Palace. Amber looked across at them and said she thought those boys were the local high spirits. The Indian man went away back into the Curry Palace. A man came out of the chip shop and stood behind the boys, watching her and Amber.

Will I film the car park? Astrid asked.

No. Film them, Amber said looking at the people standing with their arms folded across the road.

When Astrid started filming them one of the boys started coming across the road, probably to get her to stop, and Amber stood right behind Astrid with her hands on her shoulders, but the man called him back and the boys and the man went inside the chip shop and shut the door.

Died 1681. Astrid touches the hot heart with its word and numbers etched into it.

We lost that footage when the camera broke, she had said to Amber one evening in a whisper so nobody would hear and remember about the camera.

What footage? Amber said.

The footage of the local high spirits, Astrid whispered.

Amber shrugged.

Did you want to watch it again? she'd said. I didn't. Ugly little bastards.

Didn't it prove something? Astrid said.

What would it prove? Amber said.

It proved we were there, Astrid said.

But we know we were there, Amber said.

It proved we saw them, Astrid said.

But they know that we saw them, Amber said. And we know that we saw them.

It proved the thing we actually saw, Astrid said.

Who to? Amber said, and knocked her hand on Astrid's head. Knock knock, her hand went.

Who's there? Amber said.

Amber is really good at questions and their answers. That day in Norwich, after Astrid had filmed the closed-circuit camera in the station for the full sixty seconds on her camera's second-counter, she had looked up from the eyepiece and seen, behind Amber, that a man in a short-sleeved shirt and tie had come out of a door further down the platform and was watching them.

He watched them when they went to film the next camera across the station by WH Smith. Halfway through Astrid filming the third one, in the entrance hall, he was standing there next to them.

I'm going to have to ask you to stop that, he said to Amber.

Stop what? Amber said.

Stop filming, the man said.

Why? Amber said.

It's not permitted, he said, for members of the public to record details of our security system.

Why not? Amber said.

For reasons of public safety and security, the man said.

Why are you asking me? Amber said.

I'm asking you to stop filming, the man said.

Not what, why, Amber said. Why are you asking me? I'm not filming anything.

He folded and unfolded his arms. He put his hands on his hips id est he was getting really irate.

If you wouldn't mind asking your little girl to stop filming, he said.

He kept glancing up at the camera above them like he knew he was being recorded.

She's not a little girl, Amber said. And she's not mine.

It's for my local researches and archive, Astrid said.

The man looked at Astrid in total surprise, like he couldn't believe anyone who was twelve could speak never mind would have a reason for saying anything out loud.

It's for a school project on security systems in train stations, she said.

Amber smiled at the man.

I'm afraid, I imagine, you'll need to get written permission from the proprietors of each station for something like that, the man said to Amber, ignoring Astrid.

You're afraid or you imagine? Amber said.

What? the man said.

He looked bewildered.

Afraid or imagine? Amber said.

The man glanced again at the camera and wiped the back of his neck with his hand.

And are you congenitally unable to talk to her, so you have to refer everything to me, like I'm your secretary or a special sign-language interpreter for her, like she's deaf or dumb? Amber said. She can speak. She can hear.

Eh? the man said. Look, he said.

We *are* looking, Amber said.

Listen, the man said.

Make up your mind, Amber said.

You can't film here, the man said. That's final.

He folded his arms at Amber and kept them folded. Amber looked right back at the man. She took a step forward. The man took two steps back. Amber started to laugh.

Then she linked her arm into Astrid's arm and they went out of the entrance hall into the town bit of Norwich.

Did you see, Astrid said as they walked into the sunlight at the front of the station, how that man was really sweating under his arms?

Yeah, well. Not surprising. Pretty hot today, Amber said unlinking, and strode off ahead towards the bridge.

Astrid walks home from the village again in the sweltering heat. She swings her arms out from her sides as she walks. That's how Amber walks, with her arms kind of swinging out, as if she knows exactly where she's going and though it's quite far and you might not know where you're heading to, it'll be worth it, it's going to be really really amazing when you get there.

It is a really long day, then Amber gets back from wherever it was she went.

By the way, she says when Astrid is clearing the table that night after supper. While I was away I sorted something out for you.

Like what? Astrid says.

You'll see, Amber says.

Astrid is in bed in the horrible room on the hottest night so far. Tonight on the news it said this was the hottest day ever, since heat records began. Everything in the room smells fusty, hot. It is just before she goes to sleep.

She sees in her head Amber sitting by herself on the train to Liverpool St with the countryside going so fast past her then the train pulling into the station and Amber getting off the train and going through the little turnstile and across the concourse and down the steps and the escalator and getting on the tube and sitting on it then getting off the tube again and walking the rest of the way from the station up past the deli and the shops and across the park and up the road then all the way up Davis Rd to the junction and across it to outside Lorna Rose's mother's house. But what if Lorna Rose wasn't in? What if she was at her father's? Amber knocks on the door but there is no answer. So. So she goes to Zelda Howe's house and rings the bell and someone comes to the door and it is actually Zelda Howe and Amber slaps her hard across the face.

Surprise, Amber says.

Then maybe Amber goes to Rebecca Callow's house and knocks on the door and a woman answers, probably their au pair, and Amber says she is Rebecca's teacher from school come about something so the au pair lets her in and shows her through the house and into the big back garden where Rebecca is sitting in the white swing chair they have in their garden and another girl is in the garden too doing a headstand on the lawn and doesn't see Amber coming in and the first thing Amber does is get her by the legs like she is helping hold her up and the girl says who are you? And Amber says to her are you Lorna? And the girl says yes and Amber says then believe me I am your worst nightmare welcome to hell and swings her legs so she falls over. Then she goes to Rebecca, who is watching with her mouth open, and she gets hold of either side of the swing chair and pushes it hard backwards so that Rebecca falls out of it on to the lawn. Then while Rebecca goes running inside she gets Lorna's mobile out of Lorna's hand – she is sitting on the grass looking dazed trying to phone someone – and she says now watch this very carefully and she puts it on the path and she stamps on it hard so it breaks into pieces. Next time, she says to Lorna Rose, it'll be your hand I do that to. And then she goes through the house and Rebecca Callow is in the kitchen crying on the phone to someone in a real state of fear and the au pair is in the hall on another phone and Amber pulls Rebecca's long hair once really hard and says how do you like it, being treated like that? and the au pair is still in the hall shouting in her Croatian or whatever accent and Amber walks round her giving her a really wide berth and lets herself out the front door and lets it slam shut behind her.

Then Amber goes to a research place where you can find out where people are for other people who need to know. She says to the lady behind the counter, I need to trace the whereabouts of, and then she writes down his name on the form.

The lady behind the counter nods. It won't take long, she says, because this is a quite unusual name. Can I ask if you are a next-of-kin?

No, Amber says, but I am acting on behalf of a next-of-kin person who needs to know where he is so she can legitimately contact him.

Then Amber slips the lady two hundred pounds in neatly folded cash over the counter like in a film or drama.

It's a family matter, Amber says.

The lady looks all round her to see that nobody has seen this happen.

Certainly madam. I won't be long, the lady says.

She disappears through the back where the computers are which have all the details on them of everybody, like where they are in the world and what it is they're doing there.

Astrid dreams of a horse in a field. The field is full of dead grass, all yellowed, and the ribs are showing on the horse. Behind the horse an oilwell or a heap of horses or cars is burning. The sky is full of black smoke. A bird which almost doesn't exist any more flies past her. She sees the shining black of its eye as it flashes past. It is one of the last sixty of its species in the world. All over the field at Astrid's feet people are lying on the yellowed grass. They have bandaged arms and heads; there are drips attached to some of them. A small child holds out a hand to her and says something she

134

can't understand. Astrid looks down at her own hand. There is no camera in it.

She is nearly asleep in the stifling hottest-ever heat when she hears a door across the hall open and close, then hears her own door open and someone come into the room and the door close again.

She pretends to be asleep. There is someone there in the dark, someone not moving so you can't be sure, but some different filled kind of silence definitely there in the room.

Astrid knows the scent, clean, like clean leather and a little like oranges, clean skin, talcum powder, maybe wood, pencil shavings, a pencil that's just been sharpened is what she smells like.

She stands over the bed for a long time before she moves. The bed shifts as she gets into it. Astrid keeps her eyes shut. She pulls in closer, slides in close to Astrid's back. She blows warm breath into Astrid's hair, right into her head. She wraps her arms one around Astrid's middle and the other over her shoulder round her front, and breathes the same warm breath into the back of Astrid's neck.

Astrid feels her own bones underneath the warm breath, thin and clean there like kindling for a real fire. She thinks her heart might combust right out of her chest id est the happiness

the middle of dinner with
everybody there listening she says: *if you're going to give
anybody a hard time, give it to me*.

Then she winks at him, right at him, right in front of his
mother, right in front of Michael, who haven't a clue. A hard
time! Give it to me! Then winks right at him. Magnus feels
the reddening rise of his prick thickening against his jeans,
his heart a hot hole into his chest, his head burning, his face,
a burning feeling all up the back of his neck.

Magnus, his mother says a moment later. You've really
caught the sun today.

Uh huh, Magnus says. He can hear himself mumble. He
sounds like a stupid child. Too much in the sun, he says.

Ha! Michael says as if Magnus has said something very
clever. His mother says he'll go a nice shade of brown
tomorrow. Astrid doesn't say anything, is being quiet so as
not to attract attention to herself. Magnus knows the tactic,
she learned it from him. Look at them all. They know
nothing. A minute ago they were arguing about something
pointless, Astrid losing a camera that cost a lot of money.
But Amber covered for her. It is what Amber is like.

Amber = unbelievable.

He can't look over at Amber or he will go an even worse colour of red.

He looks at his mother instead, who is telling Amber about when she was a girl again. His mother has been twittering all evening like one of those little birds that people who live in Mediterranean countries keep in cages outside their windows, the songbirds that start singing when the sun hits their cages in the afternoon or the early evening. *We sang I Love To Go A-Wandering, we sang Had a little fight with my mother-in-law, Pushed her into the Arkansaw, Little old lady, she could swim, Climbed right out to push me in. We were a generation of girls strung between these types of expression. One minute it was Calypso Christmas carols, the next it was nymphs, shepherds, Flora's holiday, I actually used to imagine someone called Flora packing her case for going on holiday when we sang This is Flora's ho-li-day.*

Ha! Michael says again like everything's a great in-joke. Amber is leaning on her elbow at the table. She yawns without covering her mouth. His mother = small bird blinded by sunlight into forgetting it's still in a cage.

It makes Magnus feel something, to think this. The feeling is equivalent to a kind of sorry. He feels it too, though he doesn't know why, for Michael sitting forward in his seat, peeling back the petals of that small salad flower so carefully. He feels it for Astrid sitting next to him, lost. But she isn't lost at all – she's right here. There's nothing wrong with her. But something feels lost. He can't explain it.

He puts a piece of bread in his mouth. He wishes he could put a stone or something in his mouth, something that wouldn't just dissolve, that wouldn't alter because of humans having digestive juices that rot everything, something he could concentrate on without it changing. But stone =

Lapidary Club = the sorriness dwarfs him, towers up out of him, as big as what? as a lighthouse on a rock with a glare of light coming out of it hitting each of the people at the table. Magnus has to look away because of what it lights up.

His mother = broken. There is something broken about the way she says what she says, the way she leans forward so brightly at the table saying *it's such a lovely night, it's been such a lovely day, it's such a lovely supper.* Michael = what? His glasses are on squint. His body is at an awkward angle. He looks dated. He looks like an Airfix model put together by a boy not concentrating properly, so a wing got stuck on a little crookedly, a wheel got superglued out of joint with the others; dull blobs of too much glue on it in all the wrong places.

Magnus glances at Astrid.

She looks back at him, right in the eyes.

What? she says.

Astrid isn't totally broken yet. But if a window could throw a brick at itself to test itself that's what she'll do, she'll break herself, Magnus thinks, then she'll test how sharp she is by using her own broken pieces on herself. Everybody at this table is in broken pieces which won't go together, pieces which are nothing to do with each other, like they all come from different jigsaws, all muddled together into the one box by some assistant who couldn't care less in a charity shop or wherever the place is that old jigsaws go to die. Except jigsaws don't die.

Magnus's stomach starts to really hurt.

What? Astrid is still saying, making a face at him. What? what? what? what? what? what? what? what? what? what? what? what? what?

Astrid, Eve says.

What? Astrid says.

138

Amber laughs. Eve laughs too. Stop it, she says.

Stop what? Astrid says.

Everybody laughs except Astrid.

I didn't actually do anything, if anyone actually cares, Astrid says. It's him who was looking at me funny.

In a funny way, Astrid, Eve says.

What? Astrid says.

Looking at me in a funny way, Eve says.

I am *not*, Astrid says. It was *him* looking at *me*.

No, not *at me*, I mean the way you said it, Eve says. You said: looking at me funny. You should have said: looking at me in a funny way. Ask Michael.

Amber puts the flat of her hand on top of Astrid's head, takes it off again. Astrid sinks back in her seat, rolls her eyes, sighs. It is Amber who makes things okay. If Amber is a piece of broken-up jigsaw too, Magnus thinks, then she is several pieces of blue sky still joined up. Maybe she is a whole surviving connected sky.

Idiom, Michael says suddenly like a mad person, looking up from the flower on the end of his finger. He shrugs. Attic, he says. He shrugs again. Amber smiles a lopsided smile at Magnus over the table so that he can't not think about her broken-open mouth moving there above him next to his own eyes, then his own mouth, open too, totally amazed at what the rest of himself is doing below, pressed hot right into her.

You're very quiet, Saint. What are you thinking about? Amber says across the table. (In front of everybody.)

Nothing, Magnus says.

What exactly were you thinking about it? Amber says.

About what? Magnus says.

About nothing, Amber says.

Everybody laughs.

No, Magnus says. I was thinking, um, lighthouse. If you

wanted, for instance. I was trying to work out, to measure the total inside area in cubic metres it would be really difficult because of the changing size of it as you went further, uh, further up inside.

Magnus has gone a really really red colour, Astrid says.

God, yes, darling, his mother says shaking her head. Is it sore? Run upstairs, Astrid, get the aftersun. It's in my soapbag.

No, Magnus says. I'm fine.

I think you should definitely use it tonight, Eve says.

It's all right, Magnus says.

It looks very raw, she says. Weren't you using any protection?

Amber looks straight at Magnus, raises one eyebrow. She laughs out loud. Magnus can't not laugh. He laughs too. In front of everybody, still nobody getting it, nobody knowing, nobody even beginning to work it out. They all start laughing along anyway, even though. They laugh like a family all laughing together at something.

Amber = what?

The Jordan Curve Theorem. Every simple closed curve has an inside as well as an outside. Amber's bare breasts hanging down above his head were two perfect bell curves. She is a torus. Inside her is curved space. It was late afternoon. He came out of his room. Amber was whistling, standing on the upstairs landing looking at the ceiling like she was some kind of house expert off a tv programme.

Wait here, she said. Don't go away.

She fetched a stick from the garden to shift the loft hatch open. She gave him a leg-up into the loft. She climbed on to the banister to get in after him. He leaned out, helped pull her up. The floor is bare boards up there, unvarnished. There is a small skylight blackened with old dirt. There is a lot of stuff in boxes, a lot of dust. It is even hotter than the rest of the house. Amber wiped her hands on her shorts, crouched on the floor for a minute, looked right at him. What about here? she said. He didn't know what she meant. He didn't know what he was supposed to say. While he was trying to think of something she slipped away down through the hatch again.

He noticed how his heart sank. Her going felt like he'd done something wrong. But she came straight back below the hatch with a blanket coverlet kind of thing out of one of the bedrooms.

She was pretty fit for someone quite old. She balanced on the banister again, reached for his hand. She levered herself up barefooted off the wall. She slid the door-cover across the hatch with her foot. She straightened up. She looked round, still holding his hand.

This'll do, she said.

Dark, he said.

She let go of his hand. But then she took off her t-shirt. The tips of her breasts were white around the nipples. She took off her shorts. Parallel postulate. Incalculable x. She took his hand again. She put it on her thigh, then put it further up her thigh. Point of contact. She undid his belt. It leapt out, it formed a parabolic curve (roughly speaking $y = x$ squared). She squeezed him. It shot out, like out of a spot.

Then she said, lie down here.

Manifold = aggregate.

Aggregate = formed of parts that make up a whole.

Infinity = never-stopping.

A sequence which repeats itself at regular intervals, once, then again, then again, then again = periodic.

Point of intersection. She made him lie on his back,

she was perpendicular, right-angled. She added herself to him.

The line going from Amber's eyes to his at one precise moment had the most unbelievably beautiful gradient in the world.

Inside her was like going inside a boxing glove, or a room made of pillows, or wings. Magnus exploded into a billion small white feathers.

The smell of the hot summer attic, the smell of them both, stuck with amazing sweat. The lean of her up against him afterwards, laughing against his ear. The lean of her whole body as she walks, as she talks, as she sits saying nothing at all, smiles at him across the table over supper with nobody else knowing. Her hidden miraculous curves.

Amber = angel.

They have sex in the loft three more times. Twice when the house is too full of people they have quick (quite sore) sex in the garden behind the bushy hedge. Once Amber comes to Magnus's bedroom after everyone has gone to bed. This is one of the best times.

It is unbelievable.

How wet it all is is a little shocking. Magnus had no idea. He is also always a little shocked, no matter how many times he sees it, by Amber having hair, like that, down there. It simply hadn't occurred to him women would. It is of course obvious when you think about it. Of course they do. Presumably they remove it with hair-removing products before they go online or have their photos taken or are filmed. Or maybe, like boys, like men, some women just have it, some just don't. Maybe older women have it. He looks at his mother as she walks across the garden. He wonders if she removes it, or if she hasn't any, or if she has a lot. He wonders in what area of cm squared. Then he has to blink a lot, he can hardly think straight.

I'm taking St Magnus for a walk into the village, Amber announces to Eve. We'll be away about an hour, long enough for me to ravish him sexually then bring him back safely, is that okay?

Magnus feels all the colour drain out of him. When he can hear again he can hear Eve, Astrid too, laughing like they think it's a hilarious joke.

We'll be reasonably private, Amber is saying. We won't alarm the good people of the village, not this time anyway. Will we?

Mmphgm, Magnus says looking at the ground.

Can I come? Astrid asks.

No, Amber says. But if you're good today I'll take you shoplifting tomorrow.

Have a nice walk, Eve says not looking up as they go. Don't go too far.

Amber = genius, Magnus thinks. Amber = genius squared for thinking to find a man who has a key to the church in the middle of the village. The next time she goes to London she gets a copy of the key made. This is genius to the power of three.

They go there most days after that. They aren't disturbed once.

Why do you always wear that stopped watch? he asks Amber one afternoon in the church. Amber, kneeling on the floor between his legs, has just finished taking the tip of him in her mouth, coaxing him out of himself again. As she did he saw the flash of her arm with her watch on it that always says seven o'clock no matter what time it actually is. For example it is about five o'clock now.

Amber leans back against the pew, pushes her hair back off her face with her hand.

I need to keep an eye on the time, she says.

Yes, but it's always the wrong time, Magnus says.

That's what you think, Amber says.

Then, with her watch hand, she reaches down. What she does next blanks his mind completely of time.

Time is nothing at a time like that.

Afterwards they sit on the village green, on the village bench. People go past. Amber says hellos to them all. They all say hello back like they know her. They all smile. They are the Village People. Magnus doesn't tell Amber that they call them this. Eve is never rude about the village for some reason, neither is Michael, in front of Amber.

Look how long their shadows are, Amber says as two cyclists pass them. She waves at the cyclists. They wave back. Magnus watches the shadows waving their strange-angled arms on the road surface.

People are nothing but shadows, he says.

You're not fucking a shadow, you know, Amber says. Or if you are, then this shadow likes it fine, even if that's all I am, just a shadow.

He is embarrassed that he might have offended her. But she doesn't look offended in the slightest. Instead, as usual with Amber, it is an astonishing way of looking differently at things. It makes him momentarily brave.

It keeps getting dark when it's light, he says. I mean, when it's not meant to be dark.

Does it? Amber says.

She thinks about it.

Persistence of vision, she says. You must have seen something so dark that it's carried on affecting your vision even though you're not looking directly at it any more.

But how? Magnus says.

Exactly the same as if you saw something too bright, she says. God you're stupid for someone who's supposed to be so clever.

Magnus sits up. (Situation = possible light as well as possible dark.) An old lady goes past.

How are you today? Amber says. Hot, isn't it?

Oh it's a hot one all right, the old lady says. The rhubarb's dead. The leeks are dead. The geraniums are dead. The lawn's all dead. It was the heat that did it. You're a good girl, you, aren't you, always at the church, day after day, him too, always there with you. It's grand to see.

Ah, it's not me, it's him making me go, Amber says. He's a saint, you know.

You're a good boy, you, the old lady says to Magnus. There's not many boys as'd go to the church like that all them days on their holidays in the time that's theirs. You'll make someone a good husband one day.

Where's your own husband today then? Amber asks.

Oh yes, my husband, he's dead my love, the old lady says. I had one, I had him for fifty-six years, he was a good enough lad while he was here, but he's dead now.

Amber waits until the old lady is well up the road before she turns to Magnus.

It was the heat that did it, she says in his ear.

Amber = angel, though maybe not quite in the way Magnus first thought when he saw her all lit up that first time in the bathroom when he was up on the side of the bath.

She'd caught him as he came down. She'd steadied him. She'd sat him on the rim of the bath. She'd looked up at the shirt arm swinging above them from the shirt tied round the beam. Then she'd unbuttoned her shorts, sat on the toilet. She was urinating. Do angels urinate? He looked away, shut

145

his eyes. It was quite noisy. When he opened his eyes again she was buttoning up her shorts.

You're very polite, she said.

She pressed the flush handle.

You could really do with a bath, you know, she said.

She turned on the taps. Water came out of the showerhead.

Stand up, she said.

She undid the button on his jeans.

Where've you been? she said. In the river?

She knew everything. He turned his back to her. He slid his wet jeans down his legs. He stepped out of them on the floor. When he sat in the bath it was with his back to her. She reached the showerhead down. She showered him. Then she soaped his back, then his chest, his neck, then she put her hand down underneath, soaped round his balls, all round his prick. He was ashamed of himself, when she did that.

She adjusted the taps, showered the soap off him with warmer water. Then she soaped his hair, rinsed it off. She turned the taps off. He stood up. He was shivering. She held out the towel. While he dried himself with his back to her she stood on the side of the bath, reached up, untied the shirt from the beam. She jumped down. She was so light on her feet. She put the shirt to her nose then screwed it up in her hands, folded it inside the jeans all in a damp bundle which she put into his arms.

Maybe some cleaner clothes, she said.

She was sitting on the top step waiting for him when he opened the door of his room again, clean now, cleanly dressed, to check if she was still there or if, as he suspected, he'd totally made her up.

The television is full of the news about Saddam's dead sons. The Americans killed them in a shoot-out a couple of days ago.

The tv shows the photos of them again, the ones taken directly after the killing. Then it shows the photos the Americans took after they shaved them to make them look more like they're supposed to look, like they looked when they were recognizable. The photos taken after that prove they're clearly the sons.

This is a turning point, the tv says. It has broken the back of the war, which will be over now in a matter of weeks.

Magnus looks at the photos of the dead faces on the screen. They were tyrants = all sorts of torturing, raping, systematic or random killings. A typical human being contains about one hundred billion neurones. A human being = a cell which divides into two then four then etc. It is all a case of multiplication or division.

The people on the tv talk endlessly. After the talk about the deaths there is talk about the government's popularity via the tv channel's own phone-in poll, then a report on the current political stratification of middle England, the shift of support after the killings. They say the word middle a lot. Support among the middle class. No middle ground. Now to other news: more unrest in the Middle East. Magnus thinks about Amber's middle, her waist, her abdomen, how doing it with her smells like wax melting into heated-up fruit, how the kisses taste of aquarium.

So as anyone who was a hep cat back in the swinging sixties will happily assure you, the woman on tv is saying, you can still be trendy in your own swinging sixties because what we used to think of as middle age is nowadays almost unrecognizably youthful!

A picture of Mick Jagger comes up on the tv screen. Swinging 60, the caption says.

Magnus shifts, restless on the sofa. He stands up, presses the remote. The tv is obedient, switches off. The room, however, goes on ticking round him by itself.

He walks to the village. When he gets there he walks the whole circle of it to see how long it takes him.

It takes fourteen minutes.

He circles the locked church.

The little shop with the post office is shut. Its shutters are down.

On his way back to the house he stops outside a long building. He has the feeling he's been here before. Then he recalls distinctly: he is leaning on the wall; he is trying to be sick; a man is coming out; the man is angry; he is shouting at him, helping him roughly to his feet; there are people watching him through a window.

Magnus steps over the tiny wall round the building into its empty car park. From the front he sees that the building is an old-style bingo hall. It is one of the biggest buildings in the village that's not a house. It must have been important in the life of the village at some point, though now it is pretty dilapidated-looking.

Two painters are redecorating its outside. They are painting it whiter. There is a strong smell of paint, beyond it the smell of food. The building seems to be a restaurant of some sort. No wonder the man came out shouting at him, if he was being sick outside his restaurant right in front of diners eating dinner.

Magnus remembers himself that night, a broken boy on the ground.

His mother, broken. Michael, broken. Magnus's father, his real father, so broken a piece of the shape of things that, say he were walking past Magnus, his son, sitting in the corroded bus shelter of this village right now, Magnus wouldn't recognize him. He wouldn't recognize Magnus. Everyone is broken. The man who has the restaurant, he's a broken man. Magnus remembers his shouting. Those two painters, they're broken, though you can't always tell by just looking. They must be, since Magnus knows everybody in the whole world is. The people talking on all the millions of tvs in the world are all broken, though they seem whole enough. The tyrants are as broken as the people they broke. The people being shot or bombed or burned are broken. The people doing the shooting or the bombing or the burning are equally broken. All those girls on the world wide web being endlessly broken in mundane-looking rooms on the internet. All those people dialling them up to have a look at them are broken too. Doesn't matter. All the people who know in the world, all the people who don't know in the world. It's all a kind of broken, the knowing, the not-knowing.

Amber is broken, a beautiful piece of something glinting broken off the seabed, miraculously washed up on to the same shore Magnus happens to be on.

A woman goes past Magnus in a car. She looks at him. It is amazing how many older women turn their heads at him. He feels momentary pride that he knows what to do, that Amber has taught him how.

But then he realizes it was just the cleaner who works for them in their holiday house. She was looking at him because she recognized him.

He has seen her standing spraying chemicals on to wood, rubbing at a sideboard with a lemon-scented disposable duster.

I broke somebody, Magnus says to Amber that evening when they go to the church.

So? she says. And?

She says it kindly. She unbuckles him.

So.

It is another evening. The shadows outside have lengthened. Everyone is in the lounge. Amber is doing something to his mother's knee. His mother is telling Amber information about the French Impressionist Edgar Degas. Magnus wonders why his mother has this need to tell Amber things, as if she doesn't know them, as if Amber is stupid or an uneducated person. Michael is the same, always quoting stuff as if it's instructive to her. Amber knows all kinds of things about most things. There's not much she doesn't know about. He and Amber have had discussions about how light is part particle, part wave-structure, how time is bending, speeding up so that actual minutes are shorter though we don't notice it because we don't know how to yet. Amber knows about Egyptian, Minoan, Etruscan, Aztec everything. She knows about car electronics, solar radiation, the carbon dioxide cycle, things in philosophy. She is an expert on those wasps which inject other insects with paralysis so that their own grubs can feed off something still alive. She knows about art, books, foreign films. She spoke for ages one afternoon in the attic about an Irish playwright who listened at the cracks in the floor of the room he was renting, to hear the people in the kitchen of the house he was staying in, so he could put the kind of speech that people actually used into his plays.

Right now Amber is kneeling on the floor in front of his mother while his mother holds forth to Amber, but really to the whole room, as if the room has never heard of French Impressionism, about how beautiful the Degas sculptures of horses are, how like life the Degas dancers are. She is explaining that when Degas died he left instructions that his sculptures – which were mostly made of clay but also in some cases of the stems of his paintbrushes, even grease from Degas's kitchen – were not, under any circumstance, to be cast in bronze. He wanted them to rot away. He wanted them, his mother says, to have a life cycle. But after Degas was dead his agent ignored his instructions. His agent had them cast in bronze after all. His mother is trying to get a discussion going about whether this was morally right or wrong. Amber, meanwhile, is rubbing his mother's knee gently, in clockwise circles.

360 degrees is the total number of degrees in a revolution because shepherds, who were the first astronomers, used to believe that the year had 360 days total.

Otherwise, the bottom line is, we wouldn't have them, his mother is saying. The world would have lost great art if his agent hadn't been greedy enough to.

Magnus watches Amber's hand. 360. 360. 360.

His prick twitches.

She stops the circling. She starts pressing places below his mother's kneecap.

Is that any better? she says.

His mother nods uncertainly.

From nowhere Magnus is overcome with love for his mother, for his sister watching sleepily from the sofa, for Michael at the table rustling the paper. He even loves Michael. Michael's all right. At the very same moment Magnus understands that if he ever let it be known that he feels anything at all, things will fly apart, the whole room will disintegrate, as if detonated.

There are things that can't be said because it is hard to have to know them. There are things you can't get away from after you know them. It is very complicated to know anything. It is like his mother being obsessed by the foul things that have happened to people; all those books about the Holocaust she's got piled up in her study at home. Because can you ever be all right again? Can you ever not know again?

For example. Is his mother innocent because she doesn't know about what he is doing with Amber every afternoon in the church? Is Astrid innocent because of it? Is Michael? What kind of innocence is that? Is it good? Is that what innocence is, just not knowing about something? To take an extreme example. Is it innocent, as in a state of goodness or whatever, if you simply don't know about all those people in the Holocaust? Or is it just naïve, stupid? What use is that kind of innocence anyway?

It seems to Magnus that it is no use at all, unless someone wants to feel more powerful than somebody else because one person knows something the other person doesn't.

Can you ever be made innocent again? Because up in the attic with Amber, or over under the old wooden roof of the church, fast-breathing the dusty air – held, made, straightened out then curved by her – Magnus cannot believe how all right, how clean again it is possible to feel even after everything awful he knows about himself, even though supposedly nothing about what Amber is doing, or he is doing, or they are doing together, is innocent in any way. In fact, the opposite is true.

He wishes they all, all the people in this room, knew everything about him. One of the really bad things about it is that they don't.

But one of the reasons the room is still holding together, even in this broken way, is that they don't.

There's his mother, telling Amber things. There's Amber, not-listening, 360-ing her knee. Something about Amber at the centre of it like an axis is what is holding them all together right now in this room, keeping everything going round, stopping everything from fragmenting into an exploded nothing that shatters itself out into the furthest reaches of the known universe.

Amber is ruthless with Astrid. She is unbelievably rude to Michael. *As if I give a monkey's fuck about what you think about books.* She is bored silly by his mother, makes no attempt to hide it. *Uh-huh*. So: Astrid is besotted. Michael looks more determined every time. His mother gets keener to dredge up 'interesting' things to say. It is like a demonstration of magnetic gravity. It is like watching how the solar system works.

As concerns Magnus himself, Amber = true.

Amber = everything he didn't even know he imagined possible for himself.

He will be able to remember this all his life, this losing his virginity to, learning all about it from, an older woman; the kind of thing that would happen to a boy in a classic novel or something but is really actually happening to him, the kind of thing that he will be able to tell someone over a beer in a quiet pub, leaning on the counter, speaking low, moved by his own memory of it when he is much much older, a man, in his late twenties maybe or his thirties.

Magnus catches the train to Norwich. From there he takes the train to the city with the university in it to which he was once meant to be considering applying.

He asks a taxi driver to take him from the station to the library. But the library the taxi takes him to, by mistake, or maybe because he looks like a student, is the main university library, to which, because he's not a member, he has no access. The man at the computers, at the front desk in the huge entrance hall which smells of complicated polish, treats Magnus like an imbecile for not knowing this. Well, this is fair enough. Only an imbecile would expect anything more.

The city is so beautiful, everywhere tourists taking videos. He walks back into town over a beautiful tourist-heavy bridge. He watches them videoing the beautiful yellowstone walls, the outsides of colleges to which he was once supposed to be considering applying. When he gets to the town market, a rough-looking girl at a stall selling hats directs him to the other library, the public one, behind several municipal-looking buildings next to a multistorey car park.

It smells disconcertingly of people in the public library. Even the stairwell smells of people.

The only book useful to him in the Reference part of the library, which is full of non-members (old people, poor-looking people, unemployed-looking people, foreign-looking people) all using or waiting to use the few computers, is The Penguin Dictionary of Saints. *Magnus of Orkney. D. on Egilsay, 1116, f.d. 16 April. This Magnus was a son of Erling, joint ruler of the Orkney islands. When King Magnus Barefoot of Norway invaded the Orkneys, Magnus Erlingsson took refuge with Malcolm III of Scotland and is said to have lived for a time in the house of a bishop. After Magnus Barefoot's death he returned to the Orkneys, where his cousin Haakon was in possession; at length Haakon treacherously killed him on the island called Egilsay. Magnus was eventually buried in Kirkwall cathedral, which is dedicated in his honour, and other churches bear his name; he was thus honoured because of his repute for virtue and piety, but there appears no reason why he should have been called a martyr. There is a number of other saints named Magnus, mostly martyrs, but little is known about any of them.*

Magnus reads the passage again, but not because he wants to know the story, which isn't much cop anyway, which is a bit annoying after he's come all that way specially to find it. Instead, he finds, he is totally fascinated by a single word. The word is: and.

Virtue *and* piety.

And other churches bear his name.

And is said to have lived.

It is so simple, so crucial a word.

He flicks through the saint book letting his eye stop on random sentences.

Only the names of some persons <u>and</u> places survive. It was only to be expected that miracles should be attributed to him, <u>and</u> his reputation as a wonderworker was subsequently enhanced. She made a public bonfire of her wardrobe <u>and</u> jewellery, <u>and</u> was then taken to a house of nuns. At a place called Dokkum he <u>and</u> his companions were set upon by heathen Frieslanders <u>and</u> put to the sword. But no confidence can be put in the story that she was denounced as a Christian by her rejected suitor, <u>and</u> miraculously saved from exposure in a brothel <u>and</u> from death by fire. This story, which gained immense popularity, is not heard of before the seventh century <u>and</u> there is nothing to suggest that she was anything other than imaginary.

Outside the library roadworkers or builders are breaking up the road surface with a pneumatic drill. Inside the library non-members are still queueing to use the computers.

Inside the library non-members are still queueing *and* outside the library roadworkers are using sheer air pressure to break up rock or tarmacadam.

Air *and* rock! The word *and* is a little bullet of oxygen. And Magnus, who came to this learned city to read about his namesake, to research the nickname he has been given by the very experienced older woman spending her summer seducing him every afternoon on the wooden seats of an old church, and the Christian name originally given to him by a father he can barely remember and about whom he doesn't really give a monkey's fuck (though his little sister feels much more strongly and emotionally about their lack of connection), is suddenly high as a kite, breathing again with the whole of his lungs as if he's been for a long time cramped

155

in a small and dark and suffocating space not big enough for the proper recognition of a small word.

And?

And, Magnus says out loud.

He must have said it too loudly because a few people in the queue turn and look. The man on the nearest computer stares at him. A librarian at the low desk raises her head as if Magnus might become a problem.

Magnus closes the book and looks the librarian in the eye. He wonders if she fancies him. He wonders what she'd be like in bed. The first computing machine in the world, he tells himself as he leaves the library, was invented by Pascal in the 1640s, and that was before Pascal was even twenty years old!

Magnus glows all the way back to the station along the streets of the glowing city. On his way he stops to breathe in, to take the summer air in, but only for a moment because if he stops for any longer than a moment he will miss Amber at the church later this afternoon. That's if she's there. That's if she turns up. He might stop for longer, actually, maybe just stand here casually for longer. Maybe he'll miss the train. Maybe Amber will be waiting in the church and it'll be Magnus who doesn't turn up today.

He has stopped beside a tree planted outside shops. It is nothing but a nondescript tree. A nondescript tree and Magnus. Its leaves, Magnus can note to himself now, are connected to its twigs are connected to its branches are connected to its bigger branches are connected to its trunk and its trunk to its roots and its roots to the ground. Its species is connected to other members of its species and to other trees related by species and to other trees by virtue of being a tree and to other plants and living things by virtue of being things which respond to photosynthesis = all food, fossil, fuels in both the past and the present: and if there's a past and a present then there's probably (and definitely possibly) a future, and the notion of a future and Magnus and all.

It is really raining. They can hear it on the roof of the church. Magnus is telling Amber about what Wittgenstein said about rain, about how there was no point in trying to count separate raindrops and that the correct answer to the question of how many there were wasn't an actual exact number but was just many. In maths, Magnus explains, correctness is sometimes relative. Some error is tolerable. It isn't the same as making a mistake.

Right, Amber says. And sin, if I remember correctly without error, equals opposite over hypotenuse, right?

Eh yes, Magnus says. That's right. But it's said like sign.

He is momentarily annoyed that she knows so much about things he knows about. And she is being ironic about something though he can't think what or how.

But he shifts a bit to be more comfortable in her arms, in the musty smell of the church with the rain drumming (allowably inexactly) on the roof and his head on the old-smelling kneeling-cushion and the curves of the tubes of the little organ visible above their heads if he looks to the left past Amber, and the tatty cardboard numbers upside down on the wall in their number-holder announcing the hymns for a service held God knows when, past or future, maybe past and future, who knows? 7. 123. 43. 208. He wonders which hymns they are. He knows from his and Amber's lunchtimes, afternoons, late afternoons in the church that whoever chooses the hymns leaves the numbers in their neat little divided cardboard piles of 1s and 2s and 3s and 4s and 5s and 6s and 7s and 8s and 9s and os under the ledge of the pew at the front. He knows the taste and smell of the church inside and out, and the brown of the old seats, the white of the walls and the brown and white of the pulpit. He has read, unseeing, so many times in the last couple of weeks, the plaques on the walls dedicated to the dead reverends. He knows, now, why people go to church. It is a simple calculation but you have to believe it. Because what does o = ?

I think I prefer you when you're a bit darker, Amber is saying. Could you maybe dim yourself a bit?

Magnus has no idea what she means but he nods and burrows his head into her shoulder and continues his calculation in his head. o = additive entity such that o + a = a. For example o + 1 = 1 and that's all you need to know about o, not what it means, or anything about it at all, more than the fact that it responds to certain given rules.

He feels Amber drift, bored, above him. She shifts herself physically over him, hurries him up. He looks up into her eyes. He is at the angle of elevation. He feels himself stiffening again. So in a moment they'll be making that breathing noise they helplessly make again, the noise that he hadn't realized was even a word, the same word breathed out and in, over and over:

and

and

and

the middle of the mundane
Norfolk night Michael sat up in the bed. Eve was sleeping.
Everything round them was silent, quite still, deceptively
ordinary, deep-down-prosaic – exactly the same as every
other night. But something strange had happened to
everything, something that came as formed, velvet, disdainful
as a cat. Change had happened. Everything rhymed now.
Yes, ab was following ab, and then the way cd followed cd,
ef, gg . . . Because he taught this sort of thing all day he tuned
straight to it, like a radio frequency:

Michael's world had become a sonnet sequence(y).

Disdainful as a cat etc. not adequate to describe what was happening, really. KO'd by a heavyweight. Shot through the chest. Earnest surgeons opening his unconscious like a splayed ribcage. Heart an open flower, beautifully petalled, beating, symmetry. Shock and heat and art had seared off all his skin, then he'd been metalled over with a new self and six new senses, a new tongue that could speak only in lines that were pentameter, intelligences that swore it was all poetry and signs:

a girl called Amber walked across a room
and everything became a new-made poem.

Amber was an exotic fixative. Amber preserved things that weren't meant to last. Amber gave dead gone things a chance to live forever. Amber gave random things a past. Amber could be worn as an amulet. Gypsies used amber as a crystal ball. Fishermen braved oceans with just a net to harvest amber. (Amber, in the hall,
walked past Michael as if he were invis
ible, a piece of nothing, unbegun.)
Greek and Roman legend had it the piss
of a wild lynx produced amber. She shone,
hardened and perfected by heat and time.
Cat urine everywhere became sublime!

Were Amber's eyes anything like the sun?
Listen, they overexposed him like a Lee
Miller / Man Ray solarization.
He glowed the moment he was looked at. He
glitzed like one firefly in the dark, then like
a whole architecture of fireworks
spelling her name and the words I love. Mich
ael sputtered out his crescendo in jerks
and flares she didn't notice, being quite
so bright herself she eclipsed everything
that shone back at her with a lesser light.
Because she was light itself. Amber, walking
through the world, lit the world, took the world, made it,
and after her everything in it faded.

But sonnets shouldn't be so damned one-sided.
They implied, at least, dialogue. He found that
no one spoke back. No one. Michael persuaded,
argued with, no one but himself, looked round at
a family that wasn't his and saw
a lot of faded colour, then he sat
in his car, stared at an empty field, raw,
stony, bleached, like he was; sat in the heat
watching it dry up. He was such a sucker.
He knew her turn of head, her hands, her laughter.
He realized that he would never fuck her.
He realized that he would never have her.
He was a very ordinary bloke.
He turned from sand to glass and then he broke.

Million a tesserae was shattered he
no possible,no with together putting
back . Front,sides,of splinters a splintery
self,remainder of a,a window shutting –
glass that so fell smashed and out look ! fuck damn
on stones the there lay if as malevolent
bare feet for unnoticing – with a slam
eh ? what ? a pieces in man,in a meant
fragments,heart,rags skin instead of a .
Overcasing the state ? was he ? know,you –
mosaic means bits. So do tesserae
before done the work, to make them,what ? do
things together ? Is a ? make do ? to whole
(denied a man in love fragments his soul) .

Disdainful   cat   urine   everywhere.

A   family that
                    wasn't   fragments   soul.

Deceptively   splayed dead gone things   denied.

Earnest   gypsies   sat
                         in
                           his
                             car,
                                  made signs.

An
  amulet hardened his crescendo.

An   field,   of a
       empty   remainder   flower.

SO BRIGHT the heart opening
                                with a   slam.

A new self   b r o k e n   took the world –
                                    n o o n e .

Heart   rags frag ments   metalled   no one spoke
                                                    back.

Deep-down a
                new tongue ec lips ed through the world.

He realized he was not adequate.
                         A sonnet beautifully beating broke.

A whole   arch it   ecture   was dark itself.

                    And after her, poetry overexposed.

Fuck poetry. Fuck books. Fuck art. Fuck life.
Fuck Norfolk. Fuck his job and fuck his wife.
Fuck teenagers who think they know it all.
Fuck that girl walking past him in the hall.
Was there corollary in love and fuck?
Was there corollary in gave and took?
Was there a point in any written book?
Was there a point in anything at all?
Was there a push that ever came to shove?
Was there a rhyme that ever came to love?
Was there a way to discipline a sigh?
Was there a place where pop songs went to die?
Was there a girl who'd never ever ever?
Was there an artery that wouldn't sever?
Did the heart fuck the mind with all its slummings?
Did Shakespeare always become e.e. cummings?
Was the end always sonnetary ruin?
Did Shakespeare always turn into Don Juan?

Michael went to the village for a walk.
That was the kind of thing a chap like him did,
holiday stroll to the village, hands in pock
ets, casual, professional, on a whim, did.
He sat outside a church and got a shock.
It sounded more strenuous than a gym did!
People were clearly fucking in that church.
It was the sound of Michael in the lurch.

It was the sound, to Dr Michael Smart,
of tragedy, a bloody song of goats.
That's what it was, a goat-song. Was it Sartre
said tragedy was those who got their oats
when others didn't, or something like thart?
Michael was tired of being a rubbish poet.
Tired of a language that barely suffices,
words that could call this All a *mid life crisis*.

Michael had fallen for a bit of rough
who'd happened past their Norfolk holiday home.
There was no doubt about it. It was luff.
He swelled with false hope, like the Millennium Dome.
He fucked his wife instead. Not good enough.
Like the Millennium Dome, nobody'd come,
they couldn't find it, it was off the map,
and when they did get there the show was crap.

It was New Labour love, then, him and Eve,
a dinner-party designer suit-and-tie,
a rhetoric that was its own motif,
they believed in each other, and a lie
was at the very centre of belief.
The waste it was made Michael want to cry.

He was a ruined nation, and obscene,
and nothing meant what it was meant to mean.

He put his hands over his ears, appalled.
Strangers having sex made him want to drown.
He walked back to the house, nonchalant, called
his therapist but she was out of town.
He walked twice round the garden feeling old,
did what he always did when he felt down,
he drove his car to the nearest supermarket
and looked for a good place to double-park it.

He filled the basket with selected fruit
then checked along the line of working girls
judging them for the likeliest recruit.
He chose the one with honey-coloured curls.
She looked about fifteen. He queued. He put
the grapes in front of her like they were pearls,
the oranges like she was very fine,
smiled at her dashingly, fed her the line.

The girl smiled back. He charmed her by explaining
her beauty, his amazement at her, talked her
into meeting him on her tea-break, feigning
wonder, left without paying, snapped 'I'm a Doctor,'
to stop the man he'd double-parked complaining,
flashed his ID, waited for her and fucked her
for fifteen mins (tea-break) in the passenger seat
in the nearby wood and she was very sweet

and everything but he felt nothing at all.
He felt – awful. Her name-badge said 'Miranda'.
Brave new world. He felt bad, utterly small.

He magicked all his cash into her hand, a
small fortune. She straightened her overall.
It was nylon. He dropped her, as if planned, a
little away from where she worked. She waved.
Brave new world. Dr Michael Smart, depraved,

wept for five hours, head on his steering wheel,
in a nondescript backlot God knew where,
miles from anywhere. Then he began to feel
hungry, so he drove back, windows down, air
flow making his eyes less red. At the meal
Astrid had lost her camera. Amber's hair
was glorious. It really was. It was.
She had hair that was truly glorious.

Afterwards Amber played this game. 'Say you
gave me something of yours, maybe a key,
a house or car key or something, something you do
quite a lot with in an everyday way, see,
a house key's maybe best, I'd be able to
tell you all sorts about yourself. Trust me.'
(He sent Astrid upstairs, told her to get
his keys out of the bedside cabinet.)

Amber closed her eyes and held Magnus's ring.
She said something about truth and disguise.
Astrid refused to give her anything.
Amber told Astrid she should use her eyes.
Eve gave her – he had no idea – something
and she told Eve something Eve thought was wise.
His turn. She held them to her perfect nose
and he could feel her breath, she leant so close.

'You're never going to get the thing you want.
Not till you work out what it is you want.
You don't actually want the thing you want.
You only want what you can't have. You want
it blindly. What it is you think you want
is nothing like what you actually want.
You've still got to work it out, what you want
and what it is, the real meaning of want.'

She dropped his keys on to the table. Never.
She'd told him he'd never get what he wanted.
It made him want her more. It was so clever.
It left him hopeless hope, a ghost more haunted
by the living unhaveable than ever.
He'd have it. He'd have her. He wasn't daunted.
He walked around the garden and he ranted.
He wasn't daunted. He'd get what he wanted.

Months later he remembered that she knew
where the house keys were kept, after this game –
in the bedside cabinet. Months later, too,
he thought about the wanting her with shame
and not a little wryness, like a clue
right under his own nose, a clue that came
and went and told him exactly what he needed,
plain as abc, and he'd refused to read it

the middle ages she'd have
been in real trouble having all that charisma; history held
that to be quite so animally magnetic wasn't always so safe
and in a different age she'd have been publicly flayed for it
or dragged humiliatingly through the village and stuck in the
stocks, or chained to a post outside the local church with all
her hair shaved off like that girl in the Bergman film, the film
where death was following the medieval knight and the
plague was making everyone go mad. (God, those Bergman
films were such hard work. They were beautiful. But
impenetrable, and so dark. The times films like those were
dealing with were dark, she supposed. And it took dark times
themselves to produce films like that one. That particular
film was meant to be an allegory about post-nuclear paranoia
if Eve remembered rightly. Did dark times naturally result in
dark art? And did art always really reflect its own time, rather
than any other time? Eve was a member of a very nice book
group in Islington, six or seven women and one rather
beleaguered man, who met in each other's houses – one of
the pleasures of it was seeing the insides of a whole range of
other people's houses. Over the last six months the book

group had enjoyed two doorstop historical novels – both Victorian, mostly about sex – by contemporary novelists, last year's Booker winner about the man in the boat with the animals, a Forster novel, the big multicultural bestseller which most people in the group got only halfway through, and a very nice novel about Southwold. Michael disapproved of the book group. He thought it bourgeois beyond belief. But Eve was a minor celebrity at the book group, being an author herself. It gave her a definite authoritative edge, which half of the group nodded to and most of them secretly resented, she sensed.)

She watched as Amber, sitting next to Michael, filled her plate from the salad bowl, and thought about what Amber would look like with her head shaved. She'd probably still be beautiful. That was real beauty, Eve thought, beauty that could withstand humiliation, or baldness, and not David Beckham baldness but spite baldness, victim baldness, violence baldness, crowd-anger baldness. She pictured Amber, head bowed and bald as an egg, hands bound behind her back round the wooden post, thirsty and silenced and beautifully insane outside a medieval church with all the villagers jeering at her.

Astrid, she said instead, quick. You should film us all at supper tonight. It's such a lovely night, it's been such a lovely day, and it's such a lovely supper, we should commemorate it.

But Astrid being quintessentially Astrid, as well as maddening Eve by arranging and eating things on her plate in some kind of psychotic adolescent order – the meat by itself first, the bits of salad separated into leaves from the same types of lettuce next, the cucumber separately from the tomato – announced she had 'lost' her nearly-a-thousand-pounds-worth of camera 'somewhere'. Amber tried to cover for her and pretend it was her fault; more the act of an

179

adolescent schoolfriend than a grown woman; with the same sweet brusqueness Amber distracted them after supper by playing one of those psychological personality games where she claimed to be able to 'know' information about someone by simply holding in her hand some object that had belonged to him or her for a considerable length of time.

Trust me, Amber said. This talent is what enabled me to travel three continents on almost no money and always eat a reasonable supper.

Everybody laughed, except Astrid, who wouldn't join in. Amber asked Magnus to give her the ring he was wearing (the one Eve had bought him for his birthday the year before last). Magnus slid the ring off his finger. Amber held it in her hand and held her hand up, professionally, in front of her face.

This ring, she said after a moment's silence, is very very precious to you. This is because your mother gave you this ring.

Astonishing! Michael said. Totally glorious!

Eve held up her hand to quieten Michael.

It was a Christmas gift, Amber said with her eyes closed, as if listening. No, a birthday. A birthday. Fifteen years to the day after your birth, your mother gave you this ring.

Well, obviously, Magnus must have told her this. But Magnus swore he hadn't.

Shh, please, Amber said. Your birth was complex. You had the cord around your neck before you were born.

Magnus's mouth fell open. He turned to his mother and stared.

Amber raised her fist with the ring in it up to her forehead again. Someone must have told her. Michael must have told her, if Magnus hadn't. Not that Eve could have imagined Michael remembering a fact like that. But Michael was odd

180

at the moment. He was strange, changeable. Several times now, Eve had found him sitting staring into space. The other day she'd found, in his trouser pockets (turning them inside out for washing) along with the usual condoms, a piece of paper which had the alphabet scrawled on it and under this a mysterious meaningless list of words: bluff cuff duff enough fluff rough stuff tough.

Amber was good at this performance of herself. She was really very good. She was almost totally convincing. She was now saying a lot of quite brilliantly pitched and conveniently vague-sounding things to Magnus about being true to yourself and being false to yourself.

Eve slipped out to the garden. There were a few small stones under a rose bush. She picked one up. She brushed the dusty soil off it and then gave it a rub on her leg. It would do. It was yellow-white, like a sea stone, glittery in places.

Back in the house, when it was her turn, she gave the stone to Amber. Amber held it for a moment. Then she laughed.

Really? she said.

Eve nodded.

Are you sure? Amber said.

Yes, Eve said. I've had it for years. It's very dear to me.

Okay, Amber said still laughing.

What did you give her? What is it she's got? Michael said.

It's private, Eve said.

We can do this privately, yes, if you like, Amber said. She took Eve's hand and led Eve across the lounge to the sofa on the other side of the room, and this is what she told Eve, holding as proof the random stone from the garden, leaning forward confidentially like a gypsy:

You were born in a good place at a good time, at the turn of the dark decades into the lighter ones. (This was true, and easy to guess.)

You had a good early love and a good early loss. (This was true, too.)

You've led a life unthinkable to most of the generations of women and men who birthed you to freedoms and riches unimaginable to them. (Well, this was true of almost everyone.)

You've been lucky.

You've been blessed.

You've been educated, more than you understand.

Really? Eve laughed.

Amber ignored her and continued:

You've always had a safe place to sleep and good things to eat, all your life.

So what is it you could possibly want to know about yourself?

And what is it they'd ask you, what do you think they'd want to know, if they were here tonight, all those women and men and women and men and women and men that it took simply to culminate in the making of you, the birth of you, that day, squealing and furious and covered all over with your mother's blood?

Well, Eve said because her head was full of the images of herself as a small new child matted with blood and Amber had stood up, was about to leave her like that, about to go back across the room and tell Michael something about himself; he was already holding up something, a keyring or something. But you can't go without telling me the answers, Eve said to Amber, low, catching her by the wrist.

To what? Amber frowned.

To those questions, Eve said.

I don't know the answers, Amber said.

All the same, Eve said not letting go.

Amber took Eve's hand and opened it. She dropped the

little white stone, warm from her own hand, back on to Eve's palm and closed Eve's fingers over it. As she did she caught Eve's hand in both of hers and shook it as if heartily congratulating Eve.

You're an excellent fake, Amber said. Very well done. Top of the class. A-plus.

Here was a summer 2003 holiday snapshot of Eve Smart in her taupe linen suit on a summer night in the moonlit garden of the holiday home. Calm and measured. Measured and calm.

Here was a summer 2003 holiday snapshot of Eve Smart (42) working hard on her latest book all summer in the idyllic summerhouse of the holiday home of Eve and her husband, Dr Michael Smart, and look how the light caught the wet fountain-pen ink on the page as she wrote line after steady line, and how she paused for a moment to think, and how the photograph caught the moment of it, and caught that unidentifiable wraith of smoke or dusty air in a shaft of sunlight, and the way this marked the accidental fall of the light through the summerhouse window that day.

Here was a summer 2003 holiday snapshot of the Smart family standing outside the front door of their 2003 Norfolk holiday home, Eve Smart and Astrid Smart at the front with their arms round each other and Magnus Smart and Michael Smart horsing around at the back, Michael with his hand on Magnus's shoulder.

A family, all of them, smiling. Who were they smiling for? Was it for themselves, somewhere in the future? Was it for the photographer? Who took the photograph? What did it show? Did it show that Michael had come home smelling, yet again, of someone else? Did it show that Magnus was a boy so like his father that Eve almost couldn't bear to sit in the same room with him? Did it show that Astrid was infuriating to Eve, that she deserved to have no father, just as Eve had done most of her life, and was lucky to still have a mother at all?

Eve roamed the moonlit garden shocked at herself and at how very fine it felt to be this angry, smoking only half a cigarette, to keep the fen mosquitoes off, well, that was her excuse. And what kind of life was it, where she needed an excuse to smoke even half a cigarette? And were there fens in Norfolk, or were the fens somewhere else? Eve didn't know. Did that make her a fake, not to know? The girl had taken her by the hand, then called her a fake. Was Eve a fake? Was she a fake everywhere in the world, or only a Norfolk fake? A Norfake! Eve felt drunk. Her heart was beating like mad. Eve Smart had a mad heart. That sounded good. It sounded extraordinary. It sounded like a heart that belonged to a different person altogether.

The very notion that Eve Smart (42) could be something other than what she seemed was making her heart beat more than anything had, including Quantum, for years.

A couple of days before this, Eve had been looking for Amber to tell her about a dream she'd just had and ask her what she thought it meant. Eve had dreamed that Michael was being sent love letters from the students he slept with and that the love letters were printed minutely on each of his fingernails, like the tiny pages of those record-breaking Smallest Bibles In The World, the words even smaller than Your Name On A Grain Of Rice. The nails could be read, but only with a special reading apparatus which was very expensive to hire and Eve had woken up before she had managed to sign all the forms in the hire shop.

Eve had prepared, over breakfast, a version of the dream

that didn't implicate Michael or herself. Astrid had told her, over breakfast, that Amber was very good at dream interpretation. But Eve couldn't find Amber. Amber had disappeared. She wasn't in the garden. She wasn't in her car. Her car was still there, though, at the front, so she couldn't have gone very far.

She wasn't with Magnus, who had his nose in a book in the front room. She wasn't with Astrid; Eve could see her kicking about outside by herself, bored-looking under a tree. Michael had gone to the city. Eve had seen him leave. She definitely wasn't with Michael.

Eve ran up the stairs. She called Amber's name. She caught sight of someone moving below her. But no, it was just the cleaner shuffling the vacuum through into the front room, trailing its plug and flex, its unwieldy plastic tube tucked up under one arm and its bits and pieces of brush held tight under her other arm.

Excuse me, Katrina, Eve called down.

The cleaner stopped. She stood still, waiting, with her back to Eve.

You haven't on your travels seen my friend who's staying with us, have you? Eve asked. Amber, you know?

With her back to Eve, the cleaner shook her head and started her shuffle through the hall again. But as she went she said something. Eve couldn't quite make it out.

What she'd said had sounded like: *her name's a hammer.*
?

It meant nothing recognizable. The cleaner had continued, machine-laden, into the lounge.

It wasn't that Eve had been scared to ask the cleaner to repeat whatever it was she said. Not at all. It wasn't that Eve was intimidated by the cleaning girl in any way, who looked poor, who looked old before her time, who looked a bit

185

simple, who looked down or away all the time, who in fact would never look Eve in the eye, who had a habit of talking to Eve with her back to her or looking away from her which definitely signalled a refusal of responsibility and meant the curtains in the main bedroom would never get changed or laundered no matter how many times Eve asked, and who was like some dreamed-up cartoon version of a resentful cleaner in a sitcom on tv but who somehow (now how did she do it?) left Eve feeling like it was Eve who was the cartoon, like it was Eve whose life was somehow less on this beautiful summer's day than the greyed-out existence she imagined for Katrina the cleaner in whatever wallpapered living room or whatever downmarket supermarket where the goods weren't quite good enough, who, with her insolent back-turned answering-back, her answering an incomprehensible answer to a question Eve hadn't actually asked, left Eve feeling off-balance, as if challenged and beaten by someone who was supposed to, who was *paid* after all to, make life easier for Eve.

Eve had stood at the top of the stairs and the vacuum had roared beneath her.

Eve woke up in the middle of the night. Michael was asleep with his pillow over his head. It was quite light in the room because of the moon. People were gathered at the end of the bed.

Who are you? Eve said.

She shook Michael's pillow. Michael didn't wake up.

There were two men and three women. One of the women was sitting at the foot of the bed holding a very small, quite motionless child. Another of the women held up something that glinted in the dark like a broken tumbler of glass. The men behind the women looked torn-up, rough. One glistened, wet down his front and across his face. The last of the women had an old-fashioned hairstyle as if from a BBC drama about the past. She held in her hand a little baton, like a tubular stick, with light coming out of one end of it. She shone this light right into Eve's eyes. Eve put her hands up over her face. When she could see again the people had gone. Where the woman with the child had been, at the foot of the bed, there was a different, older woman. It was Eve's mother. She was wearing her dressing gown as if she'd just got out of the bath.

Hello, Eve said. Where have you been?

Look, come on, I can't. I'm dead, Eve's mother said.

Eve shook Michael's pillow again. Michael woke up.

Yes, he said like a statement.

My mother was here, Eve said.

Was she? Michael said more blearily. Where? Where was she? Where is she?

She's not here any more, Eve said.

Do you want me to do something? Michael said. Some tea?

Okay, Eve said. That'd be nice.

Michael got up and went downstairs. Eve sat in bed in the empty room, listening to the unmysterious little noises of the house. Eventually she heard Michael on the stairs again. He came in with two mugs of tea and handed her one with the handle turned towards her so that she wouldn't be burned.

Thank you, Eve said. That was nice of you.

Hardly nice of me. Was it a bad dream? he said.

No, Eve said. I think it was quite a good dream.

They drank their tea, talked for a while and then both went back to sleep.

Was dream a reality? Was reality a dream? Eve walked to the village, where she knew there was a church. She was wondering if a church might help.

But the church door was locked. A notice on it gave directions as to how to get into it.

Eve found the house of the man who had the key. A woman answered the door, presumably his wife.

Are you a genuine visitor to the village? she said.

She was a stocky woman wearing an apron. She had the same inbred jaw as Katrina the cleaner. She looked at Eve with possible malevolence.

Yes, Eve said. I'm staying at the Orris house; my husband and I have rented it for the summer.

No, what I mean is are you a genuine tourist? Do you have permanent accommodation elsewhere? the woman said.

Of course, Eve said.

Have you got an electricity bill? the woman said. Or a gas bill or something with your name and address on it?

Well, no, not right now, Eve said, not on me. I didn't know I'd need one to get into the church.

Well, you do, the woman said.

But you could phone Mrs Orris and I'm sure she'd vouch for me, Eve said. Do you know Mrs Orris?

Do I know the Orrises? the woman said. You'll be the one with the family, are you?

I expect so, Eve said.

She asked Eve's name and home address. She shut the door. Three minutes later she came back with an old mortise key on a piece of rope.

Is it for praying or are you just going in there for a bit of a look, like? she said.

Probably a bit of both, Eve said.

Now, you can have the key, but don't be giving the key to nobody who asks you for it, the woman said, because them travellers are threatening to camp out in the church, so if you give it to anybody else and any traveller gets into the church and we can't get them out then it's you that'll be to blame for that and you that'll have to pay for any sorting it out and any damage as gets done.

Right, Eve said. Got you. Guard it with my life.

And bring it back when you're finished with it, the woman called after her down the garden path between the neat pinks and the rose bushes.

Eve walked back through the murderous village to the church.

Its grounds were at least quite interestingly wild and its door reassuring and traditional in its heaviness. But inside, the church was disappointing. It was nothing special. It was blank, utilitarian and modern, regardless of its old stone walls. It was ugly. It didn't smell spiritual, whatever spiritual would smell like. It smelt of disuse; it smelt a bit seedy. It said nothing about the possibilities of anything after this life, other than more of the same small dull accountings, more of the same colour brown. Brown, Eve decided, was the real colour of the empire, of Great Britishness – the sepia colour that had set in like a dampstain in the Victorian era. Ceremonial brownness. The Union Jack should be brown white and blue. The St George cross shouldn't really be red. It should be brown on white, HP Sauce on a white plate, or an HP Sauce white bread sandwich. All the small towns and villages flew the flag. They had driven, on their way here, past repetitions of repetitions of brown-brick Victorian semis and terraces, houses and shops like extras from a post-war kitchen-sink drama, houses brown as decrepit dogs and so on their last legs that someone should really take them in hand and have them humanely put to sleep. It was the end of an era. It was the brown end of an era.

Eve sat down on the back pew and felt a bit illegal for thinking these things. She tried to think about the big subjects, but now she couldn't get a song out of her head from when she was small, by a group she had forgotten the name of who had insisted that the concrete and the clay beneath their feet would begin to crumble but love would never die and that they'd see the mountains tumble before they said goodbye. My love and I will be. In love eternally. And that's the way. That's the way it was meant to be. It was meant to be like it was on all the American tv series, where the Waltons had their lumber mill right outside the house and all the girls got married and the boys worked the mill or went to the war and came back from the war, and the eldest boy grew up to be a voiceover and kept the solemn record of their lives on Walton's Mountain, the mountain named after their family, and Laura and her sister Mary and Ma and Pa built a whole town with just their bare hands and the goodness of their family, and all went to the church they'd helped build, every week. If beautiful blonde Mary went blind, then a few episodes down the line she'd get her sight back, of course she would with beautiful big blue eyes like those, how could eyes like those not see again? Pa and Ma gave each other knowing looks as Laura saved a whole orchard of trees from something – was it a drought, or an evil woodchopper? Eve couldn't remember. Ma helped the girls (and herself) comprehend pregnancy by getting them to help their cow give birth; Ma and the cow had a special understanding. Laura ran down the hill with her arms out like a bird for the sheer joy of it again and again in the closing credits. Then she learned the truth at seventeen, like in the Janis Ian song; because presumably that child actress got hardly any parts in anything after Little House on the Prairie was over. Eve couldn't remember seeing her in anything ever again and surely she'd have been easily recognizable, unless she'd had her teeth fixed.

She put her feet up on the wood of the pew then took them off again, dusting down where they'd been with her hand. She tried to recall the words of At Seventeen: inventing lovers on the phone who murmured vague obscenities because the girl in the song was too ugly to get any valentines and do anything other than invent lovers. And then that Marianne Faithfull song about the woman so past it at thirty-seven that she'd never drive through Paris in a sports car with the wind in her hair. It was all over at seventeen. Then it was all over again at thirty-seven. Forty-two, Eve thought. I've really had it. There was the tape, too, that the German assistant teacher at school, blonde, petite, and who must have been all of twenty-two, brought to class for them to translate, a song by a German rock star. *Sie ist vierzig*, he sang, *und sie fragt sich, war es nun schon alles?* Because she'd never get to California now, would she, that forty-year-old woman, being so old? She'd never get to frolic in the sea now with Jimmy Dean and all those film stars she'd dreamed about. Abandon hope, all ye who enter here. Eve (15) looked up from her desk in the German class at Eve (42) all those desert years later, and winked. Eve (42) sat in the church with all its buried dead outside under the grasses and paving stones and wondered how her books were doing on Amazon. She wondered if there was anywhere in the village she could go online and look it up and find out.

Then she wondered how her books would do on the real Amazon, if she were to drop them into it off the side of a boat.

This vision of herself on a boat and her books in the water sinking took her by surprise and made her laugh out loud. The church rang with her solitary laughter. It wasn't respectful. When she stopped laughing the echo of herself stayed in her ears.

She locked up the church again. She returned its key to its rightful keeper.

What is it that's wrong with your knee? Amber asked Eve out of the blue one evening.

My knee? Nothing, Eve said. Why?

You always hold your right leg that way, at that angle, when you sit down, Amber said.

No, Eve said. Well, funny you should say it, though, since I did damage the knee quite badly, years ago, but it's fine now. How funny. I'd never noticed I held it like that. Probably because I'm sensitive about it I do it.

It hasn't completely healed, you know, with you holding it like that, Amber said.

It feels fine, Eve said.

It looks sore, Amber said.

She had come across the room and knelt down in front of Eve. Now she was holding Eve's knee with both her hands and pressing the muscles round it with her thumbs. Eve felt panic shoot out of her knee and up and down her body.

No, really, it's absolutely fine, she said.

Amber didn't stop. She was pressing quite hard. She had very hot hands.

It's sensitive, Eve said.

Yes, Amber said.

She began to circle Eve's knee with her hand and Eve had the peculiar sensation she usually only had when she was in an aeroplane air-bouncing in mid-takeoff, her heart in her mouth, her body sprung and fearful with her feet braced against the floor and her arms hard against the arms of the chair.

Eve started to talk. She said the first thing that came into her head.

Later, when they were getting ready for bed, Michael was strangely resentful.

You never told me you had a bad knee, he said. All these years and you never mentioned it, not to me anyway. Why didn't you?

You never asked, Eve said and lay back in the bed.

Michael: What did you do to it to damage it?

Eve: I fell off a horse.

Michael: A horse? When were you ever on a horse?

Eve: It was before I knew you.

Michael wasn't listening and didn't really care when it was. He was traipsing round the room like a petulant boy, looking for his special pillow. Eve lifted the sheet and showed him his pillow, tucked under the crook of her knee.

Eve: I need to borrow it tonight.

Michael: You know you can't. You know I need that one.

Eve: Can't you use one of the others? This one would really help me get some sleep, I need to put something under my knee after all that playing about with it, and it's just the right shape for it.

Actually her knee felt fine, but she didn't want to tell Michael this. Actually it felt very good, better than it had felt for years. Actually she was annoyed, though she knew it was irrational, that Michael had never at any point in their more-than-ten years together noticed she might even conceivably have a history of a sore knee. Instead it took some girl who didn't even know her, to notice it. How many other things didn't he notice? How many other things was she blind to, herself, because of his inadequacies?

She gave Michael back his pillow and he put the light out and positioned the pillow over his ear.

Eve lay in the dark with her hands folded neatly on her stomach. As she lay there she got angrier and angrier.

193

Very quietly, she got up and pulled on her dressing gown.
Very quietly, down she went.

Amber was lying on the back seat of the car. When she
saw Eve through the open window she kicked open one of
the back doors with her foot. She drew her legs up to her
chest so that Eve could sit on the edge of the seat.

Couldn't sleep? she said.

Eve shook her head.

Want to go for a drive? Amber said.

If you're not too busy, Eve said.

Amber laughed and shrugged her shoulders. Up to my eyes,
she said.

I mean, obviously not busy, I mean tired, Eve said. If you're
not too tired.

I'm not tired at all, Amber said. She buttoned up her shorts.
She swung herself over the front seats into the driver's seat
and opened the passenger door for Eve.

Forty miles an hour on the Norfolk backroads, the
headlights lighting up dizzied insects and the colourless sides
of the hedgerows; Eve and Amber had their elbows out of
the rolled-down windows in the warm-cool air of the night.
Eve lit a cigarette and passed it, lit, to Amber.

I feel quite renegade, Eve said.

I like driving nowhere, Eve said. It's much better than
driving somewhere.

We're just like Thelma and Louise, Eve said.

Whee, Eve said.

I was twenty-three, Eve said, and I was on a tube train in
London, and there was this boy opposite me, he was very
good-looking. He was reading a book. That's the thing, he
was reading this intelligent-looking book, but he had a name-
badge on which meant he worked for Curry's. It said Curry's,
and then underneath it said his name: Adam. So I waited

until he looked up and saw me looking at him, and I said, you'll never believe this, but I'm Eve. And he said, actually you'll never believe how many people come up to me telling me they're Eve, and he smiled, and then he looked back down and carried on reading his book as if I wasn't there. I had never done anything like that before in my life, I had never so much as said boo to a goose, never mind made a direct pass at someone I'd just seen thirty seconds ago. So I stood up to get off, but before I got off I leaned in over the top of his book, it was a book about a Polish film director, Adam was always finding things to be interested in before they became trendy and everybody else was interested in them. I leaned in over the top of it and said, yes, but what you don't realize is, I'm the real Eve, the original Eve, and then I got off the train, it wasn't my stop but I wanted to make an exit. So I went up the escalators and up to the street, and I stood in the air and I was really angry at myself, but I was exhilarated too, I was both. I kept telling myself he wouldn't have been worth it because he worked, you know, for Curry's, and I was right, because as it turned out, as I found out, he had almost no ambition, Adam, in fact you could say he had negative ambition. But there I was, standing in totally the wrong place, I had no idea where I was in the city and I was going to have to buy another tube ticket because I'd exited the station, so I turned around to go back down the steps and – there he was, standing right behind me, it was like something in a film, it was even raining, like it would be, in a film, and I said, hello, and he said, hello, and I said did you follow me all the way off the train and up the escalators? And he said, no, actually, it's my stop, and he pointed, I live here, I live just round the corner. Then he said, Are you really Eve? I said yes. And he said, well, do you want a coffee or anything? And I said yes.

Eve sat back, finished, in the passenger seat.

Isn't that amazing? she said. That he said *are you really Eve?*

God, you're boring, Amber said.

I'm – I'm what? Eve said.

Is that it? Amber said. Is that the highpoint, the true-blue, the secret-can't-be-told everything-must-go ultimate all-singing all-dancing story-of-you? Jesus God you're going to have to tell me something a bit more interesting than that or I'm going to fucking fall asleep right here at the wheel.

You are? Eve said laughing.

Next you'll be telling me the 'story' of giving birth to your babies and how hard it was or how easy or whatever, for fuck sake, Amber said.

Well, Magnus, as you know, was a complicated birth, but he was fine and so was I. To be honest, it was after Astrid that I felt so totally fragmented. I still do, in some ways. But babies smell so nice. I think I'd give everything up just for the smell of my own new baby again, Eve said.

Amber had flicked what was left of her cigarette out of the window with a degree of violence. Maybe she wasn't joking. The car was going faster. She seemed to be using the whole of her body to put her foot even more heavily on the accelerator. With each word she said she jerked more speed out of the engine.

Jesus fucking wept, all these endless endless fucking endless selfish fucking histories, she was saying.

Please slow down. Please stop swearing, Eve said.

I ought to punch you in the effing ucking stomach, Amber said. That'd give you a real fucking story to tell.

She took her hands off the wheel and then hit the wheel with the flats of both palms. The car swerved and jolted.

Don't, Eve said.

The car rattled, swayed far too far over to the right as Amber took the left-hand bend too fast.

Eve began to fear for her life.

Eve went to London to see her publisher. After Norfolk, London was unbelievably noisy and busy.

Amanda, her publisher, took her to Alastair Little in Soho for lunch, now that Jupiter could afford it. On their way, Eve stopped and gave a street-beggar a pound coin. Amanda scrambled in her bag for a coin too, to do the same. Between the publishing house office and the restaurant, Eve stopped and gave away a coin to every person who asked her, just to see if Amanda would.

Here, Eve said giving one weather-stained man a five-pound note.

The man looked astonished. Then he looked delighted. Then he shook Eve's hand. Amanda looked doubtful, then looked in the note compartment of her purse. She took out a ten, nice and new and brown.

Effing ucking ha ha ha, Eve thought.

The man did a little jig.

Thank you, ladies, he said. Have a nice day.

The restaurant was full of people looking to see who everybody else in the restaurant was.

Amanda always talked as if she had a list of the things to say to Eve memorized inside her head and she was mentally ticking them off as they spoke, seemingly spontaneously, to each other. Sixty-seven and a half thousand and rising, she was saying now that she'd ticked off the boxes beside family and holiday. Tremendous, she said. Demand for the first five is also utterly fantastic. Naturally, the question that everybody I talk to wants to know the answer for. How's the new Genuine?

197

Getting there, Eve said.

How does April sound? Amanda said looking in her diary.

April ought to be fine, Eve said.

Great, Amanda said.

I thought this time I might write about a person who dies, Eve said.

Well, of course, Amanda said.

No, I mean dies, and that's it, Eve said. Finished. Done. Kaput. End. No more story.

Well, yes, it's an interesting idea, Amanda said. Though the Genuines don't generally do that, do they? I mean, the Genuines formula is life-affirming, because they affirm life, don't they?

A Palestinian boy, I was thinking, like that twelve-year-old the soldiers shot, Eve said.

When? Amanda said. I mean, which year, roughly?

She looked confused.

Last month, Eve said.

Last month? Amanda said. Well. It cuts down the market appeal drastically.

For throwing stones at their tank, Eve said. Or what about if I wrote about someone who's alive right now, but will be dead tomorrow morning, say? In Iraq?

In . . . ? Amanda said. She looked even more appalled.

Iraq, Eve said. *You* know.

Well, it's, it's more overtly contemporaneously political than we're used to, Amanda said. Though why you'd want to change the historical focus, which is the Genuine premium, in other words which is, if you ask me, and I think if you were to ask the readers too, why they work so well, why they're so popular, why readers have just cottoned on to the formula, it's because their particular historical focus –

I haven't decided yet, Eve said. I may even decide not to write a book at all.

Of course if it's a question of advance, Amanda said.

I'm beginning to think I've maybe written enough books, Eve said.

But you just said, you just said April would be fine, Amanda Farley-Brown of Jupiter Press said looking miserable, putting down her wine glass.

It depends on the erosion of the Gulf Stream, of course, and how the relevant weather fronts perform, Eve said.

What? Amanda said faintly.

Whether April will be fine, Eve said.

Amanda looked flushed and lost. It made Eve feel bad. She didn't know Amanda very well. She didn't know what kind of life she led, what the pressures were on her life, what her reasons were for being the kind of person she was. What were the pressures on a twenty-seven-year-old with an editor's job at a small publisher that had just been taken over by a much bigger publisher? Amanda had the look of a person who's been told she'll be shot at dawn.

It's okay, Eve said. I'm just, you know, teasing you.

You are? Amanda said.

It's well under way, Eve said. April is fine.

Amanda looked visibly relieved.

Oh, she said. Good. Excellent. Perfect.

She shook her head, then ticked something in her diary.

It's a Scottish one this time, Eve said. I think it'll be quite popular. Without giving too much away, it's a land girl. On a farm.

A land girl, perfect, Amanda said nodding, writing it in her diary.

On the train out of London Eve watched her own reflection shift and change and revert to herself in the flashing-past scrubland and small towns and trees in the window, and was finally appalled; though if someone, an interviewer sitting opposite, say, or God, maybe, with a tiny dat recorder and microphone, had asked her, she'd have been unable to articulate why.

She looked away from herself. She tried to imagine that Amber didn't exist. When I get home, she told herself, it'll be summer. I'll be working on the land girl project for the next Genuine. I'll be halfway through it.

But it was like trying to imagine that there was no such thing as a question mark, or trying to forget a tune once you knew it off by heart. Or rather, off by brain; new research suggested, Eve had read somewhere, that tunes actually etch themselves, as if with a little blade, into our brains.

Michael picked Eve up at the station.

He talked about Petrarch and Sidney, structures and deviations. He was clearly in love with Amber too, and this time it wasn't the usual water off the back of the duck. Instead, the duck, wounded by a hunter and bewildered because half its head had been shot away, was still tottering about on its webby feet by the side of the pond. From the one side it looked like a duck usually looks. From the other, it was a different story.

When they got home, she walked straight in on Amber in the lounge with what looked like one hand on Magnus's crotch. Magnus stood up.

It's all right, Amber said. He's legally of age.

Amber was just helping me with my zip, Magnus said.

Astrid came hurtling in from the garden and the first thing she did was throw herself on to Amber on the sofa and give her a bear hug.

Amber growled.

Hi, Astrid said to Eve, looking out from the hug. We had a great day. Amber and I went fishing.

Fishing, Eve said. Great.

Yep, Amber said.

We went to the river and we purposefully tried not to catch anything, Astrid said. We threw lines in with no hooks on the end.

Wasn't that pointless? Eve said.

Yes, completely, Astrid said.

Literally, Amber said.

She and Amber broke into giggles and Amber, standing up, caught Eve's daughter in her arms, turned on her heels and swung Astrid round in the air.

Meanwhile, days passed. They passed irrevocably, and as if a wave of heat had actually thundered down over everything and made it hazy and blurred and submerged, underwater day after night after day.

What's it like for you now, when you think about what happened to the child? Eve said to Amber quite near the beginning of the end.

What child? Amber said.

The child, Eve said. The child. The child you. You know. The accident.

What child? Amber said. What accident?

What is it you could possibly want to know about yourself? Dream or reality? War es nun schon alles? Are you really Eve? How's the new Genuine? What child? What accident?

Amber, standing so beautiful in the doorframe of the shed, was made dark by the sunlight behind her. She came towards Eve, at her laptop, on the chair by the desk, and stood in front of her with her hands on Eve's shoulders as if to give her a good shaking.

Then she kissed Eve on the mouth.

Eve was moved beyond belief by the kiss. The place beyond belief was terrifying. There, everything was different, as if she had been gifted with a new kind of vision, as if disembodied hands had strapped some kind of headset on to her that revealed all the unnamed, invisible colours beyond the basic human spectrum, and as if the world beyond her eyes had slowed its pace especially to reveal the spaces between what she usually saw and the way that things were tacked temporarily together with thin thread across these spaces.

Amber was walking back across the garden now. She was whistling. She had her beautiful hands in her pockets making beautiful fists in the dark.

Eve shut down her laptop and closed its lid.

Michael was in the kitchen chopping food into equal-sized cubes with a knife. Astrid came running through from the lounge. Magnus had opened his bedroom door and was on his way down the stairs. Eve waited until they were all within earshot. She stopped Amber in the hall.

Goodbye, she said.

Eh? Amber said.

It's time, Eve said. Goodbye.

Where are you going? Amber said.

I'm not going anywhere, Eve said.

Mum, Astrid said.

Astrid stood as if frozen. Magnus froze on the stair. The noise of chopping in the kitchen stopped; Michael was in there with his knife held frozen in mid chop, mid air.

That's true, at least. You're going nowhere, Amber said.

Meaning? Eve said.

You're a dead person, Amber said.
Get out of my house, Eve said.
It's not your house, Amber said. You're only the tenant.
Get out of the house I'm renting, Eve said.

I am born just short of a century after the birth of the Frenchman whose name translates as Mr Light, who, in his thirties, late in the year 1894, has a bad night, can't sleep, feels unwell, sits up in his bed, gets up, wanders about the house and – eureka! Of course! The 'intermittent foot' mechanism! Like a sewing machine uses to shift material along! He commissions his chief engineer at the factory. He sits down himself to punch little holes in his own photographic paper. He and his brother design it: a wooden box with an eye. It records what it sees in shades of black, white and grey for 52 seconds at a time.

The Paris Express arrives. Audiences in the front rows duck their heads! Workers come out of their factory. Audiences marvel! A boy tricks a gardener with a hosepipe. Audiences fall off their seats laughing! People play a game of cards. Audiences exclaim at the way the leaves on the trees behind the people playing cards move in the wind! Hundreds of trains arrive in hundreds of stations. Hundreds of workers leave hundreds of factories. Hundreds of gardeners are tricked by hundreds of boys with hosepipes. Hundreds of leaves move in hundreds of backgrounds. *Special Notice to*

Workmen and Workwomen. *Why stand in the Cold and Rain when you could spend a Pleasant Hour for 1d, between the hours of 12 and 2 p.m. on Saturdays Excepted. Come and See the Events Of The Day portrayed in Living Pictures.* Man attacked by lion. A couple, kissing. Victoria's Funeral Procession, Football Finals, Grand National. Famous Airships of the World, Accompanied by the Famous Warwick's Cinephone. The Music Hall becomes the Central Hall Picture House, run by the fairground MacKenzies. They hire a woman pianist to make the place respectable. Aladdin and his Marvellous Lamp. What Women Will Do. The Rajah's Box. A woman rises out of a box in a cave and conjures up dancers all round her. A censor has painted over the bodies in each frame in red ink. Red shudders out of the too-bare necks and legs of the dancers.

Red means passion, or something on fire. Green means idyllic. Blue means night and dark. Amber means lamps lit in the dark.

Rescued From An Eagle's Nest. The Suicidal Poet. *Bombastus Shakespeare tries twelve different new kinds to commit suicide. He does not succeed in any but dies anyhow. A screamer from start to finish.* A man stands on the stage and tells the audience the story as they watch it. A little girl is kidnapped by gypsies, who take her away in a barrel. The barrel falls into the river. It heads for the rapids. A wheat speculator makes a lucrative deal that means hundreds of his workers stay poor. He falls accidentally into his own wheat shaft and the screen tints into gold as the falling wheat smothers him. The Central Hall changes its name to The Alhambra Picture House. *This House has been specially designed, in full compliance with the 1910 Kinematograph Act, for comfort and safety, and will compare favourably with any first-class, up-to-date London or Glasgow Picture*

House. It adds a tearoom. It has a full orchestra: pianist, cellist, violinist, drummer. It has seating for 1,000. It has a thirty-four-foot stage the sides of which are decorated with oriental figures. Its resident manager, Mr Burnette C. MacDonald, rattles chains in a barrel behind the screen for the chariot race in Ben Hur. Every Thursday night two brothers from the Black Isle come over on the ferry with their dogs to see the pictures and every week they sit in the same seats. One week the men don't come but one of the dogs, a grey whippet called Hector, is found sitting in his usual seat and stays for the whole show.

Fights, fires, riots, storms: Beethoven, William Tell, Wagner. Intrigue, burglars etc.: Grieg, Liszt, Beethoven. Love or sentiment: Dear Old Pal of Mine, Sunshine of Your Smile, O Dry Those Tears. Kissing: everyone in the cheap seats whistling at the screen. You know a film is a good one when its surface is covered with scratches like heavy rain. Chaplin is king of a rainy country. His cane has little notches down it like the bony nodes of a spine. He tips his hat to whatever he's just tripped over on the road. He stops to examine a hole in his shoe. A car drives past and sends him reeling into the dust. Another car going the other way sends him head over heels again. He gets up. He brushes himself down with a little clothes-brush. He sits down under a tree. He buffs his nails before he eats a piece of old black bread. *Several cinema managements have reported that after two weeks of Chaplin comedies it has been necessary to tighten the bolts in the Theatre seats since the audience had laughed so hard the vibrations loosened them.* Goodnight, Charlie, the boys in the audience shout at the end of the Chaplin short. Then the heroine tied to the conveyor belt heads steadily towards the buzz-saw. *Men are but boys grown tall*. The past appears right there in the room, the woodland glade, the dead person right there in the room. *You coward. You ran away when you knew the truth! Your son will never know you if I can help it.* Jesus saves the blind child. *Oh – oh yes – I think I can see the light.* The Love-Light. Mary Pickford tells the nun she wants the child back. The nun shakes her head. *I know, Sister Lucia, you think I'm crazy. But I'm not.* The police shoot the striking miners dead. *The pagan Chink gets a taste of the result of two thousand years of civilization.* Lillian Gish is about to have her head cut off in the French Revolution. *When a woman loves, she forgives.* Constance Talmadge lives in the mountains and refuses to marry. Blue Blood and Red. The Ten Commandments. The Campbells Are Coming. The Pride of the Clan. A woman takes a bath in a Cecil B. De Mille feature. Bathroom fashions all over the world change overnight. Puritan Passions. Enticement. Playing With Souls. Don Juan. The Adventures of Dorothy Dare, a Daughter of Daring. Ruth of the Rockies. Pearl of the Army. The Archduke gets down from his state car. The Archduke's chauffeur steps round to the front of it to check the damage from the bomb. *A Nation Gone, Borders Wiped Out, A Fertile Land Made a Desert, A King in Exile – and Pathé News Cameramen Are There.* Seven or eight men climb out of a trench. One slips down, slumps dead. The Alhambra Picture House, Luncheon Room, Tearoom and Car Park. *If I Had A Talking Picture – Of You.* At the end of it the audience sits in stunned silence. The orchestra is out of work. European films stop. American films triple. There are six cinemas. It's only a small town. The queues at each cinema are two hours long. The Empire the Palace the Playhouse the Queens the Plaza the Alhambra. There are wood-backed cushioned seats. There are art-deco walls. There are pillars. There is A P H in swirling letters round the tops of the pillars in gold. There are gold curtains whose voluptuous curved ruches go up and up in unthinkably sensual repetitions. There are lights so high in the double-domed ceiling that no one but God can change a bulb. A retired Great War sergeant-major sprays a pneumatic chrome-plated Scentinel Germspray canister up and down the aisles to *keep the air antiseptically clean and fragrant, session after session, day after day. Give your place a modern air. Have Scentinel freshness everywhere. Scentinel Sales New Hygiene Ltd., 266–268 Holloway Rd, London N7.*

Upstairs costs more money. Downstairs shouts at the screen in American accents. Upstairs and downstairs shout together at the British films with people in evening dress saying strangled-sounding things to each other. Cartoon, short, newsreel, forthcoming attractions, B movie, big picture, God Save the King. People bring their sandwiches. *Around the World in Sound and Vision on the Magic Carpet of Movietone.* 4d to get in to see The Good Earth, same price as a loaf. The World Changes. I Am A Thief. Lady from Nowhere. Woman Against Woman. Let's Get Married, showing with A Dangerous Adventure. March of Time. International Settlement. All six cinemas close for a fortnight in case of the invasion. They re-open a week later. All six black out their neons. The Great Dictator. Boy Meets Girl. The manager of the Alhambra, Mr O.H. Campbell, walks onstage in the middle of a Frank Sinatra film. Victory in Europe. Everybody cheers. Victory over Japan. Great Expectations. Gone With the Wind. Crying children are carried out of Bambi in the middle of the forest fire. People buy their own tvs and watch their own coronations. The screen gets three times bigger. Cinerama. Cinemascope. Widescreen. NaturalVision. A lion leaps out at the audience. The Greatest Show On Earth. Ben Hur, again. The Ten Commandments, again.

An ant crawls up a blade of grass growing out of a crack

in the tomb of Cecil B. De Mille. The Plaza stops showing films. The Queens burns down. The Empire closes. The Playhouse starts Bingo. Barefoot in the Park. Far From the Madding Crowd. Natalie Wood and Robert Redford laugh on their way home from the movies in This Property Is Condemned. Demolished. Demolished. Bingo club. Demolished. Bingo club. Seventh-Day Adventists' church. Demolished. Demolished. Open-air car sales. Demolished. Supermarket. Demolished. Furniture store. Demolished. Church. Demolished. Night club. Demolished. Demolished. Nightclub. Demolished. Restaurant. Listed façade. Bingo club. Demolished. Demolished. Demolished. Demolished. Steve McQueen's Porsche crashes on the racetrack. Will he be all right? The Bradford Empire. The Plumstead Empire. The Willesden Empire. The Penge Empire. The Colchester Hippodrome. The Glasgow New Savoy. The Aigburth Rivoli. The Dingle Picturedrome. The Kirkwall Phoenix. The Harrogate Scala. The South Shields Scala. The Leeds Coliseum. The Kirkcaldy Rialto. The Clapham Majestic. The Darlington Alhambra. The Perth Alhambra. The Luton Palace. The Largs Palace. The Stroud Palace. The Bristol Palace. The Maida Vale Palace. Fade to circle. Fade to black. They knock down the walls and all the films stand up out of their dead selves, transparent as the superimposed souls of the dead getting up out of their corpses.

Burt Lancaster kisses Gina Lollobrigida on the trapeze high above the crowd.

A roomful of society people breathes a sleeping gas pumped through the ventilation system of a grand old house. They all fall down.

A man loading a Great War plane with bombs holds them up for us to see. The bombs curve at their heavy ends like the naked breasts of women.

The dead on all the battlefields get up and walk. They walk and walk, they become a great crowd. Limping, bandaged, pale, carrying each other, not like zombies, like real shattered people, they walk to the houses of the living and they stare in through the windows.

A woman conducts a tiny orchestra whose players are no bigger than her hand.

A country girl stands under a shower of golden coins. A minute ago she was too poor for food. A door opens in front of her. It leads to a magic land.

The agents appear out of nowhere in the middle of the room. They're told what the house-owners want – to move everything to another house across the city. They nod – and disappear into thin air, there one second, gone the next. The house-owners are bemused. They shake and scratch their heads. But then the books climb down by themselves from the shelves. They jump on to the windowsill. They throw themselves out of the window. They jaunt off up the street below, waving their pages. The plates climb down off the dresser. They strut in a line to the window and jump. The cups follow. They throw themselves out. None of them smashes. The cutlery ups and walks. The chairs jump out of the window. The clothes float out of the wardrobes. The shoes, largest first, down to the children's tiny boots, walk themselves out of the house. The carpets roll themselves up and out. The house empties itself.

Palais de luxe, Alhambra, place of my conception, for which I was named.

The workers go home through the factory gates. It's the end of the long, long day.

The end

of the world. Even if it is just
1 km wide, which sounds quite small, and travelling at just
20 km a second, which sounds quite slow, it will still be the
end, the absolute end. Say it hits somewhere like America
and people elsewhere don't mind because they're nowhere
near America. Say it hits America and then the burning crusts
of the big hole it makes in America are flung up into the sky
and they shower down on to, among other places, England.
The whole of England, not just London, not just Islington,
will be burning. Norfolk will be burning. Stratford will be
burning. Richmond and Kew, and that place near Bedford
where they sometimes have to go because Michael's parents
live there, will be burning, and Hebden and all the other places
Astrid hasn't been to will be burning. Astrid is two vowels
short of an asteroid. Asterid the asteroid. The Asteroid Belt is
between Jupiter and Mars. An asteroid is a pile of space rocks
welded together into one huge rock by its own gravity and can
be a km or more wide. An asteroid is a star on steroids. It is
what happened to the dinosaurs. Probably only one, only
about 10 km wide, is all it took to make them exactly that,
dinosaurs. But a lot more recently than that, only ninety-five

years ago to be exact, which is not very long in relation to history and is only a relatively short percentage of time ago, a very small, almost negligible-sized asteroid hit Siberia though miraculously there were only six people killed by it even though it had the same power of detonation as 1,000 complete WMDs. It was just insanely lucky for human beings that it was only Siberia that it landed on.

She is not afraid to imagine the end. There will be burning chipmunks and skunks hurtling through the air, glowing red in the dark like chipmunk-sized live coals, there will be skunk-firebombs and burning bits of that bridge from San Francisco or bits of film studios and that castle and the fake rides in Disneyland and the Empire State Building, glowing like huge embers, hurtling thousands of miles up into the air and down again for miles, gaining speed and then smashing into the clockface of Big Ben, smashing into the Houses of Parliament, and Waterloo Bridge, and the Eye toppling on its side and all the people in it being thrown about inside the falling capsules like they're on the inside of snowglobes, and the buildings all on fire, Tate Modern on fire, the art burning, the restaurant burning, the shop burning.

Astrid yawns.

She is up quite early.

It is morning but it is still dark out there. She is looking out of the window at the sky above the houses. It is the colour of streetlights, then dark above. The heating hasn't come on yet. It is cold. She is wearing one of the three new red pyjama tops. She has two of the new red jerseys and the new red cardigan all layered on top of each other on top of the pyjama top and the cardigan buttoned up.

You can't have everything red, her mother said. You can't have everything the same colour.

They're different shades of red, Astrid said.

216

Anyway I'm not totally convinced that red suits you, Astrid, her mother said.

Astrid sniffed and held out the red cardigan. Her mother sighed and took it to the paying desk.

Michael, however, doesn't notice or care what colour Astrid chooses and he's in charge of paying for things till her mother comes back, by which time almost her whole wardrobe will be red.

She has tucked her feet inside the ends of the pyjama trousers, which are luckily a bit big for her. She will grow into them.

A lot of people are up and have lights on in their houses though it is still so early and dark, people getting ready for work or whatever. 6.35 a.m. on the new digital radio alarm, which sends a signal to Greenwich and receives the exact correct time back. Her room smells of the new bed and all the other new stuff. The smell of new stuff is exciting at first, then a bit annoying. Everything has the smell. It is practically all new now, literally almost everything in here and almost everything everywhere in the house.

It was amazing to see the floorboards. It was amazing to see the walls. It is still amazing to think about. Getting home and walking in through the front door and it all being bare was like hearing yourself breathe for the first time. It was like as if someone had turned your breathing volume level inside you up to full.

Astrid doesn't really miss the old stuff, just some of it. She liked it best when the house was still totally empty of stuff and they came back from the three nights in the hotel and slept in the borrowed sleeping bags on the floor till the beds arrived. It was amazing that it was the doorknobs going and not something a bit bigger or more obvious, like the Aga or the computer or the first editions or the manuscripts, that finally made her mother cry. Her mother has been gone now for three weeks and three days. It is not fixed, the date of her coming back. It is a round the world kind of thing. It is apparently very necessary. Astrid thinks it is deeply irresponsible.

They'd got home from holiday and gone into the empty house and her mother stood and stared, like they all did, in the hall first and then going through to each room. Both her mother and Michael were laughing at first, kind of standing or going past each other, their eyes open like they couldn't believe it, like it was a giant practical joke. Then her mother tried to open the door to get downstairs and see what had happened there but she couldn't open the door because there was no doorknob.

Then she started crying.

They were arts and crafts, she was saying. She kept saying it, like an insane person. The doorknobs were arts and crafts.

It was doorknobs that were the end for her. The end is presumably different for everybody. Astrid thinks now that this is rather a disgusting end, doorknobs. It's the end, her mother kept saying after that. The absolute end.

The beds, the chairs, the cupboards, the doors off the wall-units, the wardrobes, all the things in all the cupboards and units and wardrobes. Even the magazine pictures of Busted etc. off Astrid's wall. Even the blu-tack that they were stuck on with. The chests of drawers, things like the scissors and the elastic bands etc. and bits of string that were in the drawers. There was nothing left. Not even a lost button. It was like all the floors had been swept clean. Not even a lost paperclip down a crack in the wood. The only thing the thieves didn't take was the answerphone. It was bleeping on the floor by the wall in the dining room with its little red light flashing on and off. They could hear it when they opened the front door, you usually can, you always could when you got home and opened the front door, so it wasn't like it was a big surprise to hear it, except that this time it was almost preternaturally loud. It sounded a lot louder because of everything else being gone. They'd taken the phone though, so Michael called the police on his mobile. The whole house, Michael said. Literally stripped. Then he phoned a hotel. His voice was weird because they'd taken the carpets, even the stair carpets, so the sound in the house was completely different. Just someone saying something, anything, out loud, sounded weird.

So, first they'd got back from Norfolk and parked the car. Then her mother had opened the door. As soon as they went in Astrid registered the bleeping noise. Then she registered that something was different. Then she registered that the place where the coatstand usually was was strange. This was because the coatstand was gone. And then she could see that something else was gone too and then she remembered what it was, it was a bookcase, because she remembered the shape of the bookcase in the hall. And then she saw that the places on the walls that looked weird were the places where pictures had been. It is funny, Astrid thinks, that it actually took a moment to remember, and sometimes was actually quite difficult to re-imagine what it was that was in the space that something left after it got taken away.

Then they went into the front room, the lounge, the playroom, the kitchen, and looked at all the things that had gone from there.

And so on.

So the only things left, apart from obviously the answerphone, are what she and Magnus and her mother and Michael all came back with, had in the four-wheel drive or had with them in the holiday house in Norfolk. The thieves took the taps off the sinks. They took the tops off the regulators on the radiators, which has proved a bit problematic because of it now being nearly November and still not sorted out with replacements and it's sometimes quite definitely cold but sometimes too warm for the radiator to be on high all the time and none of the radiators in the house can be made to change their heat level without a pair of pliers.

It had its good side, because Astrid couldn't be in trouble about her mobile any more because she said it had been in her bedside cabinet, which obviously got taken like everything else.

Her mother went round all the neighbours, but no one had seen or heard anything unusual. The Moors had seen a removal van coming and going two weeks ago. We didn't think anything of it, they told her mother and Michael. We thought you were moving. We were waiting for the estate agent sign to go up because we're thinking of having our own house valued.

Her father's letters and the photograph got taken. They were in the holdall under the bed, with the shoes and the plastic bags and posters also under the bed, which all got taken.

Astrid looks down the road. Then she looks up the road. There are a few people walking around, getting into cars etc., but nobody she recognizes. It is not as if she is expecting to see anybody she recognizes. But it is what your eyes do. They look at people who are strangers to see if they aren't strangers.

A streetlit leaf falls off a tree. She sees it hit the ground. She looks at the strip of sky above the houses again. There are more than 1,000,000 asteroids, and those are only the ones that scientists and astronomers actually know about. There could easily be loads more. Id est.

She has pretty much stopped saying things like id est out loud. It is a bit lame to. She will be thirteen in three months' time. She would, in three months' time, have been sorting through her old toys and dolls and doll's house etc. in the two toy cupboards and giving them away to younger children like the Powells and the Packenhams and the children of families not like Astrid's who end up in hospital, like Magnus was made to do with his, but they have, as it were, already been sorted and distributed for her. Though she does wonder where for instance Harry the Rabbit and the velvet-covered collection of ponies and all those bears etc. in all their various states of wornness and newness are now.

In heaven, Magnus said when she wondered it out loud.

Listen, Astrid said to Magnus a couple of weeks ago when they were out in the garden because the house was full of carpet people putting new carpets on to the stairs and back into the rooms that had originally had carpets. There's this thing, I was wondering, why would I want to do this thing?

What thing? Magnus said.

Magnus has been sitting around a lot at home doing nothing. He has two months more of suspension pending inquiry. It was one of the things on the answerphone when they got home. He and Michael sit in different rooms all day. Astrid thinks that if she was suspended or lost her job or whatever she would at least go to a library or a bookshop or the swimming pool rather than waste her day just sitting around doing nothing, which is a bit disgusting.

Say I saw an animal that looks dead, Astrid said. Why would I want to poke it with a stick?

To see if it's alive, Magnus said.

But why, Astrid said, would I want to do something that might be cruel if the animal isn't dead and is still alive and only looks like it's dead?

To see if it's alive, Magnus said again.

Astrid had unpacked her bags from holiday and found the two tapes. She had caught the bus to Dixons, where they have her model of camera wired to a display unit. It was plugged in. She had clicked it open, inserted the first tape, which happened to be the tape with the dead thing on it on the road, and stood in the shop and watched the dead thing from back then. It lay there, dead. Astrid turned the volume up. There was the sound of the country, buzzing and air and birds. Then she saw a hand that must be her own hand lifting a latch thing on a door. Then the top of the head of the woman who was the cleaner at that house and the noise of the vacuum, then Astrid's voice asking her something and the cleaner answering. Then the walk down the stairs, it wasn't very good camerawork, it was the kind you can't look at without feeling queasy, then some floor, then into blinding sunlight reflecting into the lens. Then nothing else on the tape after that, just white noise. This was majorly annoying, because Astrid had been hoping for some footage of Amber from that day, which is one of the earliest days.

She is not allowed to talk about Amber. She is not allowed or supposed to even mention her.

It's finished now, her mother said. That time's over. Let it go, Astrid. I'm warning you. That's enough.

This had made Astrid recite, every time the car came to a traffic light junction all through the rest of their time left in Norfolk and all the way home: red, amber, green, or: green, amber, red (depending on which way the lights were changing, obviously). When her mother worked out why she was doing it she went insane at Astrid and there was all sorts of shouting and demanding. So Astrid went undercover. She started saying: amb I supposed to be back by ten? or whatever. She asked Magnus questions in front of their mother about the kind of music called ambient. She talked out loud in the car about the way a cow was ambling along a field, or an old person was ambling down a road. She talked in front of her mother to the woman behind the counter in Heals about the difference between a lamp taking a three-amb or thirteen-amb fuse. According to the woman it was for more light.

Astrid, her mother said.

What? Astrid said.

Don't push your luck, her mother said.

You are disgusting, Astrid said under her breath. She changed the word amber in her head to the word red when a red car went past them. She said, out loud, what a nice red car. When she saw another she said, I like the red colour of that car.

Now her clothes are red, her bedcover is red, her toothbrush in the new holder in the ensuite is red, her carpet is a shade of red. Etc.

Astred Smart.

So her mother knew something was up, but not what.

But now her mother is away, Astrid has stopped adding the b or talking about amb or red or whatever. There's no point in doing the red thing with Michael. Astrid is planning to say something about Amber to Magnus, but the couple of times she has been about to she has for some reason decided not to. She still doesn't know why. It feels a bit mean, or a bit weird, like poking that dead thing with the stick. All the same, she is planning to say something to Michael about it at some point and to see what happens when she does.

She ejected the tape and slipped the other one into the camera, because with any luck this was the one with the dawns on it, the beginnings tape. She pressed Rewind, then pressed Play.

The shop assistant boy was standing behind her and shoved her in the back.

You, he said. Can't you read?

There was a sign on the camera display unit which said Customers Are Requested Not To Touch The Equipment. Please Ask A Member Of Staff If You Need Assistance.

Astrid pressed Pause.

Give me three good reasons to do what it says, she said.

Because it says so, the boy said.

Feeble, Astrid said.

Because I say so, the boy said. And because it's not yours. It's for sale. If you buy it, you can do what you like with it.

You don't have to be so dictatorial about it, Astrid said.

Eh? the boy said.

One: the reasons you've given me so far are really lame reasons, Astrid said. Two: it's the display model, isn't it? That means it's one of the cameras the company writes off. So you could be a bit nicer to me and let me watch my film on it. It's not as if I don't know what I'm doing. It's not as if I'm doing it any harm. And three: if you shove me in the back again I'm going to report you to the management of this chain store as victimizing a thirteen-year-old girl customer and shoving her in the back, which is actually physical abuse, and I don't want to report anyone to anything because it's lame to.

You what? the shop boy said. He looked totally amazed. Then he laughed.

You're quick for thirteen, he said. You're too young, if you're thirteen, for me to ask you out.

Like I'd go even if you did, Astrid said examining the camera.

He was all right. He let her watch her next tape on the

shop camera without bothering her or anything. But there was nothing on the tape, just a series of fast-forwarded dark skies going light, one after the other. With each edit into another day the dark crashed down again on the screen. Then it paled into white-ish, though Astrid remembers the days as a deep far blue.

There was no dawn footage of Amber. There was nothing. It was as if Amber had deleted herself, or was never there in the first place and Astrid had just imagined it.

Astrid checked twice more. Then she ejected the tape and closed the side of the camera and went to leave the shop.

Finished so soon? the boy said.

He was a lot older than Astrid, about Magnus's age.

You've left your films, he said. Don't you want them?

I've finished with them, she said.

What're they of? he asked. Are they of you?

No, she said.

If you give me your mobile number, the boy said, I'll give you three new tapes free. Go on.

I don't need tapes, she said.

Everybody needs tapes, he said.

I haven't got a camera any more, she said.

What about something else then? he said. Batteries. Earphones for your Walkman. Your iPod. What have you got? A Walkman or an iPod?

No thanks, Astrid said.

Well, just give me your number then, the boy said. Go on. I won't call it till you're fifteen. I promise. Two years next September your mobile'll ring and someone'll say hello, is that the girl with the really blue eyes? Do you remember me? Do you fancy going to the multiplex to see a film with me tonight?

I can't give you my number, she said.

Why not? the boy called after her out of the open door of the shop. What's wrong with me?

I don't have a mobile, Astrid called back.

The boy shouted over the heads of the people in the street. Hey, he shouted. I could get you a good deal on a mobile.

So by the time Astrid remembered to be disappointed about there being nothing much on the tapes, by the time she'd stopped at a shop window further along and tried to ascertain in its reflection how blue her eyes actually were, the disappointment of it wasn't as strong as it might have been if all this other stuff hadn't happened when she went to the shop.

Anyway she can remember quite a lot of things without having them on tape. The other day i.e. out of nowhere she suddenly remembered the time she and Amber were walking past a farm or somewhere and the huge dog ran out and barked at them as if it was going to go for them, really snarling, and Amber yelled right at it, stamped right over to it shouting at it and it backed off, it actually stopped barking as if it was surprised and backed away from Amber standing there on the road.

Astrid didn't even know this was still in her head.

It is hard to remember exactly what Amber looked like. It is annoying that there was footage of that cleaner but none of Amber.

She remembers Amber did something very funny, something that made her laugh and laugh, rolling on the ground, but she can't remember exactly what it was offhand. She can remember the sensation of laughing. She can remember exactly what it felt like to stand in front of, for example, the local high spirits, making them feel bad because someone had their eye on them, and this is the thing to remember, not what their faces or their clothes were like or where they were standing or how many of them there were. Nobody is ever going to ask her to prove which people in the village they were; that's someone else's responsibility, that's for someone else to do. Her responsibility is different. It is about actually seeing, being there.

Astrid can't believe, for example, that her mother has just gone off round the world etc. like she has. It is like the opposite of actually being there. It is substandard parenting. It will have consequences. It is substandard responsibility. It is the kind of thing, along with people's parents breaking up, and grandparents who either die or have Alzheimer's and come and live with people's families and are tragic and don't recognize their faces any more and can't eat properly on their own etc., that makes people at school have eating disorders or cut themselves, which is something Astrid would never do since it is so unoriginal; there are already three girls Astrid can easily think of who obviously cut themselves and only one of them is particularly intelligent, and there are possibly also another two or three who do it and keep it a bit more secret, and there are also three girls with obvious eating disorders that everybody knows about. So they are all lucky in this house and this family that Astrid isn't the kind of person to want to do that kind of thing.

Zelda Howe is one of those girls with an obvious eating disorder.

It is amazing how quick you forget, even something you think you know, even something you really want to remember. It is amazing how memory works and won't work. A face can be just a blank. But like when she remembered about what happened with that dog, sometimes things like faces or memories come into your head on their own and you can see things so clearly that you couldn't not see them if you tried. It is insane. Astrid can't really remember what she looked like. She has searched through the holiday photos, but before her mother left she must have censored them for pictures that had Amber in them. Astrid has one of the photos in her pyjama pocket, the one of her and Magnus and their mother and Michael standing at the front door of the substandard house, because it was Amber who took it.

It is interesting the way that this is said about photographs, that a photograph gets *taken*. It is interesting that it is possible to say that Amber took the photo but that Astrid still has it. Here it is, in her pocket.

Astrid can see Amber taking it right now, if she thinks about it. She stood on the driveway stones with her feet apart and the camera up at her eye and she said: ready? and they all stood, ready.

It is actually quite a good photo of Astrid, which is rare because she is not very photogenic and usually hates photos of herself. Her eyes are very blue in it, it is true. They are a kind of sunlit flash of blue across her face.

She gets it out of her pocket and bends it to see it more clearly in the light from the streetlight. She purposefully makes sure she doesn't look at her mother in it, just at Magnus, Michael and herself, and you can also see the shape of the door of the house and a bit of the driveway. It is a moment of what Amber literally saw through the tiny camera window. That is amazing to think of it like that, like them all fixed like that, standing outside the house like that forever, but really being something no more than a split second long inside Amber's head. It is amazing that a photograph is forever but is really a kind of proof that nothing is longer than a split second in time.

At that moment forever in the photograph they are all looking at Amber and Amber is looking back at them.

If Astrid thinks of it that way, as something not being seen through her own eyes, then it's okay to look at her mother.

Her mother looks nice in the photograph. She is smiling. It is a really happy smile.

The smile annoys Astrid more and more. She puts the photo back into her pocket. She stops herself having the feeling of wanting to cry. It isn't too hard to do this.

When her mother comes back, Astrid is going to go into that branch of Dixons again and see if that boy is still there and if he remembers her like he said he would. She will say she has come in to look at mobile phones. If he asks her out again she will say yes and go out with him. This will really annoy her mother, who has a weird thing about Astrid never growing up to marry a shop assistant. One night this is what Amber told Astrid in her ear in the dark in the bed in the room in the holiday house in Norfolk.

She didn't like him because when they met he worked in a shop, Amber said.

No way, Astrid said.

Way, actually, Amber said.

She pulled Astrid's hair, once, sharply.

That was sore, Astrid said.

You deserve worse, Amber said. You're as disgusting as they are. What would you prefer? I know. He gave up his career as a promising brain surgeon and already well renowned physicist although he was so young. No, I know. He was a computer genius and moved from company to company making lots of money and having a massive effect on the ways people communicated electronically. For instance, first he made a fortune inventing email spam. And then he made a fortune inventing the way that email spam could be blocked from reaching people's emails. But he soon got bored with the pointlessness and took a job in a shop instead.

What kind of a shop? Astrid said.

An environmentally friendly alternative-consumer natural and fair trade products shop in somewhere in the north called Hebden, Amber said.

Astrid nodded.

He likes the north, Amber said. That's why you and Magnus have northern names.

Astrid shrugged her shoulders, shy, warm under Amber's arm.

Actually, no, Amber said. In reality he was born gifted. His talent was a talent for cleaning things. From a very early age he was exceptionally gifted at making things shine. It made him feel good, to make things clean. When he grew up he took a job as a cleaner, which is all he really ever wanted to do. Now he cleans the houses of people all over England, moving from place to place. He makes almost no money. He only just makes ends meet. But he cleans things so beautifully that it makes life better. It makes the things and the life shine.

(Astrid Berenski.)

Don't believe a word, a single word that woman told any of you, her mother said in the house immediately after, and said it again in the car once, and said it occasionally again in the empty house and as the house filled up with new things.

Your mother's right, Michael said. I'm afraid it's true. She was a charlatan and a trickster and a liar. She was the same as a quack doctor selling remedies that don't work to sick people off the back of a wagon. She was a mountiebank.

Magnus nodded, looked sad.

Only Astrid saw red. She saw, in her head, Amber up on the back of a horse with a mountie's hat on and the bright red jacket they wear. Amber, on patrol, nodded down to Astrid as the horse clopped past.

It is good that to see red also means to be angry. Imagine everything you saw, red, like you could see in infra-red. When Astrid went back to school in September, the first time Lorna Rose dared to give her the you're a weirdo look in the middle of that English class, Astrid, instead of ignoring it or freaking out about it, stood up out of her seat and old Miss Himmel looked up from the poetry, it was a poem about the last rabbit left in England and all the people going on a special trip to see it and Miss Himmel said Astrid what are you doing, sit down, and Astrid just kept going, walked along the desks right to where Lorna was sitting and stood in front of her desk looking at her and Lorna was laughing like she was scared, looking like she couldn't believe it and Astrid stood at her desk and said, low under her breath so only Lorna could hear, I'm watching you. Miss Himmel said Astrid, sit down right now, and Astrid said I'm just telling Lorna something she needs to know, and Miss Himmel said tell whatever it is to Lorna in your own time, not mine or the class's, unless you want to tell the whole class your business and explain it to us all. Astrid said I don't mind telling everybody right now, Miss, unless Lorna would rather we kept it private, and Miss Himmel said, well? Lorna? What's this about? and Lorna said it's private, Miss, and Miss Himmel said right Astrid, for the last time sit down. Astrid looked at Lorna in the eyes one more time. Then she went back to her seat and sat down and they all got on with the poem and since then they haven't done anything to her, in fact Lorna Rose and Zelda and Rebecca have all made a kind of almost embarrassing effort at being friendly and Zelda keeps phoning her up at home and telling her the things about her grandfather living with them and how hard it is that he lives there now and how him eating makes her feel permanently preternaturally sick and how guilty she feels that it does.

But the thing is, when Astrid remembers that morning in the class, it all takes place inside her head in a kind of strange film with strange colours, everything bright and distorted, like the colours have had their volume turned up to full too.

Also, the astonishing thing is, she doesn't need her father's letters any more. They weren't proof of anything really. It doesn't matter that they're gone. In fact it is a relief not to always have to be thinking about them or wondering what the story is or was. Her father could be anything, and anywhere, is what Amber said.

Afraid or imagine.

It is strange to be thinking about Amber as if she is in the past.

But she is.

But it's not Amber that's over, Astrid thinks, looking at the photograph of Michael with his hand on Magnus's shoulder and both of them laughing, her mother smiling like that with her arm round Astrid, Astrid with her arm round her mother.

It's finished now. That time's over. I'm warning you.

(Amber's car in the drive, Amber starting its engine up. Her mother blocking the doorway of the house. The sound of the car reversing on the stones, the sound of the car wheels going off the stones and on to the road, the dwindling sound of the car. Her mother coming away from the door and going back inside. The empty place in the front drive of the house where Amber's car, moments ago, was.)

7.31 a.m. on the new digital radio alarm, correct to the millisecond.

232

The dawn is coming up red. Red sky at night, shepherd's delight. Red sky in the morning, shepherd's warning. Red sky at night means that it will be a sunny day the next day. Red sky in the morning means storms, it is an old folklore way of predicting what is coming. It is something else that is amazing to Astrid, that shepherds are traditionally the people who look after the sheep, lying under trees playing their pan pipes in the summer with the sheep all grazing round them and choosing which of their flock get butchered and which don't, and at school they sing The Lord's My Shepherd and the readings are all about how God looks after the little children and the lambs, but only some lambs, only the ones who believe in Him, and anyway people eat lamb all the time and it only takes a few months for lambs to become sheep, and butchered.

Peep for sheep. Michael and her mother being kind, playing games from the front seats of the four-wheel drive.

There were sheep in the fields all round the holiday house. They must have been new sheep, bought in from somewhere else after all the foot and mouth pyres.

When Astrid thinks of the village the weirdest details come into her head like the lamppost next to the field on the road from the house into the village and all the high grasses growing round its base. Why would anyone's memory want to remember just seeing a lamppost like that?

Astrid doesn't know.

It is a fact, it is official according to the newspaper, that the world is actually getting darker, that most places are 10 per cent darker than they were for example thirty years ago and some are nearly 30 per cent darker. It is to do with pollution, possibly. Nobody knows. It is like the dawn going backwards, like the dawns on her beginnings tape, but in one very long very slow-motion darkening rewind, the dark coming down by tiny percentages each day in the daylight, so slowly that nobody really notices it.

It is like a curtain coming down in a theatre.

Except that it isn't the end. How can it be the end of anything? It's just the beginning. It is the beginning of everything, the beginning of the century and it is definitely Astrid's century, the twenty-first century, and here she is, here she comes, hurtling through the air into it with a responsibility to heatseek all the disgustingness and the insanity, Asterid Smart the Smart Asteroid hurtling towards the earth getting closer and closer to the moment of impact and wherever her mother is in the world, she could wake up and look out of her hotel room window like Astrid is looking out of her window right now and see something coming down out of the sky like preternatural rain. She will look out of her window and she will maybe see the moment before it smashes a great big hole 10 km wide in front of her and blows all the doorknobs off the doors, blows all the furniture and stuff etc. out of her room and all the rooms and houses anywhere near it, it could come down anywhere, and it will have consequences everywhere, not just America or England, and in that moment her mother will think to herself that what she's doing is stupid, that all along she should have been watching out, and all along she should have been somewhere else, not there.

Hurtling sounds like a little hurt being, like earthling, like something aliens from another planet would land on earth and call human beings who have been a little bit hurt.

Take me to your leader, hurtling.

The sky is red, a storm is coming and all the cute chipmunks in the world are potential firebombs. But for now Big Ben is still standing, like a tower that tells what time it is, and so are the Houses of Parliament, and so is Tate

Modern, and the Eye, and the river is just the same old grey water with the sky dawning red above it, red all over the city of London, red through the window of Astrid's room

                                              the end result = Magnus has
been invited to return to school when the new term starts on
the 5th. The letters saying so came yesterday. They call what
happened 'the matter'. None of the letters mentions her name
or specifies what 'the matter' is. One letter came addressed
to Eve and Michael and one came addressed to Magnus
himself. The one Michael opened said almost exactly the
same thing as Magnus's. We ask your respectfulness and
confidentiality in the matter. We are glad to inform you.
The matter officially closed.

The end result = they've got away with it.

The end result = nobody really wants to know.

It is a Wednesday today. It is the last day of the year. It is
getting dark out there already and it's only lunchtime.
Magnus had been wandering about in the eye-hurting light
of the shopping precinct. Now he is in the auditorium and
the lights have gone down and the adverts are over and the
film is playing. Up on the screen the actor pretending to be
the Prime Minister has pretended to fall in love with the
actress pretending to be the tea-girl. This film had been just
about to start, so he had bought a ticket. It is about

Christmas. It is full of shiny-looking people and houses, like watching a very long building society advert, or an advert for something, Magnus can't work out exactly what. Watching it is like being hungry and having nothing to eat except, in fact, the kind of food sold in cinemas. The air in this cinema smells of cinema food, hot dogs and popcorn. Of course it does. Everyone with any brain knows they pump it in on purpose to make you buy food at the kiosk. It works. Most of the people round Magnus are putting food into their mouths without taking their eyes off the screen.

The escalators will still be going round and round in their grooves outside. Magnus had noticed it and then he had been unable not to notice it. He had stopped to watch the people coming down the down escalator and to watch how each step disappeared so neatly into the groove at the base of it as if folding into nothing as the people stepped off it and away into their futures, and the next step after it doing the same, and the next. One step had a piece of sticker or paper of some sort stuck into the metal at the front of it. It made the step more noticeable than the other unmarked steps. He watched for this step to come round a few times and for it to disappear. He went up on the up escalator and watched the steps ahead of him vanishing into the crack in the top of the machine and how the step he was on did the same. He was watching this so hard that the escalator threw him off it into the people ahead of him and then he was off balance so the people coming behind him stumbled into him too.

Sorry, Magnus said.

He was. He was really sorry.

He waited at the top of the down escalator until he saw the step with the sticker on it come round again. It was the label off a bottle of water, tattered with going round and round the treadmill system under people's feet. But then he had to wait for it to come round again because an old man stood on it first. When it came round again he stood on it and rode it down to the floor below. He rode the up escalator again, to do this again. But at the top of the down escalator he began to think what he was doing was a bit mad, so when he turned and saw that the floor he was on was the one with the cinema, and a film was literally about to start, he bought a ticket.

Maybe it is a really good film and because he is being Lobotomic Escalator Boy he can't actually tell whether it is good or not.

The end result = he is supposed to be relieved. Michael waved his and Eve's letter in the air at Magnus. It's okay, he said. It's over. Simple as abc. I'll phone your mother, tell her the happy ending.

The escalators carry on going round and round in their fixed direction circuit, folding mechanically into and out of themselves and carrying people on them up or down until the day is over and the precinct shuts for the night and they switch the power off until next morning when they switch the electrics back on and it all starts again. When the precinct is shut this cinema will be dark and empty, all its seats empty in their rows and the place dark as a cave, dark as the inside of a stone on the moon, dark as the inside of a human brain inside a head.

You can start to forget it now, Michael said holding the letter. You can let it go.

Simple as abc, 123: He can let it go, now that the old year is ending and the new year is beginning, because it will belong to that old year and new things will happen in this new year. He can let it go, as if it is a toy balloon filled with helium and he has been holding on to it by a piece of string, with the kind of stubbornness a small child has, and now he can

238

open his hand and it'll float off upwards into the sky and he can watch it getting smaller and smaller, further and further away, until he can hardly make it out any more. He can forget it. A simple act of subtraction. Him minus it. He can have his memory erased by a special laser pen-torch, like in Men in Black. Magnus likes Men in Black. He likes all kinds and genres of cinema, usually. At least, he did, before, when he knew what it was he was, and what it was he liked. He argued in the class debate about art, about how cinema was a greatly misunderstood art form and Citizen Kane was probably the greatest film ever made because of the genius way it was shot and framed from the different angles (though not his personal all-time-favourite, which was Bladerunner the Director's Cut). This film he is watching now is something to do with the British film industry. Another actor on the screen has just pretended to fall in love with an actress pretending to be his Portuguese cleaning lady because he has seen her take her clothes off to dive into a lake and seen her afterwards all tousled up and with wet hair, much prettier than she was the first time he saw her. Magnus looks at the edges of the screen, where the edge of light of the film meets the blackness. He wonders why the thing films are shown on is called a screen. What is it in front of?

Behind this one is probably just a blank brick wall.

He thinks about the way that human eyes take the outside world and flash it back, like an upside-down film, on to the retinal screen at the backs of the eyes, then the brain instantaneously turns it the right way up.

There are two girls a few seats along from him and they seem to be quite engrossed in it, quite enjoying it. It is a girls' film, after all, so Magnus shouldn't have high expectations of it or even expect it to interest him. It is the genre of film that you are meant to take a girl to.

He imagines Astrid here next to him watching this film. Astrid wouldn't just think it was shit, she would say it was. She would exclaim with boredom at it and people would turn their heads and tell her to be quiet. She isn't old enough yet to have to pretend to like stuff like this. He smiles in the dark. Just before Christmas she set fire to the pile of leaves against the side of the shed and the whole shed went up in flames. It made Michael react; he came, almost running, down the garden with a fire extinguisher. Then he stood in the garden with them, laughing at the blackened shed. Michael's all right. Then they all sat in the kitchen together for a while round the table and had coffee, something they'd never done before, round this particular table anyway. The table is a different shape from the old table, circular, not rectangular. It made a difference that night, that the table was a circle. Magnus wonders if Eve will like the new table when she gets home. Astrid is still refusing to speak to Eve when she calls. She even refused to speak to Eve when she phoned on Christmas day. Magnus has, however, more than once, come into the kitchen and caught Astrid flicking through the (now quite thick) wedge of postcards.

I thought you weren't reading those on principle, Magnus said the second time.

I'm not reading them, Astrid said. I had to take them off the top of the fridge to open its door to get the milk out and they happened to be in my hand and I happened to look down at them, that's all. It's not the same thing as reading them.

The end result letters came yesterday morning. Yesterday afternoon Astrid was watching a programme called Killer Hornets from Hell. Magnus sat down beside her on the sofa and she told him how the killer hornets, which are ten times the length of the bees somewhere in South America, send their scouts out ahead to track down beehives then report back. Then hornets mob the hive, kill the bees and eat the honey. But then some bees got clever and worked out that these hornets die at a certain temperature, 116 degrees. But bees also die at a certain temperature. 118 degrees. So the next time a hornet scout was spotted by the bees, the bees somehow knew to surround the scout and vibrate together as a unified bee being until they reached – get this – exactly 117 degrees. Fucking brilliant, Astrid said.

Astrid, would you just call me a wankstain? Magnus said.

What? Astrid said.

Would you mind just calling me it? Magnus said.

You're a wankstain, Astrid said.

Would you just call me it again, a few times? Magnus said.

You're a wankstain, you're a wankstain, you're a wankstain, Astrid said not taking her eyes off the television.

Is there a calculus for sadness? Calculus enables you to reach the correct answer without necessarily knowing why. Is there a calculus that lets you understand why and how you reached a wrong answer? The letters had come. It was the end result. Something was wrong with it.

That's great, darling, Eve had said when she called back, her voice coming and going and breaking up. It's (something) news. Wonderful news. Thank God. We (blank) faith in you. (blank) the school is being very sensible. Now you can put this all (something) and get on with your life. With your real life. With working (something) exams. It's (blank) this coming year (blank) repercussions (something) rest of your life.

Isn't there anything worse you can call me? Magnus said to Astrid as they watched the bees pick over the corpse of the hornet scout.

Nope, Astrid said. Wankstain is the worst thing I know.

(Astrid is not to be told anything about the school etc. Nobody is. As part of the non-expulsion agreement Magnus has agreed not to mention the name or case in public, and has been warned against mentioning it in private. Your respectfulness and confidentiality in the matter.)

You're a killer hornet from hell, Astrid said.

That's good, Magnus said nodding to himself because it implied relief. It implied that for doing the wrong thing he could be heated to death by the righteous exact calculation of innocent bees.

You're a killer hairnet from hell, Astrid said.

Magnus, in the cinema, laughs out loud. The two girls along from him turn and look at him in the dark because it is the wrong time to laugh, nothing funny is happening on the screen, no one else is laughing in the cinema. The actor pretending to be the Prime Minister is pretending to make a speech about how he disagrees with American policy. He is doing this because a moment ago in the film he caught the actor pretending to be the American President kissing the ear of the actress pretending to be the tea-girl.

He watches as people on the screen make jokes about how fat the actress playing the tea-girl is supposed to be, though Magnus himself doesn't think she's particularly large, not really, not that noticeably.

Pascal made a bet with himself that there was probably a God and therefore a heaven and a hell. He reckoned that if he bet his life on it, if he lived his life as if there were, then he'd attain heaven. But if he died and there was nothing, then it wouldn't really matter that there was nothing. There was no point, according to Pascal, in betting your destiny on nothingness rather than somethingness. That was a real waste of a bet.

I bet you there's something that you would never in a million years be able to guess about me, Magnus said to Astrid.

You think you're gay, Astrid said.

No, I mean it, he said. Something, I bet, that if you knew it about me you would never want to speak to me again or have me as your brother. You wouldn't be able not to hate me.

He said it as if he were joking, as if it were a joke.

You think I'm gay, Astrid said.

The programme about the bees ended.

I hate you anyway, Astrid said. There's nothing you could tell me that would make me hate you more than I already do.

She smiled sweetly at him. He smiled back. He was near tears. A programme about the events of 2003, now that 2003 was nearly over, had begun. The England Rugby team was standing, fists raised, in front of a huge roaring crowd. Then US soldiers sat around on regal-looking chairs in the dusty remains of a blown-open palace suite. Then there was an aerial shot of a police cordon round the edge of a small green wood. It was summer. Then in grainy magnified type, across the screen, the word sexed and the word up.

Is it something about your suspension and all that stuff being over? Astrid said.

Over. Easy as abc.

a). Magnus, pressing the button on the answerphone, sitting there as if waiting for him like a loyal dog, a dog who's found his long way home after unbelievable travels, right in the middle of the floor in the otherwise empty dining room.

Three messages. One for Michael (from the university, about the girl who was threatening the law suit). One for Eve (from the legal office at her publisher's, about the families).

The other, echoing out round Magnus into the empty room. Milton requesting that Eve and Michael urgently notify the school.

Magnus, tossing and turning in bed.

He must have been spotted leaving the computer room on the right date etc. by the school cctvs. He must have been traced from something which left a trace on the hard disk. The cleaners cleaning the upstairs corridor must have identified him as being there in the school after hours that night.

Beyond the windows of Milton's office the playing field, deserted for summer. Michael looking distant – it was the same week Michael heard about his job – and Eve clearly concerned about the way Milton kept warily glancing, like he couldn't not, at what bruising remained from the black eye she got from Amber when she told her to leave and Amber coiled back her arm, her fist back as far as her own head, then punched Eve hard in the eye. Milton telling Eve and Michael: school investigation, recent tragic suicide, local press, their son Magnus, implicated, necessary suspension while all proper investigations.

Eve and Michael nodding, dazed. Eve's arm round Magnus. Milton telling them. Jake Strothers, sitting crying on the pavement outside her house. Her mother opening the front door and taking him in and then phoning Milton.

(So it wasn't closed circuit or hard disk or cleaners at all. It was Jake Strothers that did it. It was love.)

Milton emphasizing relief. The case had had such relatively low profile in the media. (No mention of Anton. Anton, completely getting away with it.) Milton believed the family wouldn't press charges in any case. The case in any case the case the case in any case.

Everyone suddenly silent, looking at Magnus.

But it's true, Magnus said.

I did it.

b). Magnus on the way home in the back of the car, his arms round himself, inside him his own bones, inside them nothing, concavity; child made of nothing. Eve and Michael in the front, nodding a lot. The words publicity, avoidance, necessity. Eve and Michael hugging him when they all got out of the car. Magnus in bed at 6 p.m., asleep. A huge hand lifting the stone slab off his back. A huge hand finally coming down out of the air and picking him up out of the crowd, weighing him, turning him over in its palm, about, any minute now, to raise him to a giant eye in the sky and have a good look at him.

c). Magnus going for questioning and investigation at the end of November. The secretary sitting him down in Milton's office and Milton giving the speech at him. How surprised Milton had been to see, of all names, Magnus's name. How Milton literally couldn't believe. How in this case 'true' was 'relative'. How Milton understood that Magnus clearly didn't really mean. How hard the school had worked to exonerate Magnus. The importance of working hard this very important exam year. Bad influences and how to keep away from them. Contact with Jake Strothers, penalty of expulsion. Fortunate for Magnus, the unwillingness of the police to be involved in a clear case of suicide. Fortunate for Magnus, the very wise reluctance of the girl's family to press the matter further. Imperative to Magnus, a temperament founded on the properness and decency of knowing when to leave stones unturned so that 1. the terrible bereavement the school had already suffered because of this unfortunate accident could be allowed naturally to diminish. And 2. the bereaved family could be allowed to continue their everyday existence without even more grief from troubling speculation and interruption.

Did Magnus understand? this being the solitary question put
to Magnus at the interview.

Magnus understanding, nodding and complying. 1. 2.

$$(a+b)$$
$$+c$$

= the end result

= the matter officially closed.

Simple, abc. Mathematics. To find the simple in the
complex, the finite in the infinite.

Yes, Magnus said, it's about the suspension and stuff being
over.

What about it? Astrid said. What happened?

On the screen Bob Hope was telling a joke to some Second
World War troops. They were showing this on tv because
Bob Hope was dead. He had died in 2003.

Doesn't matter, Magnus said shaking his head.

Astrid rolled her eyes.

Like I want to know anyway, she said.

The Second World War troops roared with laughter.

Actually there is something worse than wankstain, Astrid
said.

What? Magnus said.

You, Astrid said.

Thanks, Magnus said.

You're welcome, Astrid said flicking channels. 2003, gone
in the flick of a button. It made him feel minimally better.
He slouched down further into the sofa.

Now Magnus, in the cinema, imagines Jake on the
pavement and the door opening behind him and the kindly
lady coming out, picking him up off the ground. She would
take him into the front room and sit him on the sofa and she
would make him a cup of hot chocolate, or tea, something
hot and comforting anyway, and bring it through and put it

in his hands, and he would be crying so much that his tears would fall in it, and she'd take the cup and put it on the table and take his hands and say, now now, come on, it can't be helped, it's okay, it's over. And then she'd get up and go through and phone Milton and say, Mr Milton, one of the boys is here who.

Or maybe she wasn't kindly at all. Maybe she was crazy and hurt and angry, her face still all lined from crying and not sleeping; maybe she got Jake by the hands and she dragged him in and threw him on to her front room floor and shouted and swore at him, and threw the cup she had in her hand at him, and threw everything within reach at him, plates, pictures, a vase, a table, everything – until they were both exhausted with the shouting and the sadness and everything broken all round them and both just sat in their own exhaustion staring at nothing until she got up and went through and phoned Mr Milton. And said – what? Hello, Mr Milton, this is Mrs ******, the mother of ********* ******, who can't be mentioned, the girl who died, remember, and one of the boys is here who.

It was the mother or the brother who found her, in the bathroom. Magnus knows what her little brother looks like. He is at Deans. Everybody at Deans knows what he looks like, and he will know who Magnus is now; everybody knows which boys were suspended.

They will walk past each other in the school corridors.

That noise Magnus can hear beyond the film's music and actors can't be the escalators. It is an impossibility. There is no way he would be able to hear them in this auditorium with its cinema-sound-level soundproofing. It must be the noise of the projector he can hear. The film is almost over now because everything is adding up in it. The actors from all the different segments of story have all met each other at the school nativity play or at the airport and smiled and waved at each other like they all live in the same world and they've known each other all along. The actress pretending to be the Portuguese cleaner has said yes to getting married to the actor most famous for being in the Jane Austen adaptation. Everybody has laughed at the fat actress pretending to be the fat sister of the Portuguese cleaner. The film is supposed to be about love. But its only message, as far as Magnus can make it out, is not to be too fat if you're a girl or everyone will think you are laughable and no one will want to marry you.

Along from him one of the two girls is crying. He wonders if she is crying because the film has moved her or because she thinks she's too fat. The girl is crying and crying. She isn't in the least bit fat. Her friend puts her arm round her. Magnus finds himself hoping that Astrid has a friend like this, who will put her arm round her if she is one day sitting crying in a cinema. But at the notion of Astrid crying in a cinema, especially at a film like this, the Astrid in his imagination sticks her middle finger up at him, and at it.

But what if Astrid came to a film like this one and was reduced by it, like this girl along from him? What if Astrid is nothing like the Astrid in his head is, when she's out in real life? She might have to be different. Girls have to be a certain way with each other, the same as boys do.

In a minute Magnus will have to leave the cinema. The credits are almost over. He will have to go back out of this place, like this place is a safe cave with its shadows flickering on its wall, where it's easy to pretend that there's nothing but the shadows. Out there, there's the escalators going round and round in their fixed directions. The things you're supposed to buy all the time. The end of the year. The people looking at people and not looking at people. What will he do when he sees her little brother in the corridor in the new term, in the new year? Will he pretend not to see him? Will he look straight through him? Will the little brother pretend not to see Magnus? Worse. Will he look straight at him?

A group of men were chained inside a cave, and all they saw, all they could see and all they'd ever seen of the world was the shadows their own fire made on the walls. They watched the shadows all the time. They spent their days watching them. They believed that's what life was. But then one of them was forced out of the cave and into the real world. When he came back into the cave and told the others about sunlight, they didn't believe him. They thought he was mad. Magnus can't remember the end of that story. Does the man who's seen the outside world go mad? Does he leave the cave, the only place he knew, and go somewhere else, exiled from his old friends and from the only life he'd known before that, inside the cave? Do the men chained to the cave floor kill him, because they're so disturbed by what he keeps saying?

The crying girl and her friend are waiting to get past him. He stands up to let them pass, then he follows them out of the cinema and into the glare of the shopping precinct. He feels protective. He walks behind them, protecting them without them knowing, all the way to the escalators and down, concentrating on the back of the one who was crying and has stopped now, is glancing red-eyed round her. Her friend is talking. She nods and answers. They both laugh. That's better. Also, it has got him to the bottom of the escalator without him having to think about the escalator.

He follows them for a bit.

He stands at the door of Accessorize, which is about to shut, and waits for them. When they come out again, arm in arm, he gives them a head start then walks behind them past the other shutting shops. They leave the precinct, cross the street with the crowd and disappear among the people going round the corner towards the tube and Magnus is abandoned standing in a winter street whose buildings seem to rise from the ground as two-dimensionally as the buildings of a fake street on a film backlot. A strong enough wind would blow them away.

She had a brother, just like Magnus is Astrid's brother.

She gave her brother the finger and swore at him and treated him like shit and watched tv slouched on a sofa, and he did the same back to her, exactly the same as him and Astrid.

She closed the bathroom door. She stood up on the bath, maybe. She had had enough. She stood herself up on the edge of the bath and she looked down, and instead of seeing someone there, she saw no one.

The end result.

=.

The equals sign, Magnus remembers telling Amber one afternoon so incredibly hot that it was even warm inside that old stone church, was invented by Leibniz.

It was? Amber said. Are you sure?

She had her hand, her very gentle hand, round his prick, which was out of his shorts, not doing anything, just her, holding him. He had his hand, gentle, half inside her, inside her shorts, the same. It was just after sex, and it was just before sex.

How do you mean, sure? Magnus said.

I mean, how do you know? Amber said.

I just know, Magnus said. It's just something I know.

He was half-hard. She was often a bit annoying like this between sex, to wind him up. Eventually, other times in the church, he'd know to just not enter into this kind of conversation. But at this point he was still a bit easy to wind up.

But how do you know it's true? Amber said.

Well, Magnus said. Assuming I read it in a book, because I can't remember exactly when or how I learned it as a fact, but assuming I read it in a book, well, then it will have been in a book, which makes it presumably true.

Why would being in a book make it true? Amber said.

Because if it was in a book it was presumably in a schoolbook, a textbook, Magnus said, and textbooks tend to have been written by people who have studied a subject for a long enough time, and well enough, to be able to teach it to people who know a lot less about it. And also. Books are edited by editors who check the facts before they publish them. And even assuming I didn't learn it from a textbook but from a teacher, then the same applies.

What, Amber said, teachers are edited by editors who check the facts before they teach them?

Magnus clicked his teeth.

You know what I mean, he said. Come on. A break, please. Give me.

All I'm saying is what if it wasn't Leibniz? Amber said. All I'm saying is what if it was someone else?

It was Leibniz, Magnus said.

But what if it wasn't? Amber said.

But it was, Magnus said.

He was hard now.

What if you're wrong? Amber said as she ran the circle of her hand up towards the tip, back towards the balls and up towards the tip again.

I'm, uh, I'm simply, uh, not, Magnus said.

What? Amber said.

Wrong in this instance, Magnus said.

Ah, Amber said.

She moved so his hand came out of her. She shook off her shorts, stepped out of them, left them on the old wooden floor.

Sure? she said as she climbed on to him.

100 per cent, Magnus said deep in the sweet heat of the moment. 100 per cent sure in the heat of the summer, unimaginable now that it's now and it's winter, 100 per cent sure in the sweet headfuck of the endless, ended time in that house, in that church, in Amber. I'm not in love, Amber had said to him. So don't forget it. It's just that men your age are naturally very suited to women my age, since I'm just coming up to my prime number but you're already in yours.

Did she really say prime number, as a kind of Amber joke, or did she just say prime and he added number on afterwards? Moping around on the internet on one of the new computers at home on one of the many suspended days, asking Jeeves on Ask.com whatever came to mind, like who killed Kennedy, and where was Osama Bin Laden, and how did Plato die, and did Shakespeare really exist, and who was Zeno of Elea, and when did Leibniz invent the equals sign, Magnus had discovered that not Leibniz after all but a Welshman called Robert Recorde had maybe possibly invented it, in the 1550s. The only other fact about Robert Recorde on the site was that he died in a debtors' prison.

After this, Magnus had typed in the sentence: Where has Amber gone? and then clicked on search.

Nuke Cops™ – Team Amber Has Gone Nuke CLear
Link to Us. Team Amber has Gone Nuke CLear . . . msnx writes
'Our site has undergone major rework since earlier days as McCop.
Gone-Amber

POETVILLE. Gone by Amber Lynn Faust copyright September 23, 2003.

Everything is gone, No one to lean on. Let alone, hard like stone.

Fenton-"Gone with the wind" lamp in Collectibles:Glass,

This lovely Amber Gone with the wind lamp stands 22–1/2 tall and was issued in 1971. The top globed can be lighted alone or the base . . .

Victoria Amber Light Fixture

Beyone Expression Antiques. This is an exquisite amber hobnail Gone-with-the-wind light fixture with jewels in the frame, and alternating . . .

Gone to Dogstar – Amber

Amber . . . My dog's name was Amber, and she was a red chow-chow female. She died of stomach cancer when she was eight year old.

Security at Sellafield goes on amber alert

Sellafield has gone on amber alert as a precautionary measure in line with a Government order for extra vigilance and protection at sensitive . . .

Amarillo Globe-News: Business: Amber Waves: Where have all the Web posted . . . Sunday, June 15, 2003 . . . 5:34 a.m. CT. Amber Waves: Where have all the cowboys gone? By Kay Ledbetter . . .

Amber Review and Walkthrough

When the outline of the PeeK unit in your inventory flashes, click on it to confirm that the AMBER device has gone online.

Ask Jeeves. Greetings, please enter your search below. Magnus typed in ********** ******.

Your search for ********** ****** did not match with any Web results. Please try your search again.

Magnus typed in C******** M*****. He counted the stars to make sure he'd got the correct number. Then he clicked the search button. Jeeves found him a guitar chord dictionary listing jazz chords, a link to an art museum in Los Angeles and a link for comic fonts and lettering.

After this Magnus had accessed the free galleries, for the first time since before. His heart was actually audible to him as he clicked on the first and it opened in front of him.

It was okay. It was just a porn site. It was pretty tame. It didn't matter.

Lezzie ass licking in the jacuzzi. Petra shows off her pretty pussy. Preimum Hardcore Site. Horny grandma wants an orgasm. Redhead sassy teen with inredible tits and a 'tude. Bitch swallows it. Teenie and her teddy bear loose in the yard. Golden girl baths in pee. Vixen shows off her pink love canal. Shaved muff redhead Rose. Big tittied bitch teases the camera. Dick leaves friction burns on babes tongue. Little titties Latina fucked.

Preimum. Inredible.

He'd emptied the history into the trash and switched the computer off. It wasn't that it was so bad, or made him a bad person, looking at the bodies. They were just bodies. It wasn't like in a psychological thriller movie where all the bodies suddenly had her face, or anything like that. They all had their own faces. None of them had her face. It was that he'd thought of her face and then had been ashamed, and what he'd been most ashamed at was the badness of the language, how stupid it was.

Magnus, leaning against the wall of Superdrug on the dark last day of the year, considers the Millet Seed Paradox of Zeno of Elea. If one millet seed falls and makes no sound, does the definite sound that a thousand millet seeds make when they fall together mean that a thousand nothings make a something? The girls on the porn sites stretch into thousands of thousands, and thousands more links to thousands of other links. To look at even a fraction of them

254

would take persistence of vision. The girls on the sites stretch
out their cracks to the crack of doom. Shakespeare.

Did Shakespeare really exist?

What was love actually?

Where did Amber go?

Amber going was a case of good riddance and bad rubbish,
according to Eve. Amber had been less than they'd imagined,
according to Michael. She had sold them down the river
(Eve). She had pulled the wool over all their eyes (Michael).
She had shown her true colours (Eve). She had taken and
taken from them in a very insidious way (Michael). Magnus
thinks of Amber, taking and taking from him in the attic, in
the garden, in the church. St Magnus. He thinks of her taking
his clothes from him that first night, after she bathed him.
He thinks of himself, lost after Amber had gone, wandering
the village, and the man from the restaurant coming out and
offering him something to eat and telling him the building's
history. He thinks of himself being sick outside the same
restaurant, just before Amber, and the same man coming out
angry at him. That restaurant, before it was a restaurant,
was an old cinema first, then when going to the cinema got
unfashionable it became a snooker hall and then a derelict
building and now an Indian, and the man said at this rate it
would soon be something else, though he didn't know what.
Amber had clearly befriended the man, like she had
befriended most of the Village People.

Sit here, the man had said patting the wall outside his
empty restaurant. You hungry? No? Eh? Pity. Lots of food in
there. Lots of good food. Nobody to eat it. You know what
someone wrote on the wall of the Gents? Muslim Jew bastard.
I'm not a Muslim. I'm not a Jew. I'm not a bastard. Well,
that's life. That's the way. Your friend. The lady. Where's
she gone? Eh? You don't know? Eh? You don't? Pity. Pity.

255

The man shook his head.

She's a fine one, that one, he said. A real lady. The real thing.

31 December 2003, quite late in the afternoon. He should go home. He looks at his watch. His watch has stopped. Its hands say ten to midnight, or noon. It isn't. It's only about four o'clock. All the shops are shutting. All the escalators in all the precincts all over the country are surely stopping. It's holiday time for escalators. All the people round him are drunk already or on their way to getting drunk, on their way into central London as if compelled magnetically. He should go home.

It will mean walking against the crowd.

In the gone summer light, the man nudged Magnus outside the empty restaurant.

Sure you're not hungry?

Magnus shook his head. The man smiled at him.

The real thing. Eh?

Magnus comes up the stairs one at a time, one foot, then the other, then the other. He stands on the landing outside Astrid's bedroom door. He takes a deep breath. He knocks.

Go away, Astrid shouts from inside.

It's me, Magnus says.

Like, who else? Astrid says.

She opens the door enough to peek out. Magnus can see just one of her eyes.

And? she says.

He sits down just outside the door on the landing carpet. The carpet is still so new that there are shreds of it in the corners.

I saw a really rubbish film today, he says.

So? Astrid says.

She is about to close the door again.

Don't, Magnus says.

She doesn't. She stands, suspicious, watching him through the few open inches. In a moment, any moment, she'll slam the door.

It was good, wasn't it? he says.

You just said it was rubbish, she says.

No, I mean, it was good when we were on holiday this year, he says.

Astrid stares at him. She opens the door properly.

It was really good, too, he says, when we got back here and there was like nearly nothing left.

Astrid sits down in the doorway. She picks at the new carpet too.

It was brilliant, she says. It was so good.

I think I liked it best when there was totally nothing, Magnus says. When you could just walk through a room and there was nothing at all in it.

And we could hear ourselves all different when we walked or talked, even just breathing was different, Astrid says.

Yep, Magnus says.

And when we spoke it sounded like an echo, all round us, like we lived in a stately historic house, Astrid says, or like we were on a stage or something because of the carpets gone, no carpets where you expected there to be carpets. So it was like we were walking out on to a wooden stage every time we went across a room.

Uh huh, Magnus says.

Except we weren't, she says, we hadn't, we were just at home, in our own house.

Magnus nods.

Catherine Masson, he says.

What? Astrid says.

It's her name, Magnus says.

Whose name? Astrid says.

Magnus says it again.

Catherine Masson.

Then he tells it all to Astrid through the opened door, or as much of it as he knows and as much of it as he can, beginning at the beginning

the end-of-pier jokes about
him, and if he couldn't stop coining them himself then
presumably everyone else would be doing it too, putting
the oral into tutorial, the semen into seminar, the stud into
student, he'd be the stock repertoire of the stud-ents, and not
just them but the schadenfreude lecherer peergroup in the
common room too, Michael was sure, if it wasn't too
egotistical of him to be imagining puns like these, puns about
him, as the whispered underscore of the department, in the
air outside the locked-tight door of his office (if it was still
his office and not already someone else's, all his books and
papers boxed up in the building's basement without anybody
telling him), as much in the air as the institutional slightly
fogey smell that hung in the corridor, the smell that you
stopped overtly noticing but that was there all the same, let
your subconscious know exactly what department you were
in. The story had only just broken and some wag had pinned
a notice on to his door on headed departmental paper next
to his seminar sign-up lists and the photocopy of the Blake
poem, the lineaments of gratified desire for God's sake. He
had gone back to his office to get his coat, that was the last

time he was in the faculty, back in October, and there it was, next to Blake, next to the official Departmental Memo telling them to see Professor Dint to be assigned a new tutor in the temporary absence of. *Departmental Health Warning. Girls: feeling a bit low-grade? In need of a good two-one-ing? Sign up here for injections from Dr Love (Boys: negotiable).*

Depart. Mental. At least someone had thought he was trendy; boys negotiable. Dint had had the notice removed by now presumably (like she'd had her own sense of humour removed years ago). Or maybe the notice was still on the door, Michael didn't know, hadn't been in. Astonishing how that was what being in a bookshop again brought back, the faculty, smells and all. Maybe Dr Love was now the only thing left on the door along with his name-plate, if his name-plate was still on it. Dr Michael Smart, official campus cliché.

Unbelievable that in that other life, a whole life ago, only half a year ago, he had planned out a new series of lectures on the subject and imagined himself giving them this very term, the term that was happening right now with its people scurrying all day to and from their tutorals, their semenars, as if nothing else in the world mattered. Cliché, as well as its clichéd meaning of hackneyed phrase or stereotypical response, also meant the fixed impression made by a die in any soft metal. Michael Smart, stamped. Bitten by the teeth of cliché. A soft metal. A marked man.

No, it was good. No, it was. It was liberating. It meant, for instance, that he could saunter into an early evening bookshop like this and do exactly as he'd just done, walk straight past the literature fiction literary criticism critical theory bays without even turning his head and go straight to the singular good monosyllabic *sports* section. Michael Smart, a real man at last. He had never in his life – in his old, unreal life – not stopped at lit and fict to see what was selling, what was stocked, what was new, what was on the tables, which volumes of his own private canon were available on the shelves, proof of whether or not the bookshop was a decent bookshop.

But for months he had been unable to go near the door of a bookshop without feeling nauseous. He hadn't even been able to pick up a book without feeling nauseous. So it was good, this. Here he was. He was back. There was more than one type of book in a bookshop.

Michael had decided, earlier that day, that he would take up rock climbing and mountaineering. He had decided it that morning when he was driving around on the M25 with the traffic and the dreary but undeniably springlike sky ahead of him, listening to Radio 4, on which a man whose name he hadn't caught was describing the sheer unpeopled wonder of being on top of the world, scaling something insurmountable, going further up than everyone else's litter. The man had seen dead bodies on the sides of the mountains he'd climbed. The unburied bodies of people who'd fallen on the way, got sick in the too-high air, lost consciousness or for whatever reason just not survived, were apparently quite plentiful on real mountains, the mountains which provided the real challenges. The man on the radio had described the act of rising above a corpse on the route as a kind of rebirth.

It was February. February couldn't help but be promisory. February was spring! All sorts of things were possible in spring. The coffee smell in the bookshop was good. He would find the right book then go for a coffee and have a look at it to see if he should buy it. Habit warned him not to drink coffee this late. Habit could fuck off and die. Habit was old, outworn, belonged to before. Michael liked being awake late. Did he have to go to sleep at any particular time? No. He was a free spirit. *Sports*. Football Hockey Horseracing

Motorracing Mountaineering. He took a book off the shelf of shiny books. It had a compass on the cover. He flipped it open. *Navigation is fun! It is a skill which you ignore at your peril.* It had chapter headings in its content list which sounded right. Mountain Weather. Technique on Snow and Ice. Security on Steep Ground. Dealing with Altitude. Leaving Nothing but Footprints. The Contents of Your Rucksack.

Yes. This was what Michael Smart was going to deal in from now on, nothing but the definite, the concrete, the scree and boulder fields described here, the different kinds of rock, loose rock and wet rock.

Loose.

Wet.

Why were all words so loaded? Why did they immediately poison themselves, turn into words which could be used against him, even by himself? Was everything a joke? Against him? A good two-one-ing. That was quite good. That was quite well put. There you go. There you have it. His problem was his openness, his own generosity, his willingness to congratulate even every little undergraduate shit who made a joke about him. Dead by the snowy side of a difficult route, a splay of waggish undergraduates and fulfilled ungrateful girls, and Marjory, and Tom, and that hag-faced dried-up lesbian from Personnel whose name he couldn't remember, like someone from a women's prison, no, worse, a tv drama series about a women's prison, sitting there long-faced at him behind the long table in the faculty office. Fuckulty office. See? He could make fun of his own demise, his own below-the-belt activity. It was hardly the end of the world. Further on, up from this, there was the breathtaking natural beauty of nature at its heights. Dead by the side of a mountain pass, Emma-Louise Sackville, not in person of course, just in file form. Letter and email correspondence form. Anyway she'd it, the head giving off energy like a lit hot lightbulb. You needed to buy overtrousers with zips so you didn't have to take your shoes off to put them on. So simple it was genius, really. Blisters were serious. A rope could be dead or alive. Here was a language alive with its own sheer usefulness – more, alive with a real, tenable hope. *There are very few mountains in the British Isles which can not be walked up*. It was promising. It was practical. It told you how to avoid invisible cliffs. Michael sipped the coffee. The coffee was foul. The cup rattled in its saucer as he put it back on the too-low table. He would go first to the Peak District, or Snowdonia, maybe to the Brecon Beacons or the Yorkshire Dales. He would drive. He would leave his car in the car park at the base of the mountain, or outside a nice guest house whose breakfasts were on the hearty side. He flicked further into the book. Lightning, apparently, was responsible for taking the lives of a small number of climbers every year. The book said climbers saw this as an Act of God and instructed its readers not to discard an ice axe that had been struck by lightning, even if it was fizzing or sparking, because you'd probably need it later. Michael wondered if the mention of Act of God was in the human ballpark or in insurance terms. He turned the page. There was a list of the names of knots. Mountaineer's coil, butterfly coil, double fisherman's. He thought of Philippa Knott. He wondered who was teaching Roth to Philippa Knott now. Who was double fishermanning her. *Mountaineer's coil*.

He closed the book.

God only knew.

There was no way on earth Michael Smart, at his age, could go up the side of a mountain.

You've been pushing your luck, Mike, Marjory Dint said to him informally (*Mike* meant informal). Having your cake,

eating it then not wanting to suffer the consequences. (Cliché!) One girl, we could have written off. One, we could have done something about. Don't think we didn't try. And don't say you weren't warned, I told you five years ago, four years ago, three years ago, two years ago and last year. Sackville is just the snowball before the avalanche. (Terrible, Marjory.) She's more than willing to let the cat out of the bag. (Terrible.) Altogether now, we've seven complaints to investigate, none of them, I will say in your favour, as well corroborated as Sackville's but mark my words, Michael (so, not informal at all, then, Marjory), this isn't going to go away overnight.

Marjory Dint, speaking lines like she'd learned them from a BBC script for a banal detective series.

So Michael liked sleeping with girls. Was it a crime? They liked him back. Was it a crime? They were all consenting adults. He was good-looking. They were good-looking, m[ost] of them. Was it a crime? Formally, in front of Tom and [the] lesbian from Personnel, Marjory Dint cautioned him. Formally, it was a stoppage of tenure and a half-pay, be[lieve-] me-we've-pulled-out-all-the-stops-for-you-to-get-any-[money] at-all, spell of *official leave*.

The core of the body. The shell of the body. The [book had] fallen open at the symptoms of hypothermia. He c[ouldn't] believe how many of the symptoms he had. He de[felt] cold and tired, he felt this all the time. He had de[felt] off and on this winter, times of numbness in hi[s] feet. Yes, there had definitely been times when [ ] Yes, he had physical and mental lethargy and [slowness] to answer questions or directions. That was [exactly] what he felt like, inside, all the time. Yes, [he had] outbursts and a lot of unexpected energy [ ] shaky, even right now. Look at that cup[ ]

She was away, probably. She was always out of town, in Rome or New York. Her husband was a psychotherapist too. They were a team. Between them they made the kind of fortune that meant they were always out of town, which made them exclusively expensive. Michael had stopped seeing her last spring, almost exactly a year ago, because they had spent the whole of one exclusively priced hour listing their top ten favourite pop songs. He had stopped being a client shortly after he'd told Eve about it and she'd nearly died laughing.

Michael, shivering in the bookshop, couldn't think who else to call.

He called home. Astrid answered.

It's me, Michael said.

Yep, Astrid said.

I'll be home in about an hour, he said. I just have to deliver some things to some, uh, students.

Yep, Astrid said.

Have you eaten, Michael said, or do you need me to bring anything?

Have *you* eaten? Astrid said. You're the one who's got thin.

Is Magnus home? Michael asked.

Yep, Astrid said.

Okay, Michael said. Home soon. Did your mother call?

Nope, Astrid said.

She hung up before he did.

He felt wretched.

He went downstairs to find Eve's books. They weren't in history. They weren't in biography. They were in fiction, how ridiculous, and they only had the most recent one, but they had about ten copies. Genuine Article, Ilse Silber. He took one off the shelf and turned it over to look at its back cover with Eve's picture on it. Eve, younger, smiling. He took deep breaths. He breathed in through his mouth and out through his nose.

So what was your song list, and what was hers, and how therapeutic was it, exactly? Eve had asked when she'd managed to stop laughing. She was sitting on the bed. Michael felt foolish, but it was quite a nice foolish. He sat on the edge of the bed too, a little ashamed, a little giggly himself. Ray Stevens, Misty. Four Seasons, December 1963 (Oh What a Night!). Chris Montez, The More I See You. Elvis Costello, Oliver's Army. Dire Straits, Romeo and Juliet. Charis Brownlee's number one had been Starland Vocal Band, Afternoon Delight. This made Eve laugh even more.

Thinking of you's working up my appetite, Eve sang. *Rubbing sticks and stones together makes the sparks ignite. Sky rockets in flight.*

Michael laughed, felt sheepish.

Was Bohemian Rhapsody on her top ten, by any chance? Eve asked.

Michael grimaced and nodded.

Eve gave another burst of laughter.

Was Imagine? she said.

He raised his eyebrows in a shrug. Eve laughed so much she literally cried. He had never seen her laugh so much or find anything so funny. He sat smiling next to her on the bed. She was beautiful laughing, and a little hateful.

(Your choice of songs reinforces what I consider your near-psychotic need, when it comes to self-belief, to refute all guilt, was something like what Charis Brownlee said. You know how Oscar Wilde put it, Michael, she said. We are all innocent until we are found out.)

Michael and Eve, back from holiday, standing in the robbed house, not looking at each other. On the floor between

268

them the answerphone, the only thing in an otherwise empty room. The voices had spoken. The answerphone was rewinding itself and switching itself off. There had been a message concerning Magnus, a message for Eve and a message, at last, for Michael.

Marjory Dint. *The game's up, Michael. It's Marjory. Phone me. Careful who you talk to. The legal department's involved.*

Whatever this is, I swear, I don't know anything about it, Michael said.

It's all right, Eve said. I know.

She nodded. She took his hand.

Michael, looking at Eve's photograph in the bookshop, understood again, like he'd understood now every day since, and every day the understanding came to him as incomprehensibly newly as it would if he suffered from a brain disease that meant he couldn't remember anything for longer than twenty-four hours.

Astonishing.

He realized Eve knew. He realized she had always known, known all along, and it had made no difference to her. He realized, too, that they had both been waiting for exactly this message.

He sat down on the floor in the corner made by the shelves in the S to T fiction bay and Eve's kindness opened above him as big as a sky.

The sky closed in, white. It became the white-tiled ceiling of a bookshop. He was on its floor. It was potentially embarrassing. As if browsing, Dr Michael Smart, on official leave, picked a book off the shelf next to him as if he'd been looking for exactly that book. Journey by Moonlight. Antal Szerb. Never heard of him. Translated from the Hungarian. 1930s. Michael liked things in translation. This looked like a book he could read. He opened it. *No joy I ever experienced afterwards ran as deep as the pain, the exulting humiliation, of knowing that I was lost for love of her and that she didn't care for me.*

He shut the book and put it back on the shelf. Everything hurt. He was ill and dying. He should go home.

Think of it this way. A pretty young woman arrives at the door. She is ragged, hungry and lost. She is knocking on all the doors of all the houses to see who'll be generous; it is a test. The innocent family, out of the goodness of its heart, takes her in, feeds her and offers her hospitality. Then the family wakes up next morning sleeping on the floor because she's stolen everything out from under them. Beds, bowls, breakfasts. Everything.

The father gets to his feet. He looks in the mirror. He looks the same as always. But his chest hurts. His back hurts. He puts his hand to a point halfway up his spine and he finds a hole in himself, in his back. The hole is the size of a small fist. Sure enough, his chest feels queerly empty. Then he understands. The pretty young woman has broken him open while he slept, put her hand in and thieved the heart out of him.

He looks at his wife. She looks the same as always. He looks at the girl, at the boy. They look the same as always. He has no idea whether their hearts have been taken too, along with his, and he has no idea how to find out. To say anything at all about it might break the spell and cause them all to collapse at his feet, hollowed out, the mere shell of a family. And then he'd collapse too, the mere shell of a man.

He knows he will have to get his heart back from wherever it's been taken, from whoever has it now, or he'll die. He thinks of the pretty young woman and how she fleered and flirted with him and how hard it was for him to deny her when she pressed him up against the wall of the house and dared him to kiss her and how proud he'd been when he'd said no, don't, I cannot, I dare not. Cliché. Was fleered a real word? It sounded like a folk-tale word, but it was possible that Michael had made it up to alliterate with flirted.

He stood up, straightened his trouser-legs at his feet. He would go to the front of the shop to see what floor the reference section was on. He would check the word. Then he would go to the cash desk and buy Eve's book. It was cheaper than the mountaineering books and it pleased him to think that it would be the first one of her own books back in the house since that woman Amber had robbed them all blind.

But there was no reference section in this bookshop.

No reference section? Michael said.

We don't do dictionaries, the boy behind the counter said. We did, but we stopped. We replaced the reference section with the foreign phrasebook section. The foreign phrasebook section is on the second floor with the travel guides.

Right, Michael said. Thanks.

What kind of bookshop didn't do dictionaries? The old Michael would have made a small scene, at least made a small comment. The new Michael got his wallet out and worried out loud that he'd left some mountaineering books he'd been looking at unshelved, upstairs in the café on one of the tables.

It's okay, the boy said. Someone'll find them and put them back. We're paid to do that kind of thing. Eight ninety-nine, please.

What kind of bookshop had no reference section? It beggared belief. Cliché. What exactly, he wondered as he paid for Eve's book and headed for the front doors, did beggars have to do with belief? Ah. See? You can take the man out of the words but you can't take the words out of the man. He stopped and coughed in the damp street. It was February. It was a treacherous month. He coughed again. He coughed like an old man coughed. This was new to him, this deep kind of cough, this cough that suggested a damp old back passage he hadn't known about, straight into his lungs. It felt tubercular. Maybe it was tubercular. Tuberculosis was back, it said so in all the broadsheets; it had developed a strain of itself that antibiotics couldn't kill. Think of Keats, dead at twenty-six, an old man coughing it at twenty-six. Keats had loved Fanny too. Ouch. Below the belt, that one, it actually hurt, like being punched. He really needed to see a doctor. He needed to go to the surgery and have a proper check-up. He could go into the faculty and make an appointment with Dr Love. *What seems to be the problem?* Well, Doctor, I woke up last week black and blue, bruises all over my arms and legs and chest, absolutely no reason for me to be covered in bruises, it's not like I ran a cross-country race or was beaten up or anything. Also, I keep understanding things. *Understanding things?* Yes, as if for the first time. Also, I can't stop making stupid puns and they're beginning to physically hurt. *A split infinitive. Nurse, make a note of that.* Also, I have no motivation. I feel bad almost all the time. *Bad?* Yes, bad. *Hmm. And how's your sleep pattern?* I can't sleep. All I want to do is drive around, day and night, all hours of the day and night, not stopping anywhere, though I try to avoid the C zone, obviously, I haven't totally lost my mind. Also, tonight, I was in a bookshop and I notice I now seem to have the classic symptoms of exposure. And now I can't stop coughing. *How's your appetite been?* Well, I'm just not that hungry. No idea why. *Right then. Let's have a listen to you.*

But what if the doctor put the stethoscope to his chest and looked up, puzzled, because there was no heartbeat there at all?

Below his feet was a glass basement cover set into the pavement and below that was a flurry of plants, weeds or something pressing up against the glass. It made him annoyed, the way they just grew. It made him feel very roughed-up indeed, weeds behind glass tiles that were six inches thick. All sorts of things like that left him outraged and helpless now. A picture of a woman's face ten feet high on a billboard looked a bit like her. A girl on a tv advert for Imodium, laughing with her father about how they'd solved the problem of diarrhoea, was mockingly like her, yet not her; a smiling woman in the commercial that followed straight after, in a bed watching tv in a spotless private healthcare hospital, was momentarily like her, then not like her at all in any way. The back of the head of a long-haired boy going down into the Underground had one night made Michael have to stop and search for his next breath. A woman who sped past him in a car going the other way on the road to the Isle of Dogs was like her, then gone. But it wasn't her car. It couldn't have been her. Those plants below that glass were like her. Not just like her. Somehow they *were* her, in a city crawling with the temporary, contaminated forever by a holiday taken six months ago out in the sticks. For instance, Michael was walking now, he was walking past the shops on Tottenham Court Road, but Tottenham Court Road was nothing but a mirage and the streets radiating off it were the product of a bereft and infected imagination. Goodge Street was a delusion. The tube map was an illusion of connection and direction. The M25 was a vicious circular joke. The real world was elsewhere, like she was.

Imagine her, systematically emptying things room by room, shifting them through the front door and across the pavement into a van in the dead of night. She was in league with someone, a man, surely. She had to be. She'd need someone to help move the heavier things; you'd need someone to help you clean up afterwards. Maybe it wasn't a man. Maybe it was that sullen cleaning woman from the holiday home in Norfolk; maybe they worked together as a team; one scouted out the holiday houses, then the other moved in on the families. Maybe they more-than worked together. He had seen them talking on the road to the village once, when he was on his way to the station.

Possible? It was possible. No it wasn't, she was a loner, she worked alone; she went round the country in that old white car like the perverse opposite of a post-war government-employed district nurse, knocking on the doors of complete strangers in the middle of nowhere to health-test the cores of their bodies, the shells of their bodies. *Coughs and sneezes spread diseases. Always use your handkerchief.*

Either of you two young ladies need a lift? he'd called through the window. I'm going as far as the station. Could drop you off anywhere in the village.

The cleaner had opened the back door of the car and heaved her hoover up on to the seat. Just his luck. Amber had waved goodbye and turned to go back to the house. He watched her beautiful shoulders in the rear-view mirror as she rounded the path to the house and disappeared. Gone. The cleaner was sitting on the back seat like the car was a taxi; she was next to the hoover with its plastic tube slung round her neck. The hoover was the kind that had a face painted on it, eyes and a smiley mouth.

Funny old world we live in, isn't it, when they anthropomorphize even the things we use to clean the house, eh? he said.

It's a Henry, the woman said. Top-of-the-range domestic. What I mean is, when they make hoovers and so on look more human, to make us choose them and not another brand, you know, when we go to buy a hoover, he said.

I know what anthropomorphize means, the woman said.

I, ah, I wasn't for a moment suggesting you didn't, he said but the woman was staring out of the side window now, uninterested.

She was quite ugly-looking, ruddy. Most of the villagers looked like that, like all their lives they'd eaten nothing but raw beets they'd dug up out of fields.

He took a deep breath.

So where can I drop you off, Katrina? he said. And where's your car today?

At the roundabout's fine. I don't have a car, the woman said.

I thought you had a Cortina, Michael said too late, before he remembered that the Cortina was a stupid joke between Eve and himself. But the woman hadn't noticed. Maybe she was a bit slow. (But she'd known the word anthropomorphize.)

Don't you find it a bit difficult, out here without a car? he said.

Out where? she said.

Well, out here, I mean, you know what I mean, I mean, transporting the bulk of this cleaning equipment, all the things you use to clean, from place to place, house to house, he said. A hard life.

It's not heavy, she said. And it's got little wheels.

I, eh, he said. Eh.

Right here's fine thanks, Mr Smart, she said. Thanks very much.

She got out of the car, lugged the hoover out after her and shut the door gently.

Here, Michael said.

He got his wallet from the inside pocket of his jacket and opened it and took out three twenties. He held them out through his open car window.

Don't know if my wife's paid you yet this week, he said.

You don't pay me. I come with the house, the cleaner said.

Every little helps, he said.

The cleaner was unsmiling. She took the money.

Goodge Street tube. Michael held his hand out in front of him. It shook, but only a fraction. Before he went through the barriers and down into the Underground in the rackety lift, he got out his mobile again. He scrolled up Eve's number.

Answerphone.

Hello, he said. It's me. How are you? I hope fine. Just a couple of things. Well, three. One, I'm not well. I'm pretty sure I've got some kind of exposure. Funny, I know. I'm not joking. Two, the legal people at Jupiter keep calling. It's about the families. Can you give them a call? Three, there's only £2,000 left in the main bank account and Astrid wants cash for a school trip and Magnus wants to go to Lourdes. Ha ha. I know. I'm not joking. Anyway I called the insurance about the house stuff. They estimate three months. Same as they said three months ago. What do you want me to do about it? Call me back. Speak soon.

Then he slapped shut his mobile, bought his ticket, walked into the lift and went down into the dark like a man who knew exactly where he was headed.

Magnus and Astrid were in the lounge watching tv. The lights were off. Michael switched the big light on.

Hello all, Michael said.

Magnus's taciturn friend Jake was round again.

Hello Jake, Michael said. How are you tonight?

Jake murmured something that sounded like fine thanks. Michael switched the big light off again.

Thanks, Astrid said.

He slumped down into the only chair left.

Jake was round a lot these days; he stayed over a lot. Michael had begun to wonder if Magnus was seeing a bit more of Jake than was normal and whether he should tell Eve about it, or whether they might be experimenting with dope, but after half an hour of listening outside Magnus's bedroom door one night and hearing them holding forth to each other about Pascal and Teilhard de Chardin and what to do about your parents' imminent divorce, he'd stopped saying to Jake at midnight, won't your mother be wondering where you are at this time of night, Jake?

The programme they were all watching in the dark was about Goebbels.

What are we watching, Astrid? he said.

UK History, Astrid said.

The guide was stuffed down the cushions of the chair he was in. Michael leafed through it until he found the right day and the right channel. He bent the page back so he could read it in the tv light.

UK HISTORY
7.0am The Nazis: A Warning From
History 8.0 The Nazis: A Warning From
History 9.0 The Nazis: A Warning From
History 10.0 The Nazis: A Warning
From History 11.0 The Nazis: A
Warning From History 12noon The
Nazis: A Warning From History 1.0
War Of The Century 2.0 War Of The
Century 3.0 War Of The Century 4.0

War Of The Century 5.0 Horror In The
East. 6.0 Horror In The East. 7.0 The
Nazis: A Warning From History 8.0 The
Nazis: A Warning From History 9.0 The
Nazis: A Warning From History 10.0
The Nazis: A Warning From History
11.0 The Nazis: A Warning From
History 12midnight The Nazis: A
Warning From History 1.0 Close

I guess we're watching The Nazis: A Warning From
History, Michael said.

You don't have to watch it if you don't want to. This house
is full of other rooms, Astrid said.

You know, you get more like your mother every day,
Michael said.

No way, Astrid said.

She flicked the channel immediately.

I meant it nicely, Michael said. I happen to like your
mother.

People on tv were doing a makeover in an empty house.
Statistics came up on the screen about how much more the
house would be worth after they'd done it.

Michael groaned.

It's just till the film comes on, for fuck sake, Astrid said.

No, I don't mind the channel, Michael said. It's just that I
feel a bit rough. And Astrid, please don't swear.

Rough how? Magnus said.

Hypothermia, Michael said. Classic case.

You need to be taken to shelter, Jake said.

Do I? Michael said. That's nice. That's nice to know.
Shelter. That's a nice word.

You need to be kept warm, and kept if possible totally like

off the ground, Jake said. You should be given a hot drink and something to eat, and people round you need to give you moral support.

It was the most Jake had ever said in public. Michael wished Eve were here so he could say so to her, afterwards, tonight, in bed.

Someone should get into your sleeping bag with you to keep you warm, Jake said.

Let's just not go there right now, Jake, Michael said.

And we have to watch you for heart failure, Jake said.

You don't know how true that is, Michael said.

And it might help if you curl into the foetal position, but with your head like sloping towards the floor, Jake said.

Magnus had gone through and switched the kettle on. He came back with tea for Michael. Michael was touched.

Do you want something to eat? Magnus said.

No, thanks, Michael said. But thank you, Magnus.

Have an egg, Astrid said. There are eggs in the fridge that need to be eaten.

No thanks, Michael said.

You should, Astrid said.

Should I? Michael said.

Eggs are beautiful, Astrid said. When you eat an egg you are eating beautifulness itself.

Am I? Michael said. What a lovely thought.

Boiled or scrambled? Magnus said.

Or raw? Astrid said.

Fried, Michael said.

Worst for you, Jake said.

Thank you, Jake, Michael said.

Magnus went back through. Michael curled himself into the foetal position. He sloped his head off the armchair. He watched the adverts upside down. It was quite a good thing

279

to do to adverts. It gave them back their surrealness. Magnus brought Michael a fried egg sandwich. The film came on. Black and white, old, 1930s. Margaret Lockwood. The Lady Vanishes.

It's a Hitchcock, Michael said.

And you told *me* not to swear, Astrid said.

Ha ha, Michael said.

The film was very clever, really. It was crazy and meandering for half the plot as if things were just meaningless comedy, then all its clues fell brilliantly into place. A lot of English people were stuck in bad weather in a hotel in the mountains of eastern Europe, then they were all travelling home on the same train. But a sweet old lady went missing on the train and the young beauty who'd been travelling with her insisted she was real, she'd definitely existed, though everybody Germanic on the train, including a creepy brain surgeon, was conspiring to make the girl seem like a lunatic. Only the sporty young English cad believed her and even he wasn't completely convinced. There were a lot of jokes about repressed sex and Freud and in the end it was a matter of national security.

The End.

Michael stretched his arms above his head and roar-yawned.

Fantastic, Magnus said.

Very good, Michael said.

Jake murmured something positive-sounding.

Michael stretched again. He actually felt quite good. Maybe it was the egg sandwich, doing him some good. Maybe it was the boys' instinctual kindness, earlier. Maybe it was the fact that the film itself was such a very good one, one that, if someone had asked him, he'd have sworn he'd already seen, he was bound to have seen before, but in reality he'd never seen and would never have guessed the cleverness of or the plot of, even though it was such an old classic and must have been running continuously somewhere in the background of his tv-watching for years.

Or maybe it was just the watching something good in a dark room, with other people watching it in the same way as he was. Whatever it was, he felt expansive, bigger than himself, about it. And he hadn't thought about feeling bad, not once, all the way through it.

It said it was filmed in Islington, Astrid said. Did you see? Did you see? It said at the end, when it said The End, that it was filmed here.

By the canal, Michael said. There was a film studio there.

No way, Astrid said.

No, there was, Michael said. Really. They did costume dramas, things like that. That's definitely where they made that film.

No way, Astrid said again.

She switched on the big light. Michael blinked in the too-bright room. The boys looked pale, awkward, young; the furniture they sat on looked piecemeal. They looked too young to be having to be so kind. Astrid was dancing around. She was all long arms and legs. She was wearing her t-shirt that said on it *I'm the girl your parents warned you about*.

Astrid, Michael said. Aren't you a bit cold wearing just that t-shirt?

The film studio that made that film, she was saying. Amazing. Right here, right here where we live, in Islington!

She swung on to the arm of Michael's chair like the child she nearly wasn't any more. The words on her t-shirt were inches from Michael's eyes and mouth. *I'm girl warned*. Then Astrid's open mouth, her tongue and her little teeth, were an inch from his face, his own mouth, as she swung over and down.

Michael closed his eyes. Cliché.

Really really really really truly truly truly? she said.

Michael pretended to rub his eyes. He leaned back in the chair, kept his eyes very shut. He shook his head, firm.

Would I lie to you? he said

the end of the road, at a
junction where the mailboxes stuck out of the ground, the
kind of mailboxes she had seen enough of by now to no
longer find picturesque, there was another smaller road and
a few miles along it there was a hidden little slip road that
she'd missed the first couple of times. It took her through to
another loop of road which coasted along next to woods all
coming into leaf and opened out at field after field of
impossibly beautiful horses. The horses were sleek and
perfected. The fields were rich and rolling and green behind
electric fencing hung with signs about the illegality of
trespassing. But where the woods stopped, and between the
stud-farms, there were houses. The houses had no fences.
Some were smooth and new and expensively designed, the
homes of the rich stud-farm owners. Others were more wood-
board weather-worn, some with their slats peeling and
splitting and their roofs warpy, made curved and precarious
by the winters or the wind. Most of them were probably
holiday homes or weekend homes. It only took two hours to
get here from the city. All of them, even the more falling-
down of them, looked like houses in a child's dream of

houses. All of them were big. All of them had porches and screen doors. All of them, even the ones that looked like they had had nobody living in them for quite a while, had stars and stripes hanging inert from little poles stuck by their doors.

Eve had parked the car on the grassy verge across the road from it. It sat, like all these houses, in its own open grassy space. The grass round this house was uncut. About three hundred yards away behind the trees there was another house and behind that there was another even huger house and behind them all, still visible in the moonlit night sky, the distant black ridge of mountains whose name she knew from her school atlas. Cat skill. Cats kill. Eve (15) had written the words on the inside cover of her rough-copy book in the middle of a geography lesson about rock layers and substructure. Eve (43) was on the right road, then. She had known the address of this road off by heart for more than thirty years.

But none of these houses had visible numbers. Two of them looked empty. This one right in front of her looked like it may have been empty for some time. Of the other two, the nearer was dark but the further-away one had cars outside. There had been lights in its windows earlier. Eve had heard people calling each other and a dog barking, or dogs.

By her calculation this house was the house her father had owned before he died, the house her other family had lived in. But it looked desolate. It might not be his house. The right house could, in fact, be any one of these houses. Those people with the cars and the lights and the dogs, for all she knew, could be family, though this was very unlikely; their house was on a different road. But they would probably have known, if she had had the sense to knock on the door and ask them at a time of the evening when someone might still be awake, which of these houses had belonged to him.

This was a country in which the light of the moon was so bright that you could even read a newspaper by it, if you wanted to read a newspaper. In a minute Eve was going to take her newspaper and go and sit on the porch of this empty house.

She got out of the car. She sat on the bonnet of it.

All round her was New York State. Those were the Catskills. It was the month of May. She was holding the newspaper she'd bought earlier that day in New York. There was a picture on the front of it of a man in a bodybag. The man was clearly dead. He had the empty clayey look of the not-long-gone. The bodybag was zipped quite far up, but you could see his bruises, his nose, his broken teeth, his upturned dead eye. Above the bodybag was a girl in military clothes. She was pretty, she was smiling and she was giving the photographer the thumbs-up sign above the dead man's face. There was a report about a woman in her seventies. One day they took her out of her cell. They snarled a dog at her and they made her go down on all fours like a dog. A soldier sat on her back and rode her round the prison courtyard like a horse. There were pictures of a lot of prisoners-of-war who were made, by dog and at gunpoint, to strip. Then the soldiers put bags over their heads. Then they were piled up, naked, one on top of the other into a hive of live bodies and the soldiers had had their photographs taken smiling as if at a family party over the top of the pile of people.

Eve knew that something quite mysterious happened the more she looked at the pictures. She knew it was supposed to happen like that, that although these photographs were a signal to the eyes about something really happening, the more she looked at them the less she felt or thought. The more pictures she saw, the less they meant something that had happened to real people and the more it became possible to pile real people up like that again anywhere you wanted and have your picture taken standing smiling behind them.

She could still clearly see it, the photograph of the dead man in the bodybag and the grinning girl soldier, even though it was the middle of the night. She didn't know what to do about the looking, whether to keep on looking or to stop looking. There was no answer to it. It was itself the answer. She was living in a time when historically it was permissible to smile like that above the face of someone who had died a violent death.

Eve had taken a gap year from her own history. She had been walking down the road in London and had seen a poster-sized advert in a student travel office window. *Q: Is there life after death?* She had been on her way to a press conference about the Families Against the Thievery of Relatives' Authenticity group. She could already see the news headlines. FATRA Lot of Good. As FATRA Would Have It. The families had got together to try to get money out of Jupiter Press and Eve. Eve's head was full of sentences which she'd been practising overnight. *Who is to say what authenticity is? Who is to say who owns imagination? Who is to say that my versions, my stories of these individuals' afterlives, are less true than anyone else's?* She was going to answer every question with a question. This would let her answers seem open, let her seem willing to be discursive, at the same time as be rhetorically cunningly closed. She had passed the travel office then stopped and gone back to its window and read the words on the poster again. *A: Why wait to find out? Take a gap year. Live now.* This had made her go in and press the button on the machine that gave out numbers to people waiting their turn to be seen. The ticket said number 6. It was noon. So few people were travelling because of the world at the moment, the woman in the office told her, that they were thinking of getting rid of their ticket machine. Does it matter that I'm not a student? Eve had asked. It'll cost you more, the woman said, but no, in terms of who you are, of course not. Anyone can take a year out. Where would you like to go in the world?

Instead of going to the press conference, Eve had gone to her doctor's surgery and booked herself in for injections. By now Eve had withdrawn money from HSBCs in many major cities of the world. She had been offered sex, mostly but not exclusively by men, almost as many times and in almost as many cities as she'd drawn out money. She'd drunk Coke in a hotel room in Rome. She'd drunk Coke in a bar overlooking a palace in Granada. She'd drunk Coke in a chalet bar up a mountain in Switzerland. She'd drunk Coke on several aeroplanes. She'd drunk Coke in a hotel bar in Nice on the Promenade des Anglais, across the road from a group of drug addicts on the stony beach. She'd drunk Coke in the air conditioning of a restaurant in a rich suburb of Colombo, through the front windows of which she had seen children living in a derelict tower with rags hanging from the holes where its windows should be. She'd drunk Coke in a filthily expensive bar in Cape Town. She'd been down a dirt track in Ethiopia in the middle of nowhere where there was nothing but scorch, nothing but flies, nothing to eat, nothing to farm, nothing but an old tyreless truck and some standing shacks, and the thin and always smiling people who lived there had welcomed her in, given her everything they had, which was almost nothing, then they'd swept her into their ramshackle bar like she was a whole festival and they'd presented her to the Coke machine, in front of which several of them had argued and nodded and clubbed together and shouted for more people until they eventually found enough money and

287

let coin after coin drop into the slot until the can thudded into the dust-covered mouth of the machine. *I am posting this from the airport*, she wrote on the postcard home. *Just to let you know I just drank my last ever Coke*.

She'd put coins in slots herself two weeks ago, in Las Vegas. Two weeks ago she'd flicked what she'd won there over the side of the Grand Canyon: meaningless small change thumbed into the biggest slot in the world. What would the payout be? what would thud down at her out of the world's most massive machine? For luck, she'd flung her phone over the edge after the coins. It was worth something. It was international-ranging. On its screen the angry red icon shaped like a telephone receiver had been flashing at her for days. You Have New Messages. Before she threw it away Eve left a message on the home answerphone.

Hello Astrid, hello Magnus, hello Michael, it's me. Just to let you know I'm at the Grand Canyon. I'm trying to think how to describe it. Actually it makes me think that every level pavement or road I've ever stood on was a kind of nonsense. I think I may feel vertiginous for the rest of my life. I'm sitting right at the edge. I'm on the south rim. The north rim is still closed, apparently. It's ten miles away, apparently. A man at the observation point told me they used to be able to see the curve of the earth from one of these observation places, you know, with special telescopes, but now it's not visible any more. There's a small fence here where I am, but you can climb over it and look right down, I just have, and from here I can see this tiny strip of green at the bottom. Apparently it's the Colorado River. There's a Japanese man in front of me now. He's having his picture taken. He's standing out on a rock. It looks a bit dangerous. He's on the edge in a way that's giving me an urge to run at him and knock him over it. Lots of birds. Lots of, ravens I think they are. I can see goats as well, Astrid, down on the rocks. It's as though I'm looking at a different planet, except for the tourists. It's as though it's earth before anyone was on it, except for the tourists. Of course, I'm a tourist too. It's a bit bewildering, to be honest. It's a bit overwhelming. It's very beautiful. Its colours keep changing with the light changing. It's so huge. Well, anyway, I'm about to throw my phone in. I have to throw something into it, and if it's not going to be me, or that perfectly nice Japanese tourist, well. And I just wanted to leave you a message before I did. Lots of love.

Not all of this had been recorded by the home answerphone, which had made the beeping noise signalling the end of the allocated speaking space at about the time Eve was saying the words *from here I can see*.

On the other side of the canyon, invisible to the naked eye, was her dead mother out on a ledge of rock, high on morphine in a hospital bed, singing hymns and songs all jumbled together. *Then sings my soul my saviour God to thee*. A nurse had come and closed the door. *Oh isle of my childhood I'm longing to see*. Her mother was forty-four, that was all. She couldn't hold her head up any more; her head rested on her chest as if her neck was broken. Her neck didn't work any more. She took Eve's hand and held it so tight that it hurt and when she let go Eve had marks in her hand from her mother's rings. She spoke to Eve, she said something that sounded like words but it wasn't words. Eve had had no idea what her mother's last message to her was.

I think you were old enough for it to be okay, Michael had told her when they first knew each other. You weren't really a child any more. You were past the stage psychologists talk about where children, because they're so young when they're bereaved, feel bereaved forever.

It was meaningless, what she said to me at the end, Eve told him.

Not meaningless, he said. It had meaning because she said it. Even though you don't know what she said, it had meaning because it went between you, from her to you.

Yes, Eve said.

It was just that the literal meaning itself wasn't immediately comprehensible, Michael said. That doesn't mean it didn't mean.

This conversation was one of the reasons that Eve had married Michael. He had seemed a man with whom the right kind of dialogue would be possible.

Poor Michael. A girl called Emma Sackville had finally sacked his ville. The truth had been waiting for them on the answerphone when they got back from Norfolk. But one of the last times she'd talked to Michael things had sounded better. He had had a series of poems accepted by a small publisher. The TLS or someone wanted to publish two of them. He sounded ludicrously happy about it. But Astrid was still refusing to come to the phone, and Magnus had been at the library with a friend, revising for his exams.

Eve: Priesthood? What kind of priesthood?

Michael: I know. I told him he'd have to convert first, that you couldn't just join and be a priest just like that, and he looked at me like I was some kind of idiot. But then, he always looks at me like I'm some kind of idiot. No, but he's fine, he'll be sorry he missed you, we're fine, really.

Eve: And how's Astrid?

Michael: Fine, we're all fine.

Eve: Is she still wearing red all the time?

Michael: Oh, you know. She's fine. Don't worry. She's perfectly safe. She's made friends. She's working on an

alternative school newspaper or something. She's
writing a manifesto for it, up in her room. Like mother,
like daughter.

Eve: A manifesto? Not like me, I never wrote a manifesto.
What kind of manifesto?

Michael: How would I know? It's not as if she'd show me.
She did let me choose a badge though. She's made badges
for herself and for her friends. She very grandly said I
could have one.

Eve: Did she? God, you're lucky. You're doing something
right.

Michael: There was a choice. A badge with the word imagine
written on it or a badge with the word afraid.

Eve: Imagine or afraid?

Michael: Imagine or afraid.

Eve: Which did you choose?

Michael: Ah. That'd be telling.

Eve: Very telling.

Michael: Ha ha.

Eve: Give Astrid, give them both, all my love. Tell them I
think of them every morning when I wake up and every
night before I go to sleep. I picture them in front of me
as if they're here with me.

Michael: Well, they're not. They're very definitely here with
me.

Eve: I know that.

Michael: I can tell because of the supermarket bills. And me
too, though? You think about me too, don't you?

Eve: Oh, I suppose so. I suppose I think of you occasionally.
What will you call it?

Michael: What will I call what?

Eve: Your poem sequence. What's it called?

Michael: Ah. Ha ha. I'd forgotten about that for a minute.

I should speak to you more often. It's called The Lady
Vanishes.

Eve: The Lady Vanishes. That's good.

Michael: It is good, isn't it?

Eve: Are they paying you a lot of money?

Michael: Ha ha. Joke.

Eve: No, seriously, how are you for money?

Michael: Well, we're still holding the fort, but the apaches
are definitely on the attack and I don't know that a
sonnet sequence is going to hold them at bay for long.

Eve: So . . . ?

Michael: So, no, I don't know what we'll do. I'm trying not
to think about it.

Eve: Because I'm nearly out, myself.

Michael: Ah. Does that mean you'll be coming home?

On the far side of the Grand Canyon was Eve's mother.
She wasn't in a hospital bed at all. She was young and
nonchalant, as if leaning against the sideboard in the kitchen
having a quiet think. She waved to Eve and Eve saw that her
mother was leaning on a thin layer of formica-covered wood
above nothing but air, and that just below her feet, which
were dangling in mid air, ravens circled and cawed. On the
far side of the Grand Canyon was the man who had been her
father. He was standing, operatic, on air, above an open
grave 250 miles long, ten miles wide and one mile deep. He
was older, bigger, balder; he was wearing a fine suit; he had
his arms open to her. He waved too. He waved to her mother.
She waved back at him. Then both Eve's parents, together at
last, smiled and waved goodbye like they were on holiday
somewhere nice, like they were having the time of their lives
and like their special relayed televised message to her had
reached its end.

No. On the far side of the Grand Canyon was the north

rim. It was shut because of the weather. It was out of season, even though it was the beginning of May. But you could see it by helicopter, if you wanted. All you had to do was buy a ticket, for God's sake.

Then she'd thought, I should go north and see where he lived, at least. I should at least see where I might have grown up.

She bought her road map with cash. She bought her car on her credit card in Las Vegas. I don't know if the card'll be accepted, she told the man in the used-car showroom. The man, in his shirt-sleeves, had taken a liking to her. He winked at her and got out his manual credit card processor. I don't trust you, lady, he'd said. But that don't matter. I'm insured.

Now Eve was sitting on the porch of the dark house with her newspaper under her arm. The porch creaked beneath her. Maybe it was rotten. Was this his house? She had no idea. Did it matter? She looked up at the mountains. Out in the dark on the ridge, silhouetted in the moonlight, were all the selves she could have been. They had linked their arms and were doing a kicky Scottish dance. One of them was an American Eve. She had very good skin and had married well. She lived in this house whose porch Eve was on, with several children, all boys, and a husband who was a stud farmer; they owned those beautiful horses, those perfect fields. The Eve next to her was a rougher American Eve, who had grown up and never married anyone and always looked out for herself; she was tanned and healthy and golden and she worked her own farm and owned her own beautiful thoroughbreds. Her hands were lined and strong. She knew how to breed and break a horse. Next to her was Eve now, but Eve as she'd have been if her mother hadn't died. She was happy. She radiated light. Next to her was the Eve who had stayed with Adam Berenski. She had a blank face. Next to her was the Eve who had never met Adam Berenski. She was unimaginable. Eve had no idea what she was like. Next to her was easier, it was the air hostess Eve had wanted, when she was eight years old, to grow up to be. She was glamorous and exact. Her sixties-style coat was buttoned to the top. Next to her was an Eve just like Eve was now, in reality, but one who buttoned the top button on the coat her daughter Astrid was wearing before she went out in the cold and rain, and felt real, good love as she did, not the kind of love that made you panic but the kind that made you happy.

The Eves stretched all along the black ridge. They waved at the real Eve like her dead parents had, and kicked their heels and danced as if at any point in a life you could simply have changed your mind and chosen another self.

Eve shook her head. She thought of the man in the bodybag whose dead face, made of minuscule dots of print, had been reproduced millions of times and sent all round the world and was, right now, folded under her arm, already outdated. She thought of the smiling girl soldier. She thought of the girl's own eyes, her erect obscene thumb. They were reproduced in the same kind of ink and in the same kind of tiny dots as the man's dead eye. The dead weren't the problem. The dead could look after themselves. Eve was beginning to grieve for the living.

Was there any point in it, sitting outside on the porch of a dark empty house with its rag of a flag hung by its front door? Was it even his house? Say it was; would there be anything that she really wanted in there, or that anybody in the world really needed, if she were to break in? anything more than, say, an old mouldy coffeepot that hadn't been washed out properly, an old scum-ringed cup in a sink that someone now gone might once possibly have drunk something out of?

What had she ever expected would happen? Did she think that, like in a story made up to make people feel better, she'd approach the house of her father and the house would instantly light up like a giant table-lamp, would suddenly blaze out of its dark and illumine the whole countryside with itself, that its door would open as if by magic and all the rose bushes would bow to her and offer their flowers to her as she came up its garden path? What was happy? What was an ending? She had been refusing real happiness for years and she had been avoiding real endings for just as long, right up to the moment she had opened the front door on her own emptied house, her own cupboards stripped of their doors, her own unpictured walls and unfilled rooms, no trace of her left, nothing to prove that Eve Smart, whoever she was, had ever been there at all.

She saw her children clearly, as if she were far above them, as if she were one of those black Grand Canyon ravens flying over the top of them. From here she could see that they were each on separate roads, on separate maps, and the maps were mere graphics, like the diagram maps in the Highway Code which explain how road junctions work. Hundreds of these junctions and all their possible connections to other junctions stretched away ahead of them both like a web of lit synapses. But as each of them came to the next clear junction and made the decision about which way to turn, whole huge areas of the maps under their feet snapped into darkness. Worse, the maps were made of nothing but paper. They were newspaper-thin, laid like primitive animal traps over a drop as deep as a mile. At any moment, if either of her children stepped too heavily or put a foot wrong, the maps might rip or buckle, or might just be blown away.

But right then, right in front of Eve's eyes, a huge cat, a wildcat of some sort, loped across the moonlit road on to the grass in front of the empty house. It had a rabbit or some other sort of small creature hanging dead from its mouth. It saw Eve on the porch of the house. It stopped a few feet away from her and stood and looked at her.

Then it turned its head and continued on its way at the same uninterested pace across the grass towards the back road, disappearing into the trees.

Fuck, Eve said under her breath.

She got up off the porch and looked to see if she could see where it had gone. There was no sign of it. There was nothing, either, to tell her it had really happened, but it had, she knew, because of the way her heart battered her chest. She had never, except in a zoo or in pictures and films, seen a real cat bigger than a domestic cat. It had been a bobcat, or a cougar, or something she didn't know the name of, as big as a large dog, with visible tufts of fur at the tips of its ears. Its look had been calm and measured. It had been five whole seconds long.

She went back across the grass to her car. She got in. She dropped the newspaper on to the passenger seat and reached forward to start the engine and drive back to New York on the highway that smelt of skunk and burnt tyres.

But she rested her head on the steering wheel instead. She thought about Astrid, her girl, and Magnus, her boy. She imagined them here in the car, Astrid grumpy and annoying in the back, Magnus fiddling with the radio or peering at the night sky through the windscreen in the front. She imagined she was driving slowly enough along one of these back roads and that there in front of them, just crossing the road with its big paws, was that wild cat.

Astrid would love it.

Magnus would know exactly what type of cat it was.

She fell asleep in the driver's seat and when she woke up again it was light.

Hello, Eve said.

The woman was cool but flustered. She was holding an old dog by the collar. She was blonde, thin, very well dressed and so extraordinarily hostile that Eve found herself taking a step back away from the opened door.

You're late, the woman said.

I am? Eve said.

I expected you at eight sharp, the woman said. Next time use the back. This is the front door. Rebecca, she yelled. Come down here and take this dog.

A small blonde girl in a t-shirt and jeans came down the stairs behind the woman and slipped past her without touching her.

Hello, Eve said to the girl.

The girl dragged the old dog out past Eve and round the outside of the huge house. The woman had turned, walked along the hall of the house and stopped. She made an exasperated noise. Eve followed her into the house.

Officially I just want to make it clear that I don't find an hour's lateness in any way acceptable, the woman was saying still with her back to Eve as she walked on down the hall past the stairs, which swept upwards like stairs in a film. I'm not an unlenient person, she was saying, but I have standards I will expect you to meet.

Several sentences began in Eve's head. *Who exactly is it that you*, and *I'm not the*, were the gist of all of them. But out of nowhere, instead of any of these things, she said:

What if I told you my car broke down?

What happens to your car, the woman said, is simply not my problem.

The kitchen they now stood in was huge. A set of stoves took up the whole of a wall. There was a breakfast bar with dishes all over it and there were more dishes in the sink. The woman spoke without looking directly at Eve. She spoke to a spot about six inches to the right above Eve's head.

Dishwashers. Here, the woman said. Detergents. Here. Utensils. Floor and surface detergents. Here. The supplies the agency requested are in the laundry cellar, and you will have brought everything else you need with you. You will have discussed the itinerary with Bob at the agency. If you'd like to show me your copy we can talk it through.

I'm afraid I don't know anything about your itinerary, Eve said.

You don't know anything about?

The woman looked astonished, then furious, then so disappointed that Eve actually felt sorry for her.

Well, she sighed. I think I'll need to speak to Bob at the agency. Your name? she said.

It's Eve, Eve said.

The domestic help is here, a child's voice shouted from somewhere further back in the house.

I can see that with my own eyes thank you very much Rebecca, the woman called back. And how do you take your coffee, Steve? she said.

Oh, Eve said. How nice. Lovely. Black, thanks, no sugar. Thanks.

The woman poured some coffee from a standing jug into a clean cup. She emptied the coffee from this cup into another cup. She put the empty first cup, still steaming, down in front of Eve and gestured towards the dishwasher.

The answer to that question is, you don't take your coffee at all. Not on my time, the woman said.

Then she left the kitchen, carrying the coffee in the second cup out in front of her like a ceremonial trophy.

Eve began to laugh. She stacked plates from the sink into the first of the open dishwashers until the woman reappeared in the kitchen. Her neck, below her made-up face, was very red. She had a young Latin American woman with her and two blonde children by her side, the same girl who'd collared the dog and a boy a few years younger who looked like the retarded dwarf in Disney's Snow White.

The woman came forward and took both of Eve's hands in hers.

Steve, the woman said. I'm so, so dreadfully sorry. You really must forgive me. I'm so, so dreadfully embarrassed. I can't believe I.

I've loaded this dishwasher, Eve said to the Latin American woman. I hope I did it the right way, but they're pretty much the same the world over, aren't they, dishwashers I mean?

The Latin American woman said nothing. She looked down at the floor, noncommittal. She was in enough trouble as it was.

Take our visitor through to the master living room, please, Rebecca, the woman said.

Why is she called Steve? the boy asked. Why is she called a boy's name?

Nathan, sweetest darling, the woman said. Go to the family room and watch tv.

Eve followed the girl back into the hall.

This is the foyer, the girl said. This is the staircase. This is the master living room. We have three other living rooms on the ground floor. If you'd like to see them, you can.

The master living room will do fine, thanks, Eve said.

You can sit there, the girl said waving her hand at a sofa big enough for five or six people.

Thanks, Eve said. She kicked off her shoes. Tell me something, Rebecca, she said.

The girl was watching Eve from a sofa the same as the one Eve was sitting on, over on the far side of the room. She looked at Eve's shoes. She looked at Eve's feet. She looked at Eve as if Eve were a circus freak.

I've been travelling, Eve said. I've come a long way. Help me with the answer to a question. Who lives in that smaller house, the one that looks a bit ruined, down by the road?

The girl pretended she didn't hear. She opened a book and pretended to read.

Little Women, Eve said. Which are you, then? Married, tomboy, vain or dead?

A laugh burst out of the girl, then silence again.

Any idea who lived in that house? Eve said. Or who lives there now?

The girl looked coolly back at her. She shrugged.

Thanks, Eve said. Big help.

The sofa she sat on was opposite a glass wall that looked out over a decking scattered with tasteful wooden loungers in front of an expanse of grass as big as a small London park, and finally, behind that, on to one of the fields of flawless horses.

Does your mother look after those horses? Eve asked.

We have people to look after our horses, the girl said without looking up from her book. My mother is an architect. She designed this house.

Your mother is an absolute nightmare bitch from hell, Eve said.

The book fell away from the girl's face. The girl stared at Eve, open-mouthed.

Ha ha, Eve said. Got you. But it's true. You know it is.

What's true and who knows it is? the woman said.

She had come into the room with a small tray loaded with cups, plates of crusty bread, biscuits, cheese, thin layers of meat. In her other hand she held the same coffee jug from the kitchen.

Nothing, the girl said. No one.

She looked terrified.

Coffee? the woman said.

I don't know if it's permitted to me to drink my coffee on your time, Eve said.

The woman gave Eve a warm confidential smile.

Mother, may I take Sonny to the woods? the girl said.

Keep him away from the Dunlops' geese, Rebecca. And when you get back, you'll have to smarten yourself up considerably, the woman said.

The girl left the room.

You're like me, the woman said. Black, no sugar.

You remembered, Eve said.

Jerry isn't arriving till quite late this afternoon, I'm afraid, the woman said. He has to pick up his eldest from college. In fact we held Richard's eighteenth birthday out here last fall, though I don't think I recall you being here for that occasion.

No, Eve said. I was probably in Europe at the time.

She saw out of the corner of her eye the girl peeking at them through the window, round the edge of the outside wall. When the girl saw herself be seen she stepped back out of sight.

The truth is, you really are very, very early, the woman was saying. To be honest we aren't expecting anyone till this evening at the earliest and most people are arriving late tomorrow.

That's me in a nutshell. First late, then early, Eve said.

Which explains my *faux pas*, the woman said. Again, I hope you'll forgive me.

No, Eve said. It's unforgivable, the way you behaved. And not just to me.

The woman waited for Eve to laugh. When Eve didn't, she laughed anyway.

Well, Steve, she said, it's great to have you here. I'm afraid I have a horribly busy schedule, but you're welcome to rest in your room until later, or to do whatever you'd prefer, explore wherever you – Oh! Did I hear you say that you had a problem with your car?

It's just down the road. I left it on the verge by the first house, the house by the swamp, Eve said.

You have such a great accent, the woman said.

Thanks, Eve said.

It's so classic, the woman said. It sounds like – it sounds like – I can't say what exactly it sounds like –

Is it the BBC? Eve said.

Yes. The BBC, the woman said.

When the woman left the room Eve packed as much of the food off the plates as she could into the pockets of her jeans and her jacket before a different older Latin American woman, carrying a thick wedge of what looked like new white towels, came to take her up the main staircase and along a glassed-in modernist walkway, then along a more traditional corridor. She led Eve through a door. She left the towels on a chair in the gleaming ensuite.

Thank you, Eve said.

You're very welcome, ma'am, the Latin American woman said.

She shut the door after her. The noise the door made as it shut was decorous.

302

Eve stood in the middle of the room and put a sandwich together from the bits of food she'd folded into her pockets. She ate it. She made another. She ate it. She arranged the rest of the food on the bedside table.

The room was fashionably spare. It had a large fan in its ceiling. Its walls were wood-lined; the whole house smelt of this same sweet wood. One wall had two windows overlooking a swimming pool, a set of stable buildings and a field so green it was somehow shocking. Its other walls were hung with photos of people with horses, or people on horses. Eve recognized the blonde woman in three of them. She was with a man, quite handsome, unsmiling.

Jerry.

The girl was in only one of the photos. She was much younger in it and almost unrecognizably joyful.

The other photographs were all shots of the dopey small boy dressed as a cowboy, with guns and a waistcoat and stetson, on the back of a white-maned pony that was too big for him.

There was no photograph of anyone who might match Richard (18) being picked up from college this afternoon. Son from an earlier marriage, Eve thought.

She made another sandwich with the slices of food and bread, and ate it. She sat on the edge of the perfectly made bed.

She decided she'd sleep in the car.

I was born. And all that. My mother and father. And so on.

Never mind that. Imagine the most beautiful palace. It's the most beautiful palace in the world. Now imagine it multiplied. It's a palace made of palaces. Its palaces are honeycombs of layered stone and light. There are courtyards, arches, galleries, whole rooms of constellations, because artisans cut stars through rock hundreds of years ago and the sun is still spilling stars all over the floors and walls of the palaces. There's a beautiful fountain. Stone lions carry it on their backs. There's a ceiling like a heaven made of broken curves of light. At a distance the walls look like they're made of intricate lace. From close up you can see the intricate lace is made of stone. Carved in the arches of a gate there's a hand and then a key. Carved in the palace walls, the words: no conqueror but God.

It's real! It's in Spain. Book early, it's time-allocated. Three hundred and fifty people can see it every hour. Bits of it are more than a thousand years old. The film director Ray Harryhausen recorded a lot of The Seventh Voyage of Sinbad in it because it looks like Old Baghdad. It was Moorish. It was Arab. It was Berber. It was Muslim. It got ruined. They

restored it. It was very briefly Jewish. It was very briefly
Gypsy. The Christians threw the Muslims out. The Catholics
kept the palace but put a church on top of the mosque. Poets
loved it. Writers loved it. Painters loved it. Nineteenth-
century tourists loved it. They chipped bits off its walls and
took some of it home with them. The writer John Ruskin
said it was too un-Christian to be art. The designer and
architect Owen Jones studied it, then built the Crystal Palace.
The circus promoter P.T. Barnum built himself a mansion
based on it. The mansion didn't last. It burned down in the
end. The people who built cinemas gave some cinemas its
name. Like the one I was conceived in. Now we're back at
the beginning.

Heaven on earth. Alhambra.

It's a top-of-the-range but still-affordable five-door seven-
seater people-carrier with a 2.8 litre engine that can go from
0–62 in 9.9 seconds.

It's a palace in the sun.

It's a derelict old cinema packed with inflammable
filmstock. Got a light? See? Careful. I'm everything you ever
dreamed.